RC BOLDT

CHOOSE ME

Copyright © 2019 by RC Boldt

Editing: Tamara Mataya; Editing 4 Indies; Diamond in the Rough Editing

Proofreaders: Deaton Author Services; Judy's Proofreading Services

Cover design: Cover Me Darling

Photographer: Sara Eirew

This is a work of fiction. Names, characters, places, brands, media and incidents are either products of the author's imagination or are used fictitiously and are not to be construed as real. Any resemblance to actual persons, living or dead, events, or locales is entirely coincidental. The author acknowledges the trademarked status and trademark owners of various products referenced in this work of fiction, which have been used without permission. The publication and use of these trademarks is not authorized, associated with, or sponsored by trademark owners. Any trademarks, service marks, product names, or named features in any media form are assumed to be the property of their respective owners, and are used only for reference. There is no implied endorsement if one of these terms are used in this work of fiction.

Visit my website at www.rcboldtbooks.com.

Sign up for my mailing list: http://eepurl.com/cgftw5

DEDICATION

To Matty,
I'm so glad you chose to marry the loud, cackling Italian girl with
fluffy hair. Otherwise, this thing called life would be pretty damn
boring.
P.S. I still love you more. Especially since you were my eyes for this
book.

A,
You're my favorite girl in the whole wide world and universe. Also,
your use of sarcasm at age five is stellar and impresses me to no end.
Keep making me proud, lovebug.

PROLOGUE

HOLLIS
Fairhope, Alabama

I tug at the tie strangling me. Or it could be anxiety's invisible grip tightening around my throat.

Dammit, what the hell was I thinking? I can't do this. I rake a hand through my hair, not giving two shits that I'm mussing it.

Just a few minutes ago, I sneaked into her childhood bedroom to see her—to have one final moment with just the two of us. She looked so goddamn beautiful. The veil cascading down her back from her sparkly headband. That dress made her look like one of those princesses she used to talk about when we were younger.

I wrote her a letter—one I never intend to give her. There's no way I'm a big enough bastard to confess my feelings on her wedding day when she's minutes away from pledging her life to another man.

I ease away from the crowd and lean against one of the rear posts of the enormous pergola. I'm not claiming one of those chairs because I'm man enough to admit the odds of me lasting through the entire ceremony are slim as hell. I reach inside my suit jacket for the flask tucked there. Sliding it from the inner pocket, I twist off the cap and take a swig of whiskey before pocketing it again.

The backyard overflows with guests. Neat rows of white wooden fold-out chairs line each side of the walkway leading to where her grandfather stands, chatting with Ms. Margie, the owner of the local diner. A trio of violinists stand poised off to one side.

This wedding might be in the backyard like she always claimed she wanted, but it's far larger. It's not small or intimate; it's turned into a bit of a circus. But she's getting her wish of having her grandfather officiate and her stepdad walk her down the aisle.

The violinists play the first few notes of the wedding march, and my entire body stiffens with a mixture of anxiety, nausea, and pain. A thousand-pound weight settles on my chest and grows even heavier as I watch Magnolia's stepfather usher her along.

She's getting her happily ever after.

The one constant in my life, my best friend, and the only woman who's ever owned my fucking heart and soul is getting married today.

With every step she takes, her beauty robbing me of breath, bringing her closer to him, more anger unfurls deep inside me. I should've manned up long ago.

I wish I'd had the courage to ask her to choose me.

As soon as she turns and is halfway down the aisle to him, I hightail it to my truck. I can't do this. I can't stick around and listen to her exchange vows with another man while I wish like hell I were in his place.

Within minutes, I'm yanking open the door to the old diner. I hesitate as soon as I'm inside, the *Seat Yourself* sign on display since it's not too crowded at this time. In the end, nostalgia wins out, and I slide into what I'll always think of as our booth.

I order a coffee from a young waitress I don't recognize. Luckily, she leaves me alone, and I discreetly pour some whiskey into my cup. The hefty swallow of spiked coffee doesn't do much to soothe me.

Staring into the dark brew, I'm bombarded with the memory of Magnolia and I coming here so often that Ms. Margie would place a *Reserved* sign on this booth for us after home football games on Friday nights.

More memories flit through my brain. The first time Magnolia introduced herself. When we built the treehouse. Battling bullies and her insecurities. Navigating high school relationships. College. We'd been inseparable for years. Sure, there've been some rough patches, but we've always been friends.

Now, I can't deny it any longer. I need to move on. Sell the damn house and cut ties with this place altogether. There's nothing left for me here.

The hot coffee sears my throat, but I pay it no mind. I'm lost in the past.

In how it all began.

1

HOLLIS

EIGHT YEARS OLD
Fairhope, Alabama

THIS IS THE SUMMER I ALWAYS DREAMED OF.

I get extra time with my dad before he starts his new job *and* we're building a treehouse.

Plus, we're out of Mom's hair so she can't complain about whatever bee gets stuck in her bonnet.

"What we're doin' here, son, is buildin' a cabin-style treehouse."

I peer up at my dad. "What's the difference between that and a regular one?"

"This one's more elaborate...which means it'll be a little bit more work." At my groan, he raises his eyebrows with a knowing look. "But it'll be worth it because it'll have a shingled roof, a small window, and a door."

"Really?"

He smiles. "Yes, sir." Then he gets back to work measuring the boards, and I hold them steady while he uses his electric saw to cut them along the pencil markings.

The best part about Dad's new job at the paper mill is that we moved from our apartment in Birmingham and got this great house—especially with the huge tree in the backyard—here in Fairhope. Now, Mom can stay home and be a seamstress.

After lunchtime, Dad and I start running out of steam. The heat and humidity during the summer here on the Gulf Coast are awful.

"I reckon it's almost time to call it a day." Dad raises his eyes to look at me. "What do you think?"

I heave out a tired breath. "Yes, sir."

I turn at the sound of a car pulling into the driveway of the house behind us. This neighbor's home is large—way bigger than ours—and it has a garage on the side. It's like someone drew an imaginary line between our backyards. On our side of the neighborhood, houses are smaller but still nice. The house behind us is on the other side with much bigger houses with stucco that doesn't look faded.

The other clue is the cars—all fancy, shinier ones.

A girl around my age gets out of a car with a suitcase on wheels and one arm wrapped around a sleeping bag. She hurries up to the door of the fancy house and disappears inside.

Dang. I'd been hoping there'd be a boy I could play with. Maybe there are others around here. Once Dad and I finish up for the day, I'll ride my bike around the neighborhood and check it out.

A few minutes pass while Dad and I cut the last few boards before a little voice calls out, "Hi there!"

We turn to find the same girl I just saw. She's wearing some fancy dress that has flowers on it and lace at the collar. Her shoes are shiny and pink. Her blond hair is pulled back in a ponytail.

"Hi." I force the word out and I know it's not the most mannerly, but I kinda want my dad to myself.

"I'm Magnolia Barton. I live right over there." She waves a hand to her house.

My dad smiles at her. "Nice to meet you, Magnolia. I'm Jay, and this is my son, Hollister."

I'm quick to correct him. "Hollis."

"Nice to meet you, gentlemen." She smiles, her head tipping to the side and the ends of her blond ponytail slide over the shoulder of her dress.

"Y'all are workin' mighty hard out here." Her Southern accent is thicker than molasses. "Would y'all like me to get you some sweet tea?"

I stare at her for a minute before I turn to my dad with a look like, *Is she for real?*

He smiles and his eyes crinkle the way they do when he's trying to hold back a laugh. "Why, that's a lovely offer, but I think we're good. Thank you, though."

"You're welcome." She grins, showing a small gap between her front teeth.

"Why do you talk so prim and proper?" I blurt out without thinking.

"*Son*." Dad's tone is sharp.

"Sor-ry," I mutter.

She steps closer, and I notice her eyes are a bright blue. "Mother tells me a young lady's always polite. Plus, my step-daddy, Roy always says we need to be a good example for others."

Sounds pretty boring to me, but whatever. I turn back to the boards but stop when my dad looks like he's just realized something.

"Your stepfather's Senator Barton?"

"Yes, sir," she says proudly. Then she moves in closer to me. "What're you workin' on?"

"We're buildin' a treehouse."

"*A treehouse?*" The excitement in her voice has me turning her way and I notice she smells nice. Like that coconut sunscreen my mom sometimes uses. "I've always wanted a treehouse." The way she says it in a sad kind of way bothers me for some reason.

I shrug. "When we finish, maybe you can hang out sometime."

Her eyes go wide, and her mouth forms an O. "Really?"

"Sure." *Geez*, you'd think I said I'd take her to Disney World or something. Her face brightens, and when she smiles this time, I smile back.

"I can bring over some of the sweet tea and banana bread our housekeeper makes."

"Uh..." I glance over at my dad, who looks like he's trying not to laugh. "Sounds great."

"Mr. Jay, do y'all need any help?" She links her hands behind her back, looking eager. "I'd like to pitch in somehow if I'm invited inside after it's finished."

Dad glances at her dress and shoes. "It's probably not a good idea to do much in those nice clothes, Magnolia." He gestures to his own old holey jeans and T-shirt. "Just in case."

"Oh." Her face falls.

"Plus, we're fixin' to call it quits for the day."

"What about tomorrow?" She looks up at him hopefully.

Dad turns to me, and I know he's silently asking me if it's okay to invite her to help. I'll feel like a jerk if I say no even though I really want this time with my dad to be just us guys.

I blow out a long breath. "Tomorrow, we'll be workin' on the roof, if you wanna help." Maybe she'll say no.

She blinds me with her gap-toothed smile. "I'll be here. And I'll bring refreshments."

"Great." I try to act excited, but I'm not too sure about this.

Plus, I'm not really a fan of banana bread. Chocolate chip cookies are more my thing.

All I know is, she'd better bring over some killer sweet tea.

FOUR DAYS LATER…

Magnolia comes over every morning to help with the treehouse, and each time, she wears fancy clothes.

Example: The other day, her jeans and shirt looked like they'd been *ironed*.

Not only that, but her sneakers have no scuffs or dirt stains. Basically, she doesn't wear the kind of clothes folks put on to mess around building.

She does bring over some of the *best* sweet tea I've ever had. Her banana bread isn't that bad either.

I'd still pick chocolate chip cookies over it, though.

I glance at her while I hold the electrical outlet box for Dad. We've finished the roof, and he's run electricity from his work shed that stands a few feet away from the treehouse. He said he doesn't "believe in doin' anythin' halfway." I reckon he's trying to make up for us not having a real house or backyard before.

"Where're your mom and stepdad?" I ask.

"My stepdad's at work. He had to go to Montgomery for meetin's." Her voice changes, and I'm not sure why, but she sounds beat down when she adds, "My mother's at her women's tea, plannin' some social events."

After a few hours, Dad says we need to stop for a lunch break. We're all sweaty—even perfect Magnolia. I eye her shirt.

"I can give you a shirt to wear so you don't have to worry about messin' yours up from now on." I lift my chin toward what she's wearing. "It should fit."

Her eyebrows rise, blue eyes flicking back and forth between me and my dad. "If you're sure that's okay."

Dad nods with a small smile and I tip my head toward the house. "We can run inside and get it."

My dad dusts off his hands. "Why don't we all take a break in the A/C? I'll get the fixin's for some sandwiches."

"Yes, sir." I look at Magnolia. "Come on. I'll get you a shirt or two for tomorrow."

We rush inside the house and both of us sigh when the cooler air hits our hot skin. Slipping off our shoes by the door, I tell Magnolia to follow me while Dad heads to the kitchen.

"Come on." I lead her down the hall to my room.

The instant she steps through my doorway, she gasps and covers her mouth, eyes wide in shock.

I whip my head around, looking for a Palmetto bug—which is really just a nice name for a cockroach—since they're pretty common around here. Or a ginormous spider. Something. Anything. But I don't see whatever's got her acting weird.

"What?"

She blinks and drops her hand. "I'm sorry. Your room is just so..." She trails off, glancing around.

"Messy?" I mean, it's not a pigsty, but I just flung my covers up instead of actually making my bed. Dad makes me keep my room mostly clean.

"It's the coolest room I've ever seen." She breathes this out like one of those princesses out of a Disney movie.

I'm *really* not sure about this girl.

"Uh, thanks?" I glance around at the bookshelf Dad put in my room. My favorite books are on two shelves, but on the other two are models of a 1950 GMC truck and a 1959 Chevy Impala I put together. Nothing worth gasping over.

She moves over to the models and stares at them. "Wow." Turning to me, she asks, "You made these?"

I nod. "Sure did." I step beside her. "Took me a while, but Dad told me to have patience. Said stuff that's worthwhile needs extra care and time." After I think about it, I add, "Just like the treehouse. He said it'd take a while since we were makin' it better than any of the others we've seen, but it'd be worth it in the end."

She turns her head to look at me and I realize how close we're standing. I can see her eyelashes. They're a little darker than her hair and crazy long.

"Hollis?" she whispers.

"Ma'am?" As soon as it slips out, I wince at how formal it sounds, but Dad's drummed it in my head to be polite.

Lucky for me, it doesn't faze her.

Her eyes drop to the floor for a second before darting back to mine. "Will you be my friend?"

I wrinkle my nose, confused. "I thought we were."

Magnolia's entire face brightens, like I've told her tomorrow's Christmas or something. Her smile is wide, that gap flashing at me. "Thanks, Hollis!"

She catches me off guard when she throws her arms around me and hugs me tight. *Geez*, this girl's stronger than I expected.

"The other kids aren't so nice," she mumbles, still hugging me. I pat her back awkwardly because, well...I'm not used to getting hugs from girls. Plus, Mom's never been much for them.

Or anything even close to that kind of thing, really.

Then, Magnolia whispers, "The other kids make fun of my teeth."

Anger. It's the only thing I feel when she tells me that. I don't know her well, but it's plain as day that she's nice. Without realizing it, I hug her back.

"Just ignore 'em." Then I add, "If anyone gives you trouble, let me know, and I'll deal with 'em."

She slowly backs away and looks at me with wide blue eyes. "Really?"

I nod. "You bet."

Nobody should be bullied for something they can't control. That's what Dad always says. A kid made fun of me back in Birmingham because of the scar that cuts through part of my right eyebrow. He moved away after that year, but most of first grade sucked because of him.

I tell Magnolia this, and she reaches up to run her finger over the scar. "How'd you get it?"

My cheeks get hot, and I look away. "I, uh, ran into the edge of a metal shelf in my friend's garage. We were playin' hide-and-seek, and I was chasin' after him. Cut it too close when I whipped around the shelf. Just lucky I didn't lose an eye." When I look back over at her, she winces.

"That must've hurt."

I shrug. "I had to have stitches, but that white ridge won't go away."

Her lips press flat. "Well, if anyone makes fun of it, they'll have to go through me first." She nods. "That's what friends do, right? Stick up for one another."

I grin. "I reckon so."

We stand here, and I don't know why I can't seem to look away. Her smile is happy, and I like it.

"Hollister, what're you doin' in—" My mom's voice has us whipping around to face the doorway. "Oh...hello."

"Hello, ma'am." Magnolia offers her hand to my mom who looks surprised. "I'm Magnolia Barton. I live in the house right behind y'all. It's so nice to meet you."

The look on my mom's face makes me nervous, but she gives Magnolia's hand a brief shake. Then her eyes flick to me suspiciously. "What are y'all doin' in here?"

"I was gettin' a shirt for her to wear so she wouldn't mess up hers." Then, I rush on with, "She's helpin' us with the treehouse."

Mom eyes me sharply. "How much longer will it take till it's finished?" Her tone is cold. She didn't like the idea of Dad and me working on it in the first place. No idea why.

Then again, she never seems to like anything I do.

"We're almost finished. Dad found a used air conditioner and got a cheap window for the side."

Her mouth turns down. Shoot. I thought it would make her happy to know we were close to being done.

She backs away from the doorway, looking down the hall. "I've got some more sewin' to finish." Then she's gone.

"Nice to meet you, Mrs. Barnes," Magnolia calls out after her.

Mom doesn't respond. Her rudeness makes me uncomfortable, so I shrug like it's nothing. "She's busy with a lot on her mind."

"She sews?"

"For other people. She hems pants and stuff." I dig out some old T-shirts from a bottom drawer and hand her a few. "Here you go. You can keep 'em if you want."

She looks down at the folded shirts in her hands like I just gave her fifty bucks. "Thank you so much."

I laugh a little. "They're just old shirts."

"Hollis! Magnolia! Lunch is ready," Dad calls from the kitchen.

Her blue eyes meet mine, cheeks turning a little red. She steps forward and presses a kiss to my cheek. "You're a good friend, Hollis."

Then she turns and leaves me standing in my room.

She's nice enough, but man, that kiss was just *gross*.

2

MAGNOLIA

TEN YEARS OLD

"May I please go over to Hollis'?"

I stand in the doorway of my mother's bedroom. She's sitting in front of her dressing table, sliding on her big diamond earrings. Her hair is perfectly styled, and her dress is smooth, with no wrinkles in sight. Like always.

Her eyes meet mine in the mirror, and I brace myself for what's coming.

She wants me to look and act a certain way, but I have this stupid gap between my front teeth, and my hair is never perfectly neat and straight. Plus, it's darker blond, and she says I resemble my daddy—my *real* daddy—and it's no big secret it bothers her. I know what he did was downright dirty, leaving us like he did, but it's not my fault he left.

Sometimes, I think she's trying to shove all the girly stuff down my throat because she hopes I'll become what she wants me to be. More like her.

Less like me.

It never matters what I want. And it's only gotten worse since

Roy's been elected state senator. They keep saying they want me to follow in his footsteps when I'm older.

Except I'm not that great at being social. I say what I mean and mean what I say, and that's not how things work around here. The people Roy and my mother always have around have those fake kind of smiles, and they'd tell me they love my dress even if it was a gosh darn black plastic trash bag. Just because I'm a Barton.

The only time I ever see any sign of life in the eyes of those ladies my mother hangs around with is when one of them bites off a chunk of juicy gossip.

The last bit of gossip I overheard was something about Hollis' mom being unfriendly to my mother. The other ladies said she was probably just jealous since Roy is such a "fine-lookin' man."

"Magnolia, dear," my mother starts, and I already know I won't like whatever comes next one bit. "I'm not sure this Hollis boy is the right sort of friend for you. You should hang around with the other girls."

"But he helps out Grandpa Joe at church. You always say that donatin' time and helpin' others are important."

I'm hoping this'll change her mind. Grandpa Joe's been the preacher at Holy Cross Church for as far back as I can remember. Not only that, but he's one of my favorite people in the world—aside from Hollis, of course. Grandpa Joe always sticks up for me when my mother starts going on about how I'm not "ladylike" enough, not "refined" enough, or whatever she's in the mood to complain about.

Basically, I'm never enough of anything for her. Grandpa Joe always tells me, *Be tough, Shortcake. It's not you. Your mama's always got a bee in her bonnet.*

My mother tips her head to the side. "Why don't you ever play with Lora Ann? She's a lovely little girl."

I work hard not to make a face. Just hearing that girl's name makes my stomach churn so much I about toss my cookies.

Lora Ann is wretched. The Bible verse about the wolf in sheep's clothing reminds me of her. She has perfect hair and teeth and always acts polite in front of adults, but when they're out of sight or not paying attention, that all changes. She's one of the kids who makes fun of my teeth.

As politely as possible, I tell my mother this.

She frowns. "Well, we'll be gettin' that gap fixed soon, so that shouldn't be a problem much longer." Her eyes drop to my shoulders. "And stop slouchin'."

I straighten. "Too bad Lora Ann can't get her attitude fixed," I mutter without thinking.

"Magnolia Mae! You watch that mouth of yours, young lady." Her stern expression has me lowering my eyes to the floor. "A lady never says such things."

"Sorry, Mother." But I'm not. Lora Ann is one of the last people I'd want to be friends with.

"So..." I hesitate. "May I please go over to Hollis' and play?"

A long sigh. Then she stands, turning to look at me. I work hard not to fidget in front of her. She hates that.

"Are you sure Hollis is the type of friend you should be hangin' around with?"

"Yes, ma'am," I answer. "He's really nice and mannerly. And he doesn't let anyone make fun of my teeth."

I stand taller, prouder, because he really is a good friend. The best friend I've ever had. I don't even care that he's a boy because he'll play wedding with me as long as we're inside the treehouse where no one can see. I make him practice oohing and aahing over me in my tiara and veil and fake bouquet. He's tried to play the preacher instead of the groom, but I've told him that messes everything up.

Of course, he doesn't do the whole kissing the bride part, which I'm totally okay with.

Other times, he lets me help him with a new model car he's putting together. It's fun to watch him when he's concentrating hard, because he gets this little wrinkle between his eyebrows. I'd never tell him, but he looks cute when he does that.

Most of the time, though, we're in the treehouse pretending to be the last two people on earth and on the lookout for zombies. Mother never lets me play with toy guns, but Hollis has a few that make sounds, and they're really cool.

She walks over and bends her knees to look at me eye to eye. "Now, remember what I always tell you, Magnolia."

It's really hard not to roll my eyes. "Yes, ma'am, I know." I raise my hand and tick off each thing with a finger. "Don't eat too much sugar. If I dress like a lady, I need to act like one too." I tick off more. "Hang around the right people. Go to college. Find a man who comes from a good family, has a good education and job, then marry him and live a wonderful life."

My mother's mouth lifts up into a faint smile. "I only want the best for you. For you to be happy."

I know I'm only ten, but sometimes, I wonder why what she wants for me are things that *other* people can see.

"I'm happy when I'm with Hollis. He never makes fun of my teeth or anythin'." I grin proudly. "He's my best friend."

My mother looks like she's tasting something sour. "Go play and get it out of your system. But be sure to be home in time for dinner." She turns away and mutters under her breath, "Hopefully you'll grow tired of this Hollis boy."

I frown at her back. Even though it's on the tip of my tongue to tell her I hope I *never* get tired of Hollis, I don't say a word. He's waiting on me, and I don't want to make him wait forever because he said he has a surprise for me.

So, I turn around and rush to my room to change clothes. After slipping on my sneakers, I head over to his backyard.

It's funny how much lighter I feel when I cross into Hollis' yard. I race up the ladder to the treehouse and push open the door, popping my head inside.

"'Bout time." Hollis is sitting on one of the nice cushions his dad found at the secondhand store. He's reading some magazine with a shiny car on the front. Without looking up, he says, "Thought I'd get your surprise all to myself."

I climb inside with a huff, pulling myself to my feet, and put my hands on my hips. "Now, Hollis Barnes, that wouldn't be very gentlemanly."

His dark brown eyes lift to mine and I can't see anything below them because of the magazine. The crinkles at the corners of his eyes make me think he's trying hard not to smile. "You sound like one of them old biddies at church 'bout to clutch their pearls." He drops the magazine to his lap and his grin is a mile wide. It's *so* not fair how he has perfect teeth.

I drop down beside him with a sigh and lie back to stare up at the ceiling.

"Your mom givin' you a hard time again?"

I love that I don't have to say anything. That he just knows me. And he never makes me feel like a whiny baby or a drama queen.

I close my eyes and let out another sigh. "She wants me to hang out with Lora Ann and for my teeth to be perfect." My words are snippy, but I don't have to hide that with Hollis.

My eyes spring open when he brushes my hair back from my forehead. His eyes look sad and I hate it. He has such pretty eyes for a boy, and I don't ever want him to be sad because of me.

"You're perfect the way you are." He says it like it's a fact. Like he's ready to punch anyone in the face who disagrees.

I really wish I could believe him.

I tear my eyes away and shrug. He shifts to his side and props his head in his hand. I feel him staring, and it makes me antsy.

"Stop starin' at me."

"Not until you give me that smile with the gap that makes you, *you*."

I glare at him. He just grins.

"Come on. Let me see it."

I bare my teeth, and he laughs. "I reckon that'd be good if you wanted to scare off those stray cats that hang around the dumpster behind the gas station."

I huff out a breath, and he pokes my side, knowing how ticklish I am. I squeal and shove at him.

"Come on. Give me a good smile and you can have your surprise."

"Fine." I smile. He squints like he's trying to figure out if it's good enough. I roll my eyes and laugh.

"That's it!" He grins and shoves off the cushion, grabbing something off the top of one of the small shelves. That's where we store some board games, a few of his magazines, some toys, and a few juice boxes.

I sit up and wait for him to slide back in his spot beside me. He turns to face me.

"Okay, so this has to be a secret because your mom would tan my hide if she found out."

I give him a *duh* kind of look. I never tell her anything we do. I'd never hear the end of it if she knew I'd hammered nails in the treehouse boards a few years back when I helped Hollis and his dad. Because she's told me time and again that "ladies don't get dirty or do hard labor."

Hollis smiles wider. "Close your eyes and hold out your hand."

I squint at him dangerously. "You're not fixin' to put a slimy toad in it, are you?"

He rolls his eyes. "*No*. Now, just do what I said."

"Fine." I close them. "Bossypants."

"You kiss your mama with that mouth, young lady?" I laugh at how he tries to make his voice sound like my mother's.

He puts something in my hand that feels like a small packet. "Okay, now look."

I glance down, and my jaw drops. "Hollis!" Lunging for him, I hug him tight. "Thank you!"

"Welcome."

I back away and look down at the packet of Pop Rocks candy. I've been wanting to try this for what seems like *forever*, especially since my mother doesn't let me have candy.

"And here's this." I gasp at the sight of the box he hands me. It's a model car kit. On the front is an old pink convertible. "I used some of my own money to buy it," he says proudly. "Dad helped me with the rest."

Hollis started doing chores for some of the neighbors for extra money. He says he wants to save enough to buy a truck when he turns sixteen and fix it up to look like those models he puts together.

"It's a Chevy Bel Air. It's the best pink car I could find for you." My best friend shrugs like he hasn't just given me the coolest gifts in my entire *life*. "I thought we could work on it together, if you want."

I'm so surprised, I just nod with a huge smile. Then he holds out an envelope. "And this."

"What's this for?"

He gives me a crazy look and drags out the last word. "A card for your *birthday*."

I frown. "But I thought you were comin' over for my party on Sunday and..."

He gets a weird look on his face. "Sorry, but I have to, uh"—he stares down at the floor—"go somewhere with my mom."

He's lying. He never goes anywhere with his mom.

I'd never say it out loud, but I think Hollis' mom is a witch. Not like a real one with creepy spells or anything, but with her dark hair and pale skin, the way she's always scowling and in a bad mood, she could be one.

But, still. I reckon I know why he can't spend my birthday with me.

"Hollis." I wait for him to look at me. Dark eyes meet mine, and I hate the hurt I see in them. "My mother said somethin'." It's not a question. I know by now how my mother does things.

When he gives a little shrug, like it's no big deal, I start to apologize. I need to tell him how sorry I am that my mother hurt his feelings, but he holds up a hand to stop me. He forces a smile, and I hate it.

"Open your card."

I lift the flap, slide out the card, and when I open it, a photo slips out. Instantly, I smile wide. I know exactly when this was taken.

We'd finished building the treehouse and were super sweaty. After painting the outside, we had streaks of it on our clothes and our hair was messy, but when Mr. Jay took our picture, we stood in front of the treehouse and smiled proudly.

The looks on our faces, how happy we are, makes my eyes sting, and my throat gets tight.

"You're not gonna get all girly on me, are you?"

I laugh without looking up. "Just give me a minute."

It's not just the photo that has me feeling a little weepy, but what he's written inside the card at the top, too.

To my best friend, Magnolia

We've never actually come out and said the words to each other, but now that he's written them, I feel proud. Suddenly good enough. He doesn't care that I have a gap in my teeth or that my hair gets a little frizzy sometimes. He doesn't care that I'm still learning how to climb trees or how to build those model cars he loves.

On top of that, he uses some of his money to buy me presents even when my mother tells him he's not allowed to come to my birthday party.

I rush to my feet and throw my arms around him, hugging him so tight he grunts.

Hollis had a growth spurt, so now my cheek presses against his shoulder. He wraps his arms around me and I instantly feel safer.

It's at this moment I know two things are absolute facts.

1. I officially have the *best* best friend in the world.

2. Hollis gives the greatest hugs. Ever.

We sit back, and while he opens the model car kit so we can start on it, I carefully open the packet of Pop Rocks and peer inside. They really do look like little pink rocks.

"Here." Hollis holds out a palm, and I'm careful not to spill the candy when I hand him the packet. "Open your mouth."

I open wide, and he shakes a bunch of the candy on my tongue. Immediately, the crackling sound and the odd tickling on my tongue starts up.

"Can you hear it too?" I ask excitedly. This is the coolest thing *ever*.

He nods and grins. "Cool, right?"

"It's *the* coolest." I listen to the crackling sounds until everything finally dies down.

"Want more?"

I think about it, then shake my head. "I'll save it for another time."

"You know they sell these for pretty cheap. Like three for a dollar or somethin'."

He tips his head to the side, and some of his dark hair slides over his forehead. He's let it grow longer and I like it. I think he has pretty hair for a boy, but I'd never tell him that.

"You should have 'em all. I mean, it's your birthday, Magnolia."

I frown at the packet. I'm torn between wanting to and keeping some for another time...or two. To savor it, like Mama always tells me when we're out to dinner with some important people. She says, *Savor the food, Magnolia. That way you won't end up inhalin' it like a pig from a trough. Ladies savor every morsel.*

Hollis nudges my arm with his. "Come on. I promise I'll hook you up with more." He juts his chin, gesturing to the packet of Pop Rocks. "Go ahead."

I peer at him, pressing my lips together, still not sure. "You don't mind gettin' more for me sometime?"

I hate being a bother, but my mother has eyes and ears all over the place. If I walked into the store and paid for candy, she'd hear about it long before I made my way back home. I swear, there's a special phone tree for the ladies she's friends with.

I'm not allowed to go to the dollar store, anyway. *The Barton family doesn't dare set foot inside a cheap store like that.* Those were my mother's words.

I sneaked in one time with Hollis. It had been a windy, chillier day last fall, and he'd loaned me a hooded sweatshirt. After hiding our bikes in the woods behind the store, he smuggled me inside with my hood up and I'd kept my face down. It had been kind of exciting to do that even though I'd felt guilty as all get-out. So, as awesome as it was, I'd told him I couldn't do it again.

Plus, everyone who's watched reruns of the old *CSI* shows knows repetition is dangerous.

That's another thing my mother would lose her mind about. I'm not allowed to watch garbage television. The only way I get around that is to be quick enough to flip to the Food Network channel if I hear her coming down the hall.

"All right, Hollis Barnes. I'm fixin' to hold you to that promise." I grin and raise the packet to tip the rest of the candy in my mouth.

Then I crackle for the next minute or so while Hollis sorts out the pieces for the model car set.

It doesn't matter what gifts I get at my party on Sunday, because they sure can't measure up to this.

Just like Grandpa Joe said in last week's sermon, a sweet friendship is good for the soul.

Hollis Barnes is definitely good for mine.

3

HOLLIS

ELEVEN YEARS OLD

"Fixin' to see her again?"

I stiffen at my mom's question. I hate the way she asks it, the nasty tone she uses, like *her* is a bad word.

Magnolia said she'd meet me in the treehouse at ten o'clock this morning, and I don't want to make her wait, so I quickly pull two bottles of water from the fridge. Waters gripped in one hand, I turn and face my mom because she blocks the only way out of the kitchen.

Her eyes are squinty. "Don't know why you even bother. She's too good for you."

Gritting my teeth, I try to stay calm even though it's hard to when she comes at me like this.

I used to wonder what I did to make her hate me. I used to tiptoe around her and try to do everything I could think of to get her to smile at me—to act like she liked me—but nothing ever worked. I reckon I'll never know what I did to make her treat me like this.

She steps closer and jabs a finger at the center of my chest.

"You're no good for her." Another angry jab. "You're just too stupid to see it." More jabbing, and each time her finger pokes me, it makes me feel worse.

Unwanted. Like the trash she always tells me I am.

"She's usin' you. The boy who wears hand-me-downs. You're her *project*."

She's ready to jab me again, but without thinking or realizing what I'm doing, I grab her wrist, stopping her.

"*Don't*." I drop her hand and am about to turn around when she catches me off guard.

She rears back and slaps me so hard across my face, my cheek throbs painfully.

I stare back at her in shock. She's never gone this far before. Ever.

When I raise my fingertips to my cheek, it's hot to the touch.

She smiles, and it's so far from sweet or kind that it sends chills straight to my bones. For a second, I hate that I've never seen her *really* smile at me.

I quickly shove away that thought.

"You think you're different, but you're not. You're trash. You just need to get it through your head." Her smile is pure evil now. "Maybe this'll help." She pulls her hand back, ready to slap me again.

"Paula!"

My dad's loud voice interrupts suddenly. We hadn't heard him come in from work. He rushes forward and grabs her wrist, holding her back. His eyes meet mine, and he tips his chin, gesturing for me to leave the room. He steps aside, guiding her out of the way, and mutters to me, "I'll take care of this."

My cheek still burns as I pass through the house and speed through the back door to the yard. Every step I take toward the treehouse happens in a blur.

I don't breathe easy until I drag myself up and inside. Until I see Magnolia sitting cross-legged on a cushion, flipping through one of my car magazines.

The instant her eyes flick up to mine, she freezes. Slowly lowering the magazine to her lap, her lips part when she notices the side of my face where Mom slapped me.

"Hollis?" she breathes out. "You have"—she swallows hard, her throat bobbing—"a handprint on your cheek."

I lower myself beside her but avoid her eyes. Staring at a frayed string on my khaki shorts, I can't say anything. I'm embarrassed, but now that I'm with Magnolia, I'm beginning to wonder if what my mom said is true.

I mean, she isn't the *only* one who's said it.

Magnolia's mom gave me an earful that sounded similar. Not that I'd ever tell my best friend that, though.

"Hollis." Magnolia's voice is gentle. "Please just...nod or somethin'." She drags in a deep breath. "Did she do this?"

I mash my lips together and give one brief nod. Magnolia lets out a tiny, painful sound.

"Whatever she said, whatever she did, you don't deserve it." She cautiously moves closer, and I hate that she's afraid to get closer or touch me. Any other time, she'd hug me or touch my hand or arm.

I reach for her hand that's between us and lace our fingers together. Then, I whisper, "But she might be right." When she starts to protest, I hurry up and add, "You're smart and your family has money. I'm only smart when it comes to certain things and we both know my family doesn't have money like yours."

"*Hollis.*" There's so much sadness in her voice. "You're smart. Just because you're better at writin' and do well in English class doesn't mean you're not smart in other ways, too. And I don't care about money. You know that."

She shifts and raises our hands between us. I pinch my eyes

closed, embarrassed. When she presses a little kiss to the back of my hand, my eyes sting, and I force back the tears.

I don't know what I did to deserve a friend like Magnolia, but I promise to never screw it up.

"Hollis Barnes, you're amazin'. You're the best friend everyone wishes they had. You're kind and smart, and there's no way you're not good enough for me." She sounds so sure. "If anythin', I'm not good enough for you. You've taught me so much, and all I've taught you is how to play Barbies and weddin' and not to hold your pinky out when you have proper tea."

A small smile tugs at my lips, and I brave a look at her. The way she watches me makes it seem like she's begging me to believe her. To ignore everything else.

I wish it was that easy.

Still, I don't want her upset like this.

I tease her. "Did you just *kiss* my hand?"

Her face relaxes, and she smiles, rolling her eyes with a laugh. I sling an arm across her shoulders and tug her close.

When she lays her cheek on my chest, I think back to her grandpa Joe's sermon the other Sunday. He spoke about how true friends love at all times. I admit, some Sundays, I'm either distracted by something Mom said to me or a little bored—no offense to Grandpa Joe—but that bit he did about "authentic friends" stuck with me.

Magnolia's a true friend, and I won't let anyone or anything come between us.

Ever.

She whispers, and her words are a little muffled by my shirt. "I love you, Hollis."

I freeze, in shock. I'm not sure if it's because she's saying that to me or because no one—aside from my dad—ever says it.

She pulls away, rushing to add, "But not like that." Her

mouth twists into an embarrassed smile. "I mean...you know. I love you as a friend."

My throat is tight, and for the second time, I have to fight the tingling in my eyes. No way am I fixing to cry, even though part of me wants to. Not because I'm sad, but because her words mean so much.

"I know." I tug her close.

Magnolia gets me. She's the one person on this earth who does.

"I love you, too," I whisper with a little smile. "But not like that."

4

HOLLIS

TWELVE YEARS OLD
MAGNOLIA'S PRE-BRACES BUCKET LIST
SUMMER

MAGNOLIA: I'M NOT FEELING SO GREAT, SO I CAN'T COME OUTSIDE today.

This text comes in about an hour before I'm supposed to head to the park and help Magnolia with her batting. She begged me to teach her the ins and outs of baseball, especially when it comes to hitting the ball.

We've been getting in some practice at the batting cages behind the high school. I cut grass for the baseball coach, and he seems to like me, so he lets me use it as long as I lock up after we're done.

As excited as Magnolia's been, I know she must be pretty sick to bail.

Me: You need anything?

I wait to see those three dots pop up on the screen. They show, then disappear before popping up again. With a laugh, I just press the button to call her, knowing it'll be faster.

"Hey." Her voice sounds weak.

"What's goin' on?"

"I just don't feel so great. But I'll feel better by next weekend."

I scrunch my face in confusion. "You don't think you'll feel better by tomorrow?"

"I just have..." She lets out a long sigh. "Hollis, I have girl stuff goin' on right now."

A smirk tugs at my lips, and I tease, "Like, what kinda girl stuff?"

"Hollis." Her voice is stern. "Use the sense God gave you and remember our health class and all those changes they taught us about."

It dawns on me. "Oh, shit."

"*Hollis Barnes!*" She uses that prim and proper voice I always tease her about and I can't help but smile. She never cusses, and it's not like I do it all the time, but *man*...sometimes, it just fits the moment.

"What can I do to help you feel better?"

Magnolia lets out a little sigh. "Not much anyone can do, I reckon. Just have to get through the worst of it."

"So...what exactly does it feel like?"

"I have these awful cramps and just feel gross."

"I've seen commercials where the lady usually wants ice cream or chocolate." I mentally tally how much money I've saved up from cutting grass. "Want me to get you somethin'?"

Her tone is soft. "No, but thank you. Mother wouldn't let me have any of that anyway."

"What if it's somethin' I can smuggle in pretty easy? And I'd take the evidence with me after we're done?"

There's a pause before she whispers excitedly, "Pop Rocks?"

I grin. "Yes, ma'am."

She lowers her voice, and it sounds like she's cupped her

hand over her mouth and the phone. "We have to wait until she leaves for her Women's League meetin'. She's supposed to be gone in a few minutes. And Roy's still in Montgomery."

"I'll watch for her car to leave before I head over."

"See you then."

After ending the call, I change out of my ratty shirt and shorts. The few times I *have* been inside Magnolia's house, I felt out of place and underdressed. Even though her parents won't be there, I feel like I should dress nice.

I pull on a pair of khaki pants and a polo shirt and slide on my nicer pair of flip-flops. Mrs. Barton's Audi pulls out of the driveway, disappearing down the street, and I head over.

When I cross the driveway on my way to the front door, my phone vibrates in my pocket with an incoming text message. I slide it out.

Magnolia: The front door is open, and I'm in the back den watching TV. Miranda's gone for the day.

I quickly send back an *okay*. Miranda's the housekeeper, and aside from Magnolia and Grandpa Joe, she's my next favorite person. She's not snobby toward me at all.

Quietly, I open the front door and let myself inside. I can't help but stop and glance around. This place is always spotless and elegant looking. Not one thing is out of place.

When I walk into the den, it's a slightly different story, and it's easy to see why Magnolia likes this room. She says Roy calls it his "man cave," and it's the one room that's more mellow than the rest of the house.

She's sprawled on the couch, wearing some expensive yoga pants and a T-shirt, and clutching a pillow to her stomach. Her eyes lock with mine. "Hey."

"Hey." I stop at the couch, and she curls her legs up to make room for me. As soon as I sit, I tug her legs over my lap.

"I don't need to stretch out," she protests.

"It's no big deal." I shift, remembering what I've brought with me, and tug it from my back pocket. I hand her the packet.

She smiles. "Thanks." Not wasting any time, she rips open the Pop Rocks and sprinkles some into her mouth. I grin at the crackling sounds they make and how something so simple can make her this happy.

I focus on the television. "What're we watchin'?"

When she doesn't answer, I turn and find her studying me while the crackling inside her mouth finally dies down.

"Why are you dressed"—she waves a hand, gesturing to my clothes—"like that?"

I shrug, trying to play it off, and turn my eyes back to the TV. "Reckon I fit in better here in these clothes."

Silence.

"Hollis." I don't turn to face her. "Hollis. Please look at me."

With a sigh, I turn my head. As soon as I see the look in her eyes, I shake my head, my tone sharp. "Don't. I don't want your pity."

She sits up, shaking her head. "It's not pity. I just don't want you to be like them."

I frown. "Them?"

"Everyone else." Her voice softens. "Don't be like them. Just be you, Hollis."

I huff out a breath. "I put on nice clothes. No big deal. I just want to try to *look* like I'm good enough to be around you."

She tips her head to the side, and it feels like she can read my thoughts. "But you're already good enough. It doesn't matter what you wear." Her mouth spreads into a wide smile. "I love you the way you are."

"But not like that," I finish, grinning back at her.

"Well"—I reach for what I brought along with me and set it on my lap, on top of her legs—"I could read to you if there's nothin' good on TV…"

Her eyes light up when she sees which book I have. It's a small, cheap paperback of sonnets by William Shakespeare. We're in advanced English class together, and the teacher has started introducing us to all sorts of literature. Shakespeare's work is one.

I have one page—one sonnet—marked since it's her favorite. Sonnet 130. She loves it, and even though she's never actually come right out and told me why, I'm pretty sure I figured it out.

Shakespeare talks about the woman he's in love with and how she's not perfect in the least, but it's what makes her even more beautiful to him. Her imperfections—how real she is— make him love her even more.

I know she has a hang-up over her teeth, but if she could just see herself how I see her—especially when she laughs—she'd know not to worry about it. She'd see that she's awesome just the way she is.

I read her the sonnet while she finishes her Pop Rocks until it's time for me to head back home.

"Thanks, Hollis." She gives me one of those smiles that makes the corners of her eyes crinkle. That gap between her teeth grabs my attention, and I wish she knew how much I'll miss that sucker once she gets braces. It's hard to explain, but it's just…Magnolia. It's like she's being made to get rid of something that's totally *her*.

"Anytime." I pat her legs before lifting them so I can stand. "Hopefully, you'll feel better tomorrow."

∼

A WEEK LATER
SUNDAY

"Hollis, boy! Good to see you!" Grandpa Joe booms, waving me over to him after church service on Sunday.

He tugs me in for a quick hug, patting my back affectionately. Then, he tips his head to the side, inspecting me. "I reckon you're even taller than you were last Sunday." His eyes dance merrily.

"Yes, sir. Dad measured me and said I grew two more inches."

"Boy with such good manners and looks'll have the ladies swarmin' like bees to honey." He grins and ruffles my hair like I'm eight years old all over again. He's probably the only one I let get away with that these days. Grandpa Joe's a great guy, and I wish I had a grandpa like him.

"Where's Shortcake?" He looks past me. "Y'all are always joined at the hip. Thought for sure she'd be close by."

"She's with her mom." I lift my chin in the direction of where a very bored-looking Magnolia stands beside her mother, who's talking with some fancy-dressed woman with perfect hair.

"Ah, yes. I reckon she's gotta keep a tight rein on her with you around."

I toss him a confused look, and he chuckles. With a wrinkled hand on my shoulder, he steers me closer, then dips his head, lowering his voice. "I may not agree with the way my daughter handles Magnolia's upbringin', but she's no dummy. She can see the writin' on the wall." He studies me. "She knows that y'all are close, and that worries her.

"You're a part of Magnolia's future"—his eyes grow squinty, as if he's trying hard to see something in the distance—"and she doesn't like that."

Grandpa Joe's words catch me off guard. *I'm a part of her future?* I have no idea what he means by that. That we'll always be friends?

Before I can ask him about it, his attention moves to

someone behind me. His entire face lights up, and I know who it is before he even opens his arms. Turning his head, he offers his cheek, and says, "Shortcake! Have you come to give a little sugar to your grandpa?"

Magnolia's soft laughter greets me before she darts in front of me and plants a kiss on her grandfather's cheek and hugs him.

"You're just as pretty as a peach, young lady."

She blushes, but before she can respond, someone steps up to speak to him. With a wink, Grandpa Joe turns away to greet the others.

"Hollis Barnes." Magnolia grins up at me and it's like the whole world brightens when she smiles like this.

I can't help but smile back. "Ma'am."

"So," she starts, then glances around to make sure no one can overhear, "we're still on for tomorrow?"

"As long as you feel okay." She looks better than she did last week, that's for sure.

Magnolia makes a face and lays a hand over her stomach. "Ugh. That was awful." Her face brightens. "I feel much better."

"I'm glad."

"Plus"—she lowers her voice—"I've been practicin' my form in the mirror." She repeats what I've coached her on. "Legs apart, elbows out but not too much. Grip comfortably tight."

I can't suppress a chuckle and lay a hand on her shoulder. "You've got this. Don't overthink it."

Something draws my attention, and I find Mrs. Barton's sharp eyes on where my hand touches Magnolia.

I immediately drop it.

Magnolia peers up at me before turning to see where my attention strayed. When she turns back, she looks a little sad.

"Guess I should get back over there." She doesn't sound the least bit excited about it. Her smile isn't as bright, but it's still sweet. She lifts to her toes, the corners of her eyes crinkling, and I duck my head for her to whisper in my ear. "Love you, Hollis."

We both lean back, and I say what always comes next.

"But not like that."

We grin at each other before she turns away, heading back to her mother's side.

∿

"Nope. No girls allowed." Chase Beckford's face scrunches up nastily as he eyes Magnolia.

She tenses beside me and murmurs, "Hollis, it's all ri—"

I step toward him. "Bet you she'll hit a home run."

Chase sneers. "Reckon she couldn't hit much of anythin', let alone a home run."

Magnolia moves forward, fists clenching at her sides. "Ready to put your money where your mouth is, Beckford?"

Chase rolls his eyes and glances around at the other guys gathered around us near home plate. There are always baseball games on this field in the old park down the street from our neighborhood.

Chase and the others live in a neighborhood not too far from us. They go to our school but don't talk much to me these days. Mainly, it's because I hang with Magnolia. But I'm not heart-broken over not hanging out with them, though. The comments they made about me being friends with her, about me being her charity case, really pissed me off.

Magnolia taps the bat to the dirt at our feet, her lips pressed in a thin line. "If I hit a home run, y'all will let me play another time." She takes a step closer to Chase. "If not"—the edges of her lips curl up slightly—"then I'll wait at least a month before I ask again."

Chase glances around at the others, and some of them

shrug. Finally, he rolls his eyes. "Fine. But no favors. You get the same pitches as anyone else."

She grins. "Wouldn't want it any other way."

The guys take their places, Chase taking the pitcher's mound, and I turn to Magnolia and lower my voice. "Remember, keep your eye on the ball. Don't chase it. Let it come to you."

Her expression is fierce and determined. She nods. "Got it."

She walks over to the mound, and I move aside to watch. My palms are sweaty and nervousness spreads through me while she looks calm as can be.

Chase winds up and sends the first pitch, which is ball one. I study Magnolia's form and find myself holding my breath on the next pitch. It looks good—Chase is a pretty darn good pitcher— and everything happens in slow motion.

Magnolia swings, her bat connecting with the ball in the perfect spot, the loud crack echoing, and the ball whizzing through the air. She takes off, running as fast as her legs can carry her, and rounds the bases as one of the outfielders chases after the ball that's landed on the other side of the fence that encloses the ball field. Her blond ponytail bounces with her movement. The others look stunned, like they've never seen a girl do anything like that before.

I grin so wide, I swear it probably stretches from ear to ear.

She rounds the bases, and as soon as she crosses home plate, she rushes at me, throwing her arms around my neck to hug me tight.

"I did it, Hollis!" Pride and excitement fill her voice. "I really did it!"

"Heck yes, you did!" I squeeze her back.

"I couldn't have done it without you."

She came to me a few weeks ago with a list she'd come up with of the things she wanted to accomplish before her mom forced her to get braces.

Of course, my best friend had listed *Learn how to play baseball and hit a home run so the boys will respect me* on there.

A few of the other things, like eating all the corn on the cob she could handle—bad move on her part because she ended up making herself sick—and chewing her favorite type of gum were on her list.

There's one thing on it I'm still not cool with.

"That was the *coolest* moment of my life." She sighs later on while we're relaxing in the treehouse.

The guys pretty much worshipped the ground she walked on after she proved she could hit just about any decent pitch thrown her way. I left that ball field feeling like I was a bodyguard to a celebrity or something.

Magnolia pulls a pen off one of the shelves and draws a line through item number five on her list.

There's one item left to mark off.

She turns to me, eyes pleading. "Come on, Hollis. Would you please help me with this?" She holds up the list, gently waving it. "I need to experience it. Otherwise, I'll have to wait *years*."

I roll my eyes and laugh. "People *do* still kiss when they have braces, you know."

She straightens. "How do you know?"

I duck my head and shrug. "Trust me, you're makin' a bigger deal out of it than it is."

Silence hangs between us, and I finally raise my eyes to hers. She shoots up to her feet, staring at me with disbelief.

"You kissed somebody?"

I rake a hand through my hair. "Lora Ann came over a couple of months ago and asked me for help with her math homework."

One blond eyebrow rises. "Guess that wasn't all she needed your help with." Her sharp tone has my spine stiffening.

"Hey." I glare at her, anger surging through me as I stand,

facing her. "She's the one who kissed *me*."

Magnolia flicks the end of her long ponytail back over her shoulder with a scowl on her face. "Oh, I'm sure you put up the fight of your life." Her voice drips with sarcasm.

I step closer, my tone hard. "Look, I didn't bring it up because it's not important. She kissed *me*. I'd never be caught dead kissin' someone who treats you like shit." It was bad enough my dad made me be a gentleman and help her with her homework.

Of course, after Lora Ann left and I told him why I hadn't wanted to help her—because she's one of the main people who tease Magnolia about her teeth—he felt bad and said next time he'd cover for me and give an excuse.

She stares at me and I stare back, neither of us speaking. Finally, she whispers, "You cussed."

My laugh is harsh. "That's all you've gotta say?" I shake my head in frustration and stare down at the floor.

God, this sucks. We've never fought like this before. I mean, sure, we've had disagreements, but it was something simple like whether we should go bike riding first or head to the country club pool.

Nothing like this.

Her hand finds my clenched fist, and she gently uncurls my fingers to take my hand in hers. "Hollis," she says softly. "I'm sorry."

I exhale loudly. "Me, too." I raise my eyes to hers, startled by how close she is now. Her blue eyes study me.

"I just thought—" She breaks off and looks away before refocusing on me. "Would you please just help me cross that off my list? It'll only take a second. I promise." When I hesitate, she tips her head to the side. "Or I might accidentally slip up and tell your dad you cussed."

I raise my eyebrows with a smirk. "We both know who

taught me to cuss."

With an exasperated sound, she says, "Fine. Then I'll tell your mom."

That wipes away my smirk. Because my mom's a different story. I'd rather steer clear of her altogether.

Magnolia shoves at me half-heartedly with a small smile. "Oh, for the love of all that's holy... You know I'd never say a word to your mom." Her features turn serious. "Now, please? Will you help me? All you have to do is stay still."

I scowl. "Stay still?" I tip my head to the side. "I reckon you've been googlin' the wrong thing if you think that's how kissin's done."

She rolls her eyes and closes the distance between us. Resting her palms on my shoulders, she's closer than she normally is, and it makes me nervous.

Lifting to her tiptoes, she brings her mouth closer to mine. "Just give me a sec." Then her lips press lightly over mine, and a zing of electricity shoots through me. My hands move to her waist, gently holding her in place.

This is totally different than when Lora Ann ambushed me. With her, I'd felt nothing except the wetness from her sloppy excuse for a kiss. But Magnolia... There's nothing sloppy about this.

She backs away, her eyes opening, but I stop her with my hands on her waist.

"I, uh, think you should try it again." I clear my throat, trying to play it cool. "Just because it'll be so long. Like you said."

Her eyes search my face for a moment before she nods slowly. "Okay," she says in a whisper.

I dip my head and brush my lips against hers, the contact making my heart thud like crazy in my chest. I'm not sure what's going on, but I can't stop kissing her. This might not *actually* be my first kiss, but for me, this is the real one. The kind Magnolia always talked about back when she'd make me play wedding with her. A kiss that's perfect.

I don't open my eyes, but whisper against her lips, "Magnolia, I—"

The vibrating sound has us jumping apart, and Magnolia spins around to where she laid her cell phone.

I scrub my hands over my face and wait for her to get off the phone with her mom.

"*Yes, ma'am.*"

"*I will.*"

"*Yes, ma'am.*"

"*No, I'm not too dirty.*"

"*I'll be right home.*"

Finally, she ends the call. She stares down at her cell phone for a long moment before slowly turning to face me.

"Everythin' okay?"

She nods before suddenly a sunny grin forms on her face. She snags the pen and marks off her list before meeting my eyes.

"Thanks, Hollis." She steps up and wraps her arms around me, giving me a brief hug. "You helped me mark everythin' off my list." She backs away. "I have to run home. See you tomorrow, okay?"

She disappears out the door before I can find any words.

She thanked me for helping her get through her list. Including that kiss. Her first.

She acted like it was nothing.

"Because it probably wasn't," I mutter, disgusted with myself.

I toss myself down onto one of the large cushions and stare up at the ceiling. "You got all bent out of shape over somethin' that didn't even faze her."

I need to let it go.

Even though, deep down, a small part of me tries to put up one heck of a fight not to.

5

MAGNOLIA

TWELVE YEARS OLD

I RACE THROUGH HOLLIS' BACKYARD LIKE THOSE BRAIN-EATING zombies we used to pretend were chasing after us when we were younger actually *are* chasing me. My heart races, thudding so loud it echoes in my ears.

I kissed Hollis.

I kissed my best friend.

On the *lips*.

Everyone else I know has had their first kiss.

Except me.

I trust Hollis, which is why I wanted him to be my first kiss. I knew he wouldn't make fun of me if I did it wrong or tease me afterward. It would be like anything else he'd taught me to do.

Boy, was *I* wrong.

I rush inside my house and close the door behind me. Hurriedly, I untie and remove my shoes, carrying them as my feet move quickly down the hall to my room.

Please let me avoid my mother, I chant silently. My face feels hot, and I swear, the woman is like a bloodhound. I'm afraid she'll know exactly what I just did.

"Magnolia Mae!" Her sharp tone causes me to practically skid to a stop on the hardwood floors. "Ladies do not run inside a house." Then she adds, "Least of all in filthy-lookin' socks."

"Sorry, Mother." I hesitate. "I just wanted to get a shower and be cleaned up for dinner." There. That should please her since she told me we're hosting the local congressman and his wife.

"Turn around and let me see you." She sounds suspicious, and I barely hold back a cringe.

I turn and face her, praying I don't show any sign of what I was doing just moments ago. When her eyes narrow on my mouth, panic rushes through me.

She steps closer and purses her lips. "You should really be more careful. Your lips are chapped from spendin' so much time outside with"—her next words drip with disgust—"that boy."

"I'll be sure to use some lip balm."

Her eyes snap to mine, and she nods. "You'd best do that."

"Yes, ma'am." I spin around and head down the hall to my room.

Once I'm inside my bedroom, I race to my en-suite bathroom and check my reflection in the mirror.

Oh, my gosh. Lips reddened, my cheeks are flushed, and my eyes even look a little wild.

I trace the tip of my index finger along my lips as a sense of wonder settles over me. If that's what kisses are like, I can't wait to do it again. Especially with someone I really like and who likes me back, of course.

Not like Hollis because he doesn't think of me like that. I mean, I basically begged him to kiss me.

I just hope my next kiss is even more amazing than my first.

As soon as I step out of the bathroom, I notice my mother

standing in the doorway of my room. I stop short, just now realizing what I didn't see when I'd rushed in here.

My mouth parts in a silent gasp. My entire room is...

"I thought since you're now a woman, you'd want your room to be reflective of that."

Gone. Everything I loved is gone from my room.

The small model cars Hollis had bought me for my birthdays and helped me put together. The baseball I hit the home run with when I challenged the guys at the ball fields. He'd written on it with a permanent marker and dated it.

It's all missing. Everything that meant *anything* to me. Even my bedding is different, for heaven's sake.

My throat feels like it's closing up. I force out the words. "Where are my things?"

"I had Miranda dispose of them." She wrinkles her nose in distaste. "It was mostly cheap little trinkets."

I struggle to fill my lungs with air. Both panic and an ache fill my chest at the fact she's trashed my belongings.

"Now, Magnolia"—her voice is condescending—"a young lady like you deserves keepsakes that don't come from the dollar store." She raises her eyebrows in question. "Isn't that right?"

"Yes, ma'am," I reply robotically.

An edge of her mouth lifts, pleased with my response. She turns around and heads for the door. "Please don't bring any more of that trash in this house."

When I don't immediately answer, she hovers in the doorway, back to me, but her shoulders stiffen.

"Yes, ma'am," I answer.

Without another word, she disappears from sight, leaving me to slowly inspect my room again.

It looks clean, empty of any life. Even the copy of Shakespeare's sonnets that Hollis got me for Christmas last year is gone. Most likely because it was one of the inexpensive copies.

Sadness floods me, and I press my fingers against my mouth to fight it. Hollis had written in that book of sonnets—right inside the front cover—and I cherished it.

TO MY BEST FRIEND, WHO'S BEAUTIFUL JUST THE WAY SHE IS.

I knew what he meant without him coming out and saying it. He'd always gotten so upset about my mother commenting about my teeth. He'd even told me he loved my smile with the gap. That it made *me* Magnolia.

I didn't care one bit that the paperback copy he'd given me only cost a few dollars. It was something he knew I loved, and he'd used his own money to buy it for me.

A thought hits me, and I rush to my dresser. Tugging open the middle drawer, as soon as I see the contents, my entire body deflates.

The old T-shirts Hollis gave me are gone, too.

I lower myself to a heap on the carpeted floor and close my eyes. Tears silently race down my cheeks. I wrap my arms around myself, silently asking *why*? Why would my mother do this? Why couldn't she ask me first?

Why can't she accept that Hollis is my best friend?

I'm not sure how long I sit like this until a light touch on my shoulder has me opening my eyes.

Miranda squats down beside me. She reaches out to gently brush away my tears, and whispers, "I have some of your things in my trunk."

My eyes grow wide, and my lips part, but our housekeeper shakes her head to stop me. With a quick glance at my open door, she turns back to me and whispers once again. "I'll give them to Hollis."

I nod and mouth a silent "Thank you." She nods with a tiny, sad smile before she leaves my room.

I'm able to breathe a little easier knowing my stuff will be safe with Hollis.

~

LATER THAT NIGHT...

A text comes through just when I'm crawling into bed.

Hollis: Can you open your window quietly?

I frown at the odd message.

Me: Why?

Hollis: Just do it, please. And turn off your light first.

Me: Okay, hold on.

After flicking the switch to turn off the light and quietly locking my bedroom door, I tiptoe across my room. I'm not sure what Hollis is up to, but I don't want my mother to catch me off guard. I still feel raw after what happened this afternoon.

Grateful my bedroom is on the opposite side of the house as my parents' and faces the backyard, I pull the string to raise the blinds and carefully unlock and raise my window.

I whisper-yell, "*Hollis?*" He stands there on the grass in a pair of pajama pants, plain cotton T-shirt, and flip-flops.

"*Shh!*"

He reaches for the windowsill, lifts himself up, and climbs through my bedroom window with ease. He lands on his feet, carefully closes the window, and turns to face me. The hint of moonlight peeking from behind the clouds behind him makes him look like some sort of fierce archangel.

"Miranda gave me a bag with your things." His voice is hushed. Dark brows slant fiercely.

I lower my eyes to my bare feet, concentrating on my painted toenails. I'm not sure why I feel embarrassed, but I do. I mean, I'm twelve years old, and my mother won't allow me to keep a baseball or model cars or even a copy of Shakespeare's sonnets in my room. She acted like I was hoarding drugs or something.

His fingers beneath my chin steer me to meet his gaze. When he says my name softly, in a low, gentle tone, I practically throw myself into his arms.

The thing with Hollis, though, is that I never have to wonder if he'll be ready, if he'll be okay with me stealing some comfort from him.

He always is.

His arms wrap around me tight, snug like he's not prepared to let go anytime soon. His body heat warms my palms at his shoulder blades. When he tenses, I worry that I've done something wrong only to realize I'm crying, and my tears are soaking the front of his cotton T-shirt.

He runs his hands over my back soothingly. "It'll be okay," he whispers against the top of my head, his breath feathering strands of my hair. "I've got you."

Vaguely, I realize he shifts and loops an arm beneath my legs, hefting me into his arms. He carries me to my bed and sets me down. Lifting the covers for me to get situated beneath them, he says, "Gotta get you tucked in."

I scoot in and let him tuck the covers around me. When he leans back, I panic.

"Wait!" I hiss quietly. I swallow hard. "Can you...lie with me for a minute?"

He hesitates and just when I think he's fixing to say no, he slides his cell phone from the pocket of his pajama pants. "Let me set the alarm, just in case I fall asleep."

My panic eases as he taps on the screen of his phone before circling the bed to slip off his flip-flops and settles on top of the comforter. I instantly move to curl up at his side. When his arm curves around me, holding me close, I rest a palm over the center of his chest where his heart thumps in soothing, steady beats.

"I never wanna be like her." I swallow hard. "Please promise me you won't let me turn into her."

"You could never be like her." With his next words, I detect a hint of a smile in his voice. "You're too good. Sweet. Kind. Smart." He presses a kiss to my hair. "I knew it the instant we met."

We lie here in comfortable silence while the moonlight casts shadows inside my room.

"Thanks for keepin' my stuff safe."

"I put everythin' in the treehouse. It'll stay there as long as you want."

A beat of silence passes, and my eyelids grow heavy as sleep threatens to pull me under.

"I love you, Hollis," I whisper, my words a bit slurred as I close my eyes. *Just for a moment,* I promise myself. I'll close them for a second, but I don't want to fall asleep just yet. I feel so safe right now.

"But not like that," he finishes softly. Then, with his lips pressed against my hair, he whispers, "Go to sleep, Magnolia. Everythin'll be fine."

With him holding me tight like this, I know he's telling the truth.

6

MAGNOLIA

FOURTEEN YEARS OLD

CHURCH HAS ALWAYS BEEN OKAY. NOT GREAT, BUT IT'S ALSO NOT torture. It's just...church.

Normal Sundays involve my mother having to give the final approval on my outfit and hair after I get ready—because image is everything to her and Roy—and then we drive to Holy Cross Church.

Before Hollis moved into the house behind us, I'd attend Sunday school and suffer through sitting near Lora Ann Bayer and her minions. They always preened and said all the right things in front of our Sunday school teacher, who also happened to be our school librarian, Miss Dunkirk.

Of course, when the woman was out of earshot or not paying attention, Lora Ann would toss out the zingers.

"If you smile on a windy day, does the wind whistle through that gap in your teeth?"

"*Y'all,* how much food gets stuck *in* there?"

Sometimes, they'd draw a stick person with a shaded-in

rectangle between the front teeth. And then they'd be so kind as to give it to me. Like it was a precious gift.

When Hollis started coming to our church—or more importantly, when I'd conned him into coming to Sunday school with me—things changed.

Not immediately, though, but the change was noticeable.

Back then, I'd vaguely recognized that he was a cute boy. It wasn't something that nagged at me every second of the day, but more of a *Sure, he's cute. Now, can we get back to playin' Barbies?* kind of thing.

When I showed up at Sunday school that first time with Hollis in tow, I remember how surprised Lora Ann and the others had been. Like they couldn't understand what he was doing with me.

The first time they'd made a joke about me and my teeth and looked at him, waiting for Hollis to laugh along with them, his angry glare was so harsh, it'd even had *me* rearing back.

He'd shut them down every single time they tried to say something mean.

I never told him, but that day, Hollis became more than my friend. He became my very *best* friend. And my hero. Someone who wouldn't let anyone hurt me. At least not if he could help it.

Now, six years later, not much has changed.

I grin as Hollis strides up to me with his dad a few steps behind. I stand here, with my parents on either side of me, inside the entrance to the church hallway leading to where all the Sunday school classes are held, greeting everyone.

He draws to a stop in front of me after he shakes Roy's hand. Holding out a hand to me, I roll my eyes with a little laugh and shake it. He winks and moves on to my mother.

"Good mornin', Mrs. Barton." He flashes her a polite smile, and she begrudgingly eyes his nice dress pants and button-down shirt.

"Good mornin', Hollis." Her tone is cool, which is the usual for her when it comes to anything related to Hollis.

He tips his head to the side. "Would you mind if I walked Magnolia to class?"

My mother's mouth parts, and I know even before she says a word that she's about to say no. But Roy beats her to it.

"That's nice of you to offer, Hollis." My stepdad grins at Hollis' dad. "Fine young man you're raisin', Jay."

I slip past my parents and out of the greeting line before my mother can protest. Grabbing Hollis' hand, I practically drag the poor boy down the hall to our class.

"Where's the fire, Barton?" He laughs, tugging on our joined hands to slow me down.

I glance at him with a smile. "Thanks for savin' me."

"Anytime."

We enter the room and take our usual seats, and the relief at having him by my side is replaced with something that makes my stomach churn. The other girls start flirting with him, and it makes me really uncomfortable.

"Y'all are just friends, right?" Lora Ann asks with an overly sweet smile.

Hollis eyes her cautiously, much like one would watch a rattlesnake a few feet away from where they stand. "You know Magnolia and I are friends."

She lays a hand on his arm. "Of course." She laughs even though she didn't say anything funny. "Silly me, thinkin' anyone would have a crush on *her*."

Hollis' lips part—probably to defend me—but then Miss Dunkirk announces the start of class, and everyone quiets down.

I work hard to shove that entire conversation out of my mind, but the thoughts linger, taunting me.

It hurt when Lora Ann acted like no one could have a crush on someone like me.

Even more than that, though, is how I find a tiny part of me wondering if Hollis agrees.

"What're you doin' after the game on Friday?" Lora Ann asks Hollis after Sunday school's over and we're all headed to the church for service.

He shrugs, his tall, lanky form towering at my side. "Usual."

"Oh, that's right." Her condescending tone gets on my last nerve. "You meet Magnolia Mae at the diner afterward, don't you?"

Her smile is snide. "Aren't you just too precious for words?" Her tone has my spine stiffening. *Someone needs to lay hands on her and exorcise the evil.* "Shame you can't find anyone else to hang out with you."

Hollis' jaw clenches while he slides his hands in the pockets of his slacks. The edges of his lips curve up, but it's humorless.

Not that she's smart enough to pick up on it.

"The lesson today was about not judgin' others." His smirk widens. "Wouldn't want you to be one of those weeds instead of the good plants, now, would we?"

Lora Ann's mouth drops open in either shock or surprise—no telling which. He takes advantage of her lack of response to pick up our pace. His hand is at my lower back as he guides me to the section of pews where we normally sit.

"Hurry up," he mutters under his breath, "so we can get a seat and pray for her black soul."

I bite my lip to stifle a laugh and breathe a sigh of relief when there's still no sign of Lora Ann once we take our seats.

When my mother slides in beside me, I refuse to let it stifle my happiness. As long as I have Hollis by my side, everything seems that much easier.

Simpler.

Happier.

An hour and a half later, we file out of the church—quicker this time since Roy has meetings first thing Monday morning and needs to head up to Montgomery—and my mother tells me she has plans for the afternoon.

"Now, remember you're not to have anyone over while I'm gone."

"Yes, ma'am."

"Not even that Hollis boy."

I barely restrain my face from screwing up when she says "that Hollis boy." I wish she'd just accept that he's my friend and stop being so judgmental. Heck, she goes to church right along with me each Sunday. How she comes away from it and does nothing to change her ways burns me up.

"Did you hear me, young lady?" my mother prompts when I don't respond.

Internally, I roll my eyes. "Yes, ma'am."

With Mother gone, this means I'll get a tiny bit of freedom without her constantly assessing and critiquing me.

This is what has me moving to the car much quicker and with more pep in my step than before.

"Hi there. *No...* Hey, y'all! *No, no, no,*" I correct my reflection in the mirror. I sound like a crazy person, talking to myself in my bedroom like this.

Flipping my long hair back over my shoulder, I pose in front of my full-length mirror. With a hand on my hip, I thrust my chest outward. The crop top I have on is really just a cotton shirt I've gathered and tied up to bare my midriff. The cotton shorts are a pair of my sleep shorts, but all the girls wear them when they want to get a boy's attention. Especially in PE.

I jut out a hip and attempt a pouty look like the models on the covers of magazines in the grocery store checkout lines. I don't look sexy when I try that kind of expression, though.

I heave out a frustrated breath and throw myself back on my bed and stare up at my ceiling. I'm doomed. No boy will ever find me the least bit pretty. My braces are a huge strike against me. My lack of sexiness just increases my chances of winning the *I'll live alone the rest of my life and die a virgin* award.

My phone vibrates with an incoming text. I groan and snag it from my bedside table.

Hollis: You celebrating having the house to yourself?

Me: Not even. I'm way too lame.

Hollis: Do I have to come over there and cheer you up?

Me: I can't have anyone over while they're both gone.

Hollis: If I sneak through the window, and no one sees me or hears me, then did I really ever come over there? Kinda like the whole "if a tree falls and no one's around to hear it" thing.

I hesitate because I don't want to get into trouble, but I could also really use some time with Hollis right now. Maybe he can tell me what to do to look prettier even with my brace face.

Me: If you come over, you have to promise two things.

Hollis: What things?

Me: You have to promise not to laugh at my question and promise to help me.

Hollis: Yes, ma'am.

My best friend's response brings a small smile to my lips. Even though we're the same age, he always treats me with respect. Mr. Jay sure has raised him right.

I walk over to lift the blinds and open the window for Hollis. Less than a minute later, his hands reach up to grip the windowsill. He lifts himself up and inside and dusts off his hands with a grin.

As soon as he notices what I'm wearing, his smile drops. He immediately turns around to lower the window and adjust the blinds before closing them.

With his back still to me, he asks, "Can you put on some clothes?"

I scrunch my face in confusion and glance down at myself. "Hollis," I start. "I *am* wearin' clothes."

He waves a hand dismissively, still refusing to turn around. "I mean, clothes that actually cover your body, Magnolia." He sounds exasperated.

I plant my hands on my hips. "But that's what I need your help with!"

He heaves out a breath and slowly turns around. His eyes don't veer from my face.

"What do you need help with?"

I gesture to my body. "I'm tryin' to figure out what I need to do to look pretty like the other girls. Boys seem to like this kind of outfit, but I don't have boobs yet and—"

"Magnolia." Hollis' voice sounds tight, almost like he's being strangled.

"What?" I peer at him in confusion before pointing my index finger at him accusingly. "*You* said you'd answer my question and promised to help me."

He scrubs a hand down his face, eyes closed in a wince. "I didn't expect you to be half naked, for cryin' out loud!"

I growl in aggravation and toss myself facedown onto my bed.

"*Shit*," he whispers, and I don't have it in me to call him out on his cussing.

After a beat of silence, the mattress shifts with his weight. I turn my head and find him sitting at the far corner of my bed, his gaze focused on the wall. With my cheek against the comforter, I study his profile, realizing I never really take the time to *look* at him.

It's funny how I'm just now noticing the faint stubble along his upper lip and jawline. When he rakes a hand through his hair, the scar that bisects his eyebrow catches my attention. I've overheard other girls whispering about him in the locker room while we change for PE. They always wonder about his scar and think it makes him look dangerous.

He doesn't look dangerous to me, though. He just looks agitated, but I'm not sure why.

My voice is a whisper. "Hollis, I'm just tryin' to figure out how to look pretty." I swallow hard, trying to get past my insecurity somehow. "Like the others."

His head whips around so fast, I stiffen, my eyes going wide. His expression is fierce as he forces his words between gritted teeth.

"Don't ever try to be like the others." He shakes his head. "*Ever*. Because you're perfect the way you are."

"But the other boys don't—"

He shoves up off the bed and starts pacing. "The other guys are jerks. You're amazin'. Smart and—"

"*Oh my gosh, Hollis.* You don't have to say that just because I'm your friend. I know I'm not pretty with a mouth full of metal. I'm just..." I'm unsure of how to put it into words. "I just want to learn *how* to be."

I scramble off the bed and stop in front of him, forcing him to look me in the eye. I gesture to my chest. "I don't have anythin' here yet, but I don't know if that's a deal breaker or not." I wave toward him. "You're a guy, so can you tell me what I should do to make myself prettier?"

His expression looks pained, and it confuses me. "Magnolia." He says my name on an exhale. Stepping closer, he rests his palms on my shoulders. A shiver runs through me at his touch, which is...an odd reaction.

I shove it aside.

His dark eyes hold mine. "If you change to be more like someone else, you'll lose what makes you, *you*. And I don't want you to be different."

I frown. "But you don't understand what it's like. They have"—I glance down at my pathetic excuse for a chest—"boobs that aren't microscopic." He makes a choked sound, but I continue. "And no one with half a brain would want to kiss this." I point an index finger at my braces.

A tiny sigh spills from Hollis' lips before he tugs me close, wrapping his arms around me. I hold him tight, his soft, well-worn cotton shirt at my cheek, and breathe him in. The scent of Hollis' body wash fills my senses.

"Promise me you won't change. Not for anybody."

My shoulders slump slightly in defeat. I'd hoped he'd help me. Maybe give me pointers or something. "Fine," I say begrudgingly.

"Because if you change, then you're not my Magnolia anymore." His hand at my back glides over me in a soothing way. "My favorite person in the whole world." When I don't say anything, he prompts, "Promise me you won't change?"

With a sigh, I let my eyes fall closed and whisper, "I promise."

In typical Hollis fashion, he coaxes a laugh out of me a moment later. Convincing me to change and put on my usual pajama pants and matching button-up top, he sits beside me on the carpeted floor of my room, our backs against the bed, and we time each other's crackling mouthful of Pop Rocks.

He somehow got the best batch because his crackles for fifteen seconds longer than mine.

When my mother's text comes in that she's on her way

home, Hollis tucks both of our Pop Rocks packets in his pocket and gives me a hug before sneaking back out the window.

I'm about to lower it to lock it when his voice carries over to me.

"Love you, Shortcake." For some reason, Grandpa Joe's nickname for me sounds even sweeter coming from Hollis, and it brings a small smile to my lips.

As usual, I finish with, "But not like that."

After I lock the window and close the blinds, I quickly delete the texts from Hollis in case my mother decides to look through my phone. The agreement we have is she'd pay for it as long as it's understood she has the right to go through my phone at any time. I don't want to give her more ammunition to feed her dislike for Hollis.

I brush my teeth, crawl into bed, and say my prayers.

And just like I always do, I thank God for Hollis Barnes.

7

HOLLIS

SIXTEEN YEARS OLD

"Barnes'll tap that soon if he's smart."

I whip my head around to pin Ashton with a dark glare. "What the hell are you runnin' your trap about now?"

I tug a plain cotton T-shirt down over my head and run a hand through my damp hair, waiting for him to stop grinning and answer me.

We've just showered after football practice, and I have to rush out of here so I can head to my job at the country club.

"Your girl, Magnolia." As soon as he says her name, conversation in the locker room immediately stops.

Because he's broken rule number one: **Don't talk shit about Magnolia Barton.**

It's not like I'm cool with guys talking out their asses about girls, but let's be real. Guys can be douchebags and run their mouths about "hittin' it." It's disrespectful, and I do my best to shut that shit down.

Luckily, I've gained about fifteen pounds of muscle and

stand a half a foot taller than most of these big talkers, and usually that's enough to intimidate them into shutting up.

It's getting harder, though, because I know what's gained their attention. Hell, it's gotten my attention whether I want to admit it or not.

Magnolia's no longer the thin blonde who's been my best friend since I moved here. Over the past few months, somehow, her chest grew more noticeable. And her legs are even longer.

It sucks because it can be distracting. It makes me feel weird, and I'd like nothing more than to beat the ever-loving tar out of these guys when they start talking about her tits and how they'd love to get their hands on her ass.

Even with braces, nothing can put a damper on Magnolia's beauty. She's had to wear them longer than expected since apparently her teeth were "stubborn," as she likes to say.

I'd never tell her outright, but I hate that her mom made her get braces to correct that gap between her front teeth in the first place. I'd grown to love it. It was just...Magnolia. Somehow it made her even cuter.

I grit my teeth and shove my locker shut. Sliding the strap of my bag over my shoulder, I step closer to Ashton.

My voice is low, menacing. "Stay away from Magnolia."

As I hover in his personal space, his features tighten. "You think you're so big and tough, but you're nothin'. You don't fit in with us." He moves so our chests are nearly touching and his eyes turn cold. "You'll never be good enough for her."

I clench and unclench my jaw, hands fisted at my sides. I'd like nothing more than to knock him on his ass, but I know I'd end up facing the brunt of the punishment in the end.

Ashton's dad is a big deal at the country club, so he could easily make my life hell if he wanted.

I refuse to let even a flicker of a reaction cross my face and show him how his words ricochet inside me like a boomerang with sharp razor-like edges. I know he's right, but hell if I'll give him any sign his words hit their mark.

"She's my friend." I huff out each word on heavy breaths. "That means *nobody's* good enough for her."

A large paw of a hand shoves its way between us. "Y'all better break it up."

I get a stern look from my left tackle, Bryce Daniels. A few feet behind him, our tight end, Dallas Hampstead, looks ready to step in and play referee. Though he's usually quieter than the others, Dallas is still one of the rich kids and tends to hang with them.

Bryce's eyes flick to Ashton, his tone turning frigid. "If you think you're good enough to breathe the same air as Magnolia Mae, I reckon you might wanna work on what comes out of your mouth." His brows slant down. "Her daddy's in politics, so you better watch yourself."

Ashton's eyes narrow to tiny, angry slits. He shoves away and stomps to grab his things with a muttered, "Fuck this shit."

When the door of the locker room falls closed behind him, the tense atmosphere relaxes, and everyone resumes their conversations. Dallas shakes his head without a word and turns back to his locker.

Bryce slaps me on the back. "Ready to head out?"

I nod. "Yep."

We exit through the side entrance of the locker room leading to the school parking lot where I parked my truck. The minute we leave the air-conditioning and enter the faint humidity of the early evening, I breathe out a sigh.

My truck isn't brand new like most of the vehicles the other students have, but it's mine. I worked my ass off to buy it, and Dad's helped me restore it when he's not working. It's my pride and joy.

Bryce walks over to his Lexus SUV parked beside me and he

unlocks it with a quick press of his key fob. "Can't let that asshat bother you." He tugs open a door, tosses his bag inside, then turns to me. "You know that's all he wants, right?"

I give a short nod. "Yeah."

"Don't let him rile you up." He studies me for a moment. "You know he was talkin' shit..." He trails off, head tipping to the side. "About you not being good enou—"

"Yeah," I cut him off. "I know."

It's a lie, but I'm not getting into it with him. Not interested in having some Dr. Phil moment with my teammate in the damn school parking lot.

The truth is, I know I'm not good enough for Magnolia. Not good enough for her to continue to give me her time and friendship. Sure as hell not good enough to be her best friend. Her mother and mine have been determined to remind me of that.

Mrs. Barton strikes when I cut their next door neighbor's grass or at church with one of her plastic smiles to cover the fact that she's hissing at me while others are out of earshot. My mom's got free rein, though, since her comments are pretty much nonstop when I'm around and she sure as hell doesn't care who hears.

Bryce looks like he wants to say something else, but I hurry up with, "Gotta run and head to work. See you tomorrow." He gives me a two-fingered wave, and we get in our vehicles and exit the parking lot.

On the way to my shift at the country club, my mind wanders. Magnolia and I have been practically inseparable since we first met. Once school started, our last names—Barnes and Barton—ensured when a teacher seated us alphabetically, we'd be nearby one another. As it turned out, no one had a name between ours, so we usually ended up in the same row, with me in front of her.

Magnolia's the one who'll straighten the back collar of my

cheap, plain white polo—part of the public school dress code. She'll mother me, and...well, no one else would get away with doing that to me. But growing up with a mom who's never been much of a nurturer, and Magnolia who's one of the kindest people around, I allow it.

Hell, if I'm being honest, I secretly love it.

She cares about me. The boy whose family isn't wealthy and sure as hell doesn't waste money on hiring a landscaping service. The boy whose clothes are inexpensive and purchased on clearance—*if* I don't find them at the local secondhand store. Compared to the brand-new designer khaki pants and polo shirts most of the other students wear, I stick out like a sore thumb.

But Magnolia never makes me feel inferior. When she looks up at me, I feel like I belong.

She almost makes me believe I'm good enough.

"Nice to see you, son." Grandpa Joe flashes me a welcoming smile.

Mom doesn't come to church with Dad and me—at least not after the first time. She said she couldn't stand to be around so many snobs with more money than they knew what to do with. I mean, she's not completely off base, but a lot of people who attend Holy Cross Church are hardworking folks just like Dad and Mom.

"Good to see you, Joe." Dad shakes Grandpa Joe's hand with a smile, and the two start up a conversation about the message from today's service and then about the upcoming men's retreat.

I tune them out as soon as I catch Magnolia's eye from where she stands in the back of the church. Her stepdad and mom are on either side of her like they're her own personal bodyguards. I swear, they've always been like that. Watching her like they think she'll try to break free and run off or something.

I wink at her, and she grins, her silver braces flashing in the lights overhead. She looks really pretty in that dress. It's light blue, and the hem stops at her knees. I realize now that it shows off her body more than the everyday polo shirt and khakis uniform we wear to school.

I tug at my collar. It feels like the air isn't circulating in here enough. Maybe they're having problems with the A/C unit.

Magnolia's smile fades, and she leans in to say something to her mother. The woman glances over at me, and if I ever wondered what it might be like to be on Antarctica in a frigid ice storm, this is it. With an icy look, face tight, her lips still form that fake half-smile when I know she'd rather snarl at me.

I just smile back as casually as possible. You attract more bees with honey and all that.

It doesn't work, but I can't say I'm surprised. Her eyes narrow on me and I know what she's silently saying.

You're not good enough for Magnolia. Stay away from her.

Hell, she says it aloud every time she corners me. But I go against the woman's wishes for one reason: Magnolia.

Sure, it's selfish, but I've never had a friend like her before. And I have a feeling I'll never find anyone else like her. She's irreplaceable. I know she's too good for me, but I'd sooner die than hurt her.

Magnolia approaches my side and bumps her shoulder against mine. "Fancy meetin' you here." Her blue eyes are bright and happy. She tied her blond hair in a low ponytail with a ribbon matching the color of her dress.

She's just too pretty for words.

I grin and lean in to tease, "I only come here for the gossip."

She laughs softly, and the sound calms me instantly. "Oh? Pray tell. What did you learn today?"

"Well," I whisper conspiratorially, "I found out that Marilynn Jeffers thinks her husband has a problem with porn because she found the *Sports Illustrated Swimsuit Edition* in his office."

Her eyes flash with amusement. "Not that," she whispers back. "Just *scandalous*."

I nod, continuing with my teasing. "And then there's a rumor goin' around that a certain high school girl wanted to ask a certain guy to the Sadie Hawkins dance." I'm just kidding, of course, implying she wants to ask me.

Not that I would mind, though...

Magnolia freezes, her brows slanting together, lips parting in surprise. "How'd you know that? Did he say somethin' to you?"

The smile drops from my lips so fast, it would've crashed to the floor if it were possible.

"Wait, *what*?" I frown. Now, I'm confused.

"Did Dallas tell you?"

My stomach churns like the Gulf of Mexico during a bad storm. "Tell me what?" I say slowly.

"That I asked him to the dance."

There's a good chance I might hurl my breakfast right here on the worn church carpeting. I swallow hard and shake my head, forcing myself to play it cool. "He never said anythin'."

Her shoulders deflate instantly on an exhale. "Oh, thank goodness. I was worried he told you because he got cold feet or somethin'." She smiles up at me. "I asked him when I ran into him last night." Her smile fades, features drawn, and she reaches up to touch the inside of her forearm to my forehead. "Are you okay? You look pale."

Agitation attacks me at full force and I run a shaky hand through my hair, managing to drag in a much needed breath. I tip my head, gesturing to the doors leading to the parking lot. "Can we...get some air?"

"Sure." Her answer is slow and cautious.

I tear my eyes away from the concerned look on her face. She automatically holds on to my upper arm as I lead her outside. I stop a few feet away from the doors and away from the others who are mingling.

"Are you sure you're okay?"

I nod. "I'm fine."

I draw in another breath and let it out slowly without meeting her eyes. Instead, I squint against the bright glare of the sun and pretend to be interested in the people mingling around us. "So, you're goin' to the dance with Dallas, huh?"

"I can't wait." Her hand reaches for the one hanging loose at my side. "Will you help me pick out the matchin' flannel shirts? I don't want to choose somethin' too girly but still want—"

"Sure thing."

Silence. Then she gives my hand a quick squeeze.

I swear I feel it all the way to my heart.

When I turn to face her, she looks worried, so I muster up a smile. "Don't do that. You're too pretty to frown," I say gently.

Her eyes widen, her breath hitches, and I realize what I just said.

Shit. I've never said anything like that to her.

She gives me an odd look—a mix of surprise and wonder. "You've never told me I was pretty before."

I drag a hand down the back of my neck, the muscles tense and stiff, and I look away. "Come on, now." I try for a humorous tone. "You know you're pretty."

"But..." Her voice sounds a little breathless. "You've never—"

"Magnolia Mae!" Her mother's voice interrupts whatever she was about to say.

Part of me wishes I could hear the rest.

The other part is relieved I won't.

She turns her head to answer her mother, and I'm faced with

her profile. Soft features, a nose that's straight and narrow but not too narrow. Cheekbones I've heard the other girls tell her they envy. Lips that look like—

Oh, shit.

"I've gotta run. I'll see you later, okay?" I offer a quick smile to a bewildered-looking Magnolia before taking off toward my dad who's finally wrapping up his own conversation.

I don't know what the hell my problem is, but I need to regroup.

And it seems Dallas and I need to have a serious talk.

In his driveway, Dallas stands by the open driver's side door of his car. I park my truck at the curb and stride up the fancy stamped concrete drive. With earbuds in, it's obvious he's talking to someone on his phone, so he doesn't hear me approach.

He ends his call and turns, finally noticing me. I shove at him with the full force of my anger, the impact knocking him back.

I admit, it's underhanded to catch him by surprise like this. But with anxiety intermixed with anger and another emotion I don't want to admit, I've shoved aside all logical thinking right now.

"The *hell's* wrong with you?" Dallas shoves back at me.

"You didn't tell me she asked you to Sadie Hawkins," I practically snarl out.

He stares at me like I've lost my mind. "Dude, what..." His expression turns smug. "You're jealous she asked me to the dance, huh?"

I sputter, backing away. "*No.* That's not it at all."

He crosses his arms and nods with a smirk. "Might wanna tone down the whole jealous boyfriend thing, then. Plus"—he lifts a shoulder in a half shrug—"no one told me I had to ask you for permission to go to a dance with Magnolia."

My hands fist at my sides, and I speak through clenched teeth. "You better keep your hands to yourself."

He screws up his face in exasperation. "It's a dance, Barnes. People are gonna touch."

My eyes grow squinty, and he raises his hands in surrender with a sigh. "Okay, okay. Got it." He shakes his head and turns away, muttering under his breath something that sounds like, "*Asshole.*"

But I'm already walking back to my truck, feeling a little better.

It doesn't last for long, though.

Magnolia frowns and draws to a stop a few feet away from her car when I pull my truck into her driveway and slide out. I leave the engine running.

"I thought you'd stood me up."

"Just had an errand that ran a little longer." I hastily add, "Sorry."

And I *am*. Not only because I'm late, but because I hate anything that puts a frown on her face.

Her gaze is searching until her mouth finally curves up into a small smile. "You're drivin'?"

I nod. "Yes, ma'am." I rush around to open the passenger door for her. "Your chariot awaits."

She laughs, and her eyes are lighter now. I wait for her to buckle herself in before I close the door. Circling the hood, I let out a long breath, exhaling stress and worry from my body.

Once I'm inside the truck with her, it's back to normal. Just Magnolia and me.

The way I like it best.

Each couple wears matching flannel shirts for our school's Sadie Hawkins theme, so a little while later, she's finally settled on matching flannels for her and Dallas. I pull out of the parking lot of the Eastern Shore Centre, where she dragged me around to a handful of shops until she found what she deemed the "perfect" shirts.

Her shopping bag sits between us on the bench seat of my truck. My lips hitch upward because I still find it funny how the girl who has plenty of money doesn't really like to shop. Sure, she loves getting other people gifts, but when it comes to the stereotypical shop-till-you-drop mentality, she's the furthest thing from it.

Magnolia lets out a little sigh as she stares out her window.

"Feel up to one more stop before home?" I glance over and catch her eye.

Her tone is teasing. "Depends on whether you plan to feed me or not."

I grin playfully and adopt a British accent, pretending to read a Shakespeare sonnet. "My mistress' stomach loudly rumbles when she hungers."

Her laughter fills the cab of the truck and pushes all thoughts about her and Dallas aside.

"The diner?" she asks softly.

"Of course."

Luckily, it only takes about ten minutes to get to the Shore-line Diner. I park and rush around the front to open her door.

Her surprised look bothers me. "What's that look for?" I offer a hand to help her down.

She eyes me curiously and slips her hand in mine. "You usually don't hurry so fast to open my door," she says with an easy laugh.

I shrug. "Just wanna set the standards for when you're with

Dallas." I give her hand a quick squeeze. Releasing it takes more effort than I'd like to admit. I don't know what's going on, but something makes me want to keep hold of her hand.

Probably just feeling overprotective of her. *Yes, that has to be it.*

Thankfully, the diner isn't crowded, so we walk over and slide into our favorite booth. It's right in front by the large windows facing the parking lot, giving us a view of the street and anyone out enjoying a walk.

The few times we've been here after church on Sundays, we like to sit and talk a while. But when we don't feel the need to talk, we just sit and look out this window and people watch.

"Hey, y'all!" Ms. Margie, the owner, calls out to us with a welcoming smile. She sets down two menus and takes our drink order.

"I don't know why I even bother lookin' at this thing." Magnolia's eyes meet mine over the top of the menu, the rest of her face hidden by it. The corners of her eyes crinkle with humor. "I get the same thing every time." She lowers the menu to the table with a tiny laugh.

"Same here." I stack my menu on top of hers.

Ms. Margie comes back with our sweet teas and takes our food order, promising to be back with our meals soon.

I toy with the napkin-wrapped silverware, avoiding Magnolia's gaze. "So, uh...what made you ask Dallas?"

She's silent for a moment. When she answers, her voice sounds almost hesitant. "I guess I was just tryin' to be brave." Out of my periphery, I see her fingers toy with the empty paper wrapper from her straw. "He seems nice and..."

When she trails off, I lift my eyes to meet hers. She shrugs, a half-smile toying at her lips. "Honestly, I figured he'd probably be the only boy who'd go with me." She wrinkles her nose adorably and adds, "And who isn't a snobby jerk."

What about me?

I jerk visibly at the unexpected silent question.

Magnolia peers at me with concern. "You okay?"

I nod quickly. "Fine. Just...hunger pains," I lie.

She laughs, flashing her braces at me just as Ms. Margie slides our food in front of us.

We fall into easy silence while we eat, but I can't shake that unsettling question rattling in the back of my mind.

What about me?

8

MAGNOLIA

SIXTEEN YEARS OLD
A FEW WEEKS LATER

AFTER I RING THE DOORBELL, I STAND ON THE CONCRETE STEP AND barely resist the urge to fidget. I draw on all the etiquette guidelines that have been drummed in my head and attempt to exude confidence.

When she opens the door and sees me, though, a portion of that confidence goes up in smoke.

Her mouth twists slightly, and some might think it's a smile, but I know better. Hollis doesn't normally invite me inside his house, and I know it's because of his mother. I've rung the doorbell before—back before we both got cell phones—and those few times she answered, she'd sneer at me just like she is now. Like there's some inside joke I'm not aware of.

Mrs. Barnes looks past me, left then right, before settling her narrowed eyes on me. "Reckon you're lost?"

I stiffen my spine and paste the politest smile I can muster on my face. "No, ma'am. I wanted to see if you might have some fabric scraps you don't have a need for." I brighten my smile. "I wanted to make somethin' for Hollis."

She stares at me for so long, I expect her to slam the door in my face without another word. I don't understand her. I've never done a thing to this woman, yet she seems to hate me.

Then again, she seems that way toward Hollis, too, and I know my best friend. He couldn't have possibly done anything to excuse the way she treats him.

"You wanna make somethin' for him." She doesn't phrase this as a question but more like a statement. If I didn't know better, I'd swear there was a hint of a challenge in her tone.

"Yes, ma'am." I force myself not to look away, continuing to hold her gaze and stand up straight. I refuse to let her intimidate me.

Finally, after an awkward moment of her staring at me, she shrugs and opens the door wider to let me inside. "Sure. Why not."

I step inside even though an uneasy feeling settles over me. She shoves the door closed and strides down the hall as I trail behind her. I look around, expecting to see photographs of Hollis on the walls or mantel or family photos placed around the home. Instead, it's just as it was a few years ago.

Bare walls.

My chest pinches tightly. My family might drive me crazy, but at least they hang photos throughout the house. The photo they took of me with my trophy from the spelling bee in sixth grade still hangs in one of our hallways. You can walk into our house and know a family lives there. Maybe not in the foyer, where Mother insists it be decorated in a more sleek, modern way, but it's obvious everywhere else.

Here, though, there's no personality. It just feels...empty.

It's a house, not a home.

Mrs. Barnes stops at a doorway. "This is the room." She

points inside to a plastic Rubbermaid bin nearly overflowing with fabric scraps. "Take whatever you want."

Whatever I want? I can't suppress my surprise at her generosity. Even if it is just fabric scraps. "Thank you so much."

She waves me off and starts heading back down the hall. "Just don't take too long."

I stare after her for a moment before I rush inside the small room she uses for her sewing and lower myself to my knees beside the bin. Combing through the fabrics, I find a few that would be perfect and set them aside.

Once I've gathered what I need, I clutch them in my hands and stand, ready to rush out of here. Internally, it feels like there's a ticking time bomb, and I'm in fear of staying too long.

Just as I turn, one of the fabrics slips from my grip and falls to the floor beside a stack of books—*Couture Sewing, A Complete Guide to Fitting*, and a few others. When I reach to pick up the fabric, my fingertips brush against a paper that sticks out of one of the books.

Something makes me nudge the book back just a fraction to expose a bit of the handwriting on the lined paper. I can only make out a few snippets.

Your boy is

never expected

always love

Sincerely yours,

.   .   .

"You done or what?"

I snap upward, startled by her sudden appearance in the doorway. "Yes, ma'am." I rush toward where she's standing and eyeing me suspiciously. "Thank you for these. I appreciate it."

Slinking past her, I head down the hall, hurrying to the front door. Something urges me to move faster, and as soon as I pull the door closed behind me, I race back home without a backward glance.

I push all thoughts of that note to the back of my mind and get to work on my surprise for Hollis.

"*GO HOLLIS!*" I cheer as loud as I can.

I don't care that the other girls nearby cover their ears or that the cheerleaders give me dirty looks. They—especially the cheerleaders, with their captain, Lora Ann—can just deal with it. I don't care that my voice may be drowning out some of their cheering. There's no way they can possibly understand how proud I am of my best friend tonight. He's starting quarterback in this game and has already thrown two touchdown passes.

When he jogs over to the sidelines, and the defense takes the field, he pulls off his helmet and quickly scans the stands. The instant he finds me, my smile widens, and I turn to show him the back of the shirt I made. Imitating the style of his football jersey, I sewed on a fabric cutout of his number and his last name on a shirt in his favorite color, blue.

His grin when I turn back around makes the sore pads of my fingertips where I accidentally poked myself with the needle worth it.

He turns back to the field, so he won't get into trouble with his coach, and I cheer so loud for him the remainder of the game, my voice grows hoarse. He throws the winning touchdown, and I jump up and down, chanting his name. My cheeks are sore from smiling so hard.

Once the players head toward the locker room, he turns around and searches for me again. I wave and point at where I'll be waiting for him once he's showered and cleaned up. He nods and disappears inside.

I rest my hands on the cool metal railing of the stadium stands overlooking the field. Mr. Barnes sidles up beside me. "Our boy did great tonight, didn't he?" The pride in his father's voice mirrors exactly how I feel right now.

I nod. "He sure did."

Hollis' dad was late getting here. He had to work late more and more lately since they've been short-handed at the mill. I turn slightly to look at him while he gazes out over the field. He looks tired but happy.

"Well, I reckon I should head home." His eyes find mine, his smile affectionate. "Y'all stay outta trouble, okay?"

I laugh with a, "Yes, sir," because he knows Hollis and I never get into trouble.

He pats me on the shoulder before leaving, filing out with the others. I turn in the direction of the building housing the locker rooms and skip down the stairs before hurrying off to the doors.

A few cheerleaders gather around, giggling and talking in hushed voices while they eye me. Or, mainly, eye my shirt.

Lora Ann turns around, her loopy bow in our high school's colors at the base of where her ponytail sprouts from her head, and her eyes survey me from head to toe. Her smile lacks warmth, and the way she lifts her chin, as if to look down on me, makes my spine stiffen.

"Nice shirt." Her gaze flicks to the sewn-on number on my

front, and she smirks. "Were you blindfolded when you sewed that?" When the other three girls with her snicker, it eggs Lora Ann on. "I mean, it was bad enough you had that big ole gap between your teeth, but now you've made a ratty excuse for a—"

"*That's enough.*"

I pinch my eyes closed at the deep male voice. The tight, stern quality is something I've never heard before. While I love that he's come to my defense, I hate that he stepped in when I should have. I really need to learn to stick up for myself. Sure, every time she—or even my own mother—says something about my appearance, it hurts. But I need to stand my ground and make them think their words don't bother me.

Even though they do. They poke and prod through my skin and make a direct hit to my heart.

"Oh!" Lora Ann's features brighten. "Great game tonight, Hollis," she practically purrs.

Ignoring her, he steps up beside me and casually slings an arm around my shoulders. His dark eyes study me, silently asking if I'm okay.

I force a smile. "Ready?"

He nods and winks. "Yes, ma'am." Without another word, he guides me toward the parking lot and away from Lora Ann and her minions.

"Go ahead. Taste it." Hollis carefully slides his glass my way.

I grimace. "I don't know..." I'm not a huge fan of rich desserts, and he knows this.

"Trust me." He leans his forearms on the table. "It's a white chocolate shake with dark chocolate shavin's. I think you'll like it."

Reluctantly, I lean in and close my mouth around the straw.

The tiny sip of shake hits my taste buds, and I have to admit, it's pretty good.

He grins. "Good, right?"

I shrug, but just as I part my lips to begrudgingly admit it's not bad, someone steps up at the end of our booth.

Bryce rests a hand on opposite sides of our booth's seat back. "Y'all comin' to the bonfire tonight?"

Hollis hesitates, and his eyes flick to me. "What do you think?"

"I think you should come, Hollis." Lora Ann appears out of nowhere, and every muscle in my body tenses. *Good Lord, the girl seems to have made it her life's mission to get on my last nerve.*

Bryce moves aside as she all but shoves herself in the space between where Hollis sits and Bryce stands.

"Excuse me." I avert my eyes and duck out of the booth. "I'll be right back." I rush off toward the restrooms in the far back of the diner, weaving through the post-game crowd. Just earlier, I was telling myself I needed to stand up for myself, yet here I am, running away.

Right about now, I'm blessing my *own* heart.

Once I finish and wash up, I take a moment to look at my reflection in the mirror while the other three stalls are in use.

With my blond hair pulled back in a simple ponytail—and no fancy bow like Lora Ann's—I'm dressed in a pair of designer jeans—the only ones my mother would let me buy. It's super pretentious since they're ripped in some places and well-worn, but my mother's all about labels.

I let my gaze travel from my plain hair down to my home-made shirt that I'd been so excited about. Mother hadn't been pleased with it, but that's expected with anything Hollis-related. I know he liked it, judging by his initial reaction alone. But now... I grit my teeth together and bare them in the mirror, my metal mouth visible. *Ugh.*

Hollis always liked my gap.

I exhale slowly and watch as a wistful smile tugs at my lips.

A toilet flushes, jarring me from my inner thoughts, and I hurry out of the restroom to head back to the table. I slow when I spot Hollis sitting alone, toying with his straw. He swirls it around in his shake, looking lost in thought. I slide into the booth, reclaiming my seat.

His eyes lift to mine. "You okay?"

I nod.

He holds my gaze for a moment before he says, "Come here for a minute."

I eye him, trying to figure out what he's up to, but his expression gives nothing away. He merely slides over on his side of the bench seat and waits for me.

Slowly, cautiously, I move around and slide in beside him. My hand rests between us on the seat, and he covers it with his own. As soon as I feel the heat from his palm settle over top of mine, my stress over Lora Ann and my appearance all fades away. His eyes hold an odd intensity, and he leans in closer.

"Sure you're okay, Shortcake?"

"I'm okay," I murmur softly. My gaze travels along his features, over the scar bisecting his eyebrow, and down to his sharp jawline before dropping to his lips. For some reason, the curve of his bottom lip, the fullness of it, captures my attention.

"Ignore Lora Ann." I jerk my eyes up to meet his. "She's not happy unless she has someone to bitch about."

My lips part, ready to reprimand him for his language, but his smirk stops me. It's different somehow. Like it's almost...sexy?

Wait, *no*. That's not okay. This is my best friend.

"Shortcake?" His brows slant together in a fierce expression. "You're perfect. Don't let anyone tell you different."

I nod slowly. "Okay." I find myself transfixed by him. By his straight nose, the slight indentation just above the center of his upper lip, and the way he—

Crash!

The sound of dishes shattering has us spinning around in our seats. A few booths away, Bryce and some of the other guys are now apologizing to Ms. Margie while picking up the shattered pieces from the floor. Those guys are always roughhousing, it seems.

I hurriedly scoot back around to take my seat. Grabbing my sweet tea, I suck it down, and it gives me a chance to compose myself and soothe my suddenly dry throat.

What the heck was that all about?

Whatever my strange reaction was to Hollis just a moment ago, it can't happen again. *Ever.* I can't bear to risk losing my best friend. Everyone goes on about teen hormones, so I'll just chalk it up to that.

It has to be it.

"Morons," Hollis mutters under his breath with a little laugh.

I muster a smile, working hard to get myself under control and shake off the odd mood.

"What do you think? Bonfire or no bonfire?"

If we head home, we'll end up alone in the treehouse, probably talking or doing some model car kit. And, right now, with the odd way my hormones are acting, it's safe to say the last thing I need is to be alone with Hollis.

"Bonfire," I announce firmly.

He nods and pulls out his wallet, tossing down enough cash to cover our bill and tip. I know enough by now not to challenge him on this. He always insists on paying.

"Bonfire it is."

MORNING OF THE SADIE HAWKINS DANCE

"What if he kisses me at the end of the night?" I knot my fingers, anxious at the prospect of messing it up if Dallas attempts anything.

Hollis shrugs, avoiding my eyes. "Kiss him back if you want. If not, then don't." Another shrug of his broad shoulders.

Geez, I swear, he just keeps getting bigger with more muscles every time I turn around.

We're in his room, and he's taking care of his laundry, putting his clean shirts on hangers. His mom isn't home—I think she's out getting fabric or something—and his dad's at work. Suddenly, he stills and raises his eyes to meet mine.

"You know what to do if a guy tries somethin' without your permission, right?" His tone is hushed, ever so serious, and it feels like everything stills.

"Um..." I nibble my bottom lip before answering with, "I think so?" It comes out sounding more like a question than an answer.

Hollis lets out a long sigh. His fingers release the shirt, letting it fall to the bed, before approaching me quickly. My eyes grow wide, unsure of what he's about to do. His brows slant together, the crease between them more pronounced, and it draws my attention to that small scar.

"You do whatever it takes to get away from him. Use your elbow, stomp on his foot, jab your fingers in his eyes—*anythin'*. And as soon as you break free, you *run*." He lowers his chin, eyes still locked with mine. A lock of his dark hair slides over his forehead. "Promise me you'll be safe and do that"—his features turn anguished—"if somethin' happens."

"I promise." My voice comes out in a soft wisp, and I reach up to slide his hair back from his forehead. As soon as my fingertips graze his skin, a jolt ricochets through me. I draw my hand back, unsettled, and he backs away.

He returns to his laundry. With his attention on the task, he continues, "I'll meet y'all at six thirty since I have to work a short shift."

Kelsey McCallister had asked Hollis to the dance, and when he suggested we could all head there together, I agreed. Having him close by makes me feel more at ease.

I nod even though he's not looking. "Okay."

He said his boss asked him to help out at the country club for a few hours tonight, and since Hollis has been saving up to fix a few things on his truck, he agreed.

I step over to the shelf that holds his favorite books—including a copy of Shakespeare's sonnets—and I can't suppress a tiny smile when I notice the dog-eared page that I know marks my favorite sonnet. I glance over the handful of model cars he's put together—some with my help—but one book in particular snags my attention. *Auto Body Repair & Technology.*

Huh. I reckon I never realized he had such serious plans for his truck.

"I'm fixin' to get a shower and head to work, so..." Hollis trails off, and I realize I'm lingering, holding him up.

I spin around. "I'm sorry. I guess the nervousness has frazzled my brain." I pluck an invisible piece of lint from my skirt. "I'll get out of your hair."

"Hey." I jerk my head up at the gentleness in his voice. His smile is the sweet, affectionate one I'm used to. "Get over here." Arms extended, he gestures for me to come toward him. I take the few steps necessary and am instantly enfolded in his arms.

I hold him tight, exhaling a long breath. Just a simple hug from him makes me less nervous.

Hollis presses his lips to my hair, and his voice is hushed when he speaks. "You'll be just fine tonight. Don't stress over it."

I nod, brushing my cheek against his cotton shirt. "Okay."

When his arms drop from around me, internally, I pout, wanting to hug him a little while longer.

I force myself to step back. "Thanks, Hollis."

His lips tilt up. "Yes, ma'am." He winks. "Anytime."

"Thanks for agreein' to double with us." I nudge Hollis' shoulder as we walk to Dallas' SUV parked in my driveway.

We've survived a million camera flashes from our parents, who are now waving goodbye to us.

"I'm so excited!" Kelsey, Hollis' date, practically squeals. She loops her arm through his, and a sharp flash of unease ricochets through me. Probably because she's not good enough for him. I mean, *bless her heart*, the poor girl practically sleeps with anything with a male appendage.

Regardless of his date's questionable choices in allowing just anyone to frequent her lady parts, she chose a shirt that molds the muscles he's gained through football conditioning and weight lifting.

"You ready for tonight?" Dallas holds open the passenger door, and his boyish smile makes my stomach flip—in a good way. He's cute and muscular without being too intimidating.

It also helps that my mother approves of him. When I told her Hollis and his date were tagging along, her expression looked like she just bit into the sourest of lemons—like she normally looks whenever I mention him. Emphasizing Dallas would be my date and Hollis and Kelsey were just tagging along helped to smooth things over with my mother considerably.

"I'm ready. *Buuut*"—I drag out the word playfully—"are you sure you're ready for my amazin' dance moves?" I move my hands in a terrible rendition of the robot.

Good Lord *Almighty*, I'm a dork. But Dallas laughs, and when he smiles down at me, it's not in a patronizing way. He looks at me the way I've been hoping a guy would look at me someday. Like I'm pretty even though I have these awful braces, and despite the fact that I don't have many girlfriends because, well...most of them I really can't stand.

He grins wider, and I find myself envious of his perfect teeth. "I didn't realize I'd have to break out the classic moves tonight."

I try my hand at flirting and lean in closer. "I can't wait to—"

"What's this about classic moves?"

Dallas and I whip our heads around in surprise at Hollis' voice. The expression on his face is one I don't recognize. His eyes seem to silently challenge Dallas in an odd sort of stare-down.

Attempting to lighten the mood, I force a smile. "We're talkin' about awesome dance moves. Like this one." I attempt the robot again, and this time, Hollis' lips curve upward in a hint of a smile.

"Better watch it, or you'll be challenged to a dance-off tonight." His eyes crinkle at the corners.

"Bring it on." I laugh and slip inside the vehicle. Dallas closes the door and strides around to get in. Hollis sees Kelsey in on her side before getting in and buckling up.

Dallas backs out of the drive and heads toward our school gymnasium. My stomach flips with nervous anticipation of tonight. I've never actually been on a date before, so this is all new to me. I know, Hollis tried to simplify things for me earlier, but now, it doesn't seem so cut and dry to me.

When Dallas glances over with a shy smile and slides his right hand over the console, tipping his palm up, it takes me a second to realize he's waiting for me to put my hand in his.

Our palms touch and he closes his fingers around mine. His

hand isn't clammy or cold. His thumb lightly grazes my hand, and it's actually...nice.

I relax in my seat, and when Coldplay's song "Yellow" plays on the radio, I face the window. I know I'm a terrible singer and can't carry a tune in a bucket, so I don't want to subject anyone to my off-tune singing.

When the radio's volume increases slightly, I turn to find Dallas' thumb poised over the button on his steering wheel. He starts singing along, and I'm surprised he knows the words. Not only that, but he's not the greatest singer either. Actually, he's probably worse than me.

He glances over at me while singing softly, and his shy smile has me matching it with my own.

"Good thing they've got money because, good Lord in heaven, those voices..." Kelsey mutters snidely from the back seat, but I don't pay her any attention. Hollis' voice rumbles, but his voice is too low to decipher his words.

It doesn't matter, though. Because Dallas has me thinking that I might just have this whole dating thing under control.

9

HOLLIS

AFTER THE DANCE

"You're home early." My mom sneers when I walk into the kitchen to grab a glass of water. "Did she finally realize you're trash?"

I should be used to her nasty jabs by now, but they continue to find their target. I refuse to acknowledge her, hoping she'll lose interest and go back to whatever she was doing while I was gone.

With a glass in my hand, I press it against the dispenser on the refrigerator door and fill it with water, trying to buy myself time. To try to calm the intense anxiety rushing through me.

I should know better. Because nothing stops her from spewing her hate.

"Did that little whore buy that shirt for you?" She practically spits out the words, and when I turn around, my grasp on the glass is so tight, I'm surprised it doesn't shatter. She moves closer, and that's when I catch a whiff of it.

Alcohol.

My eyes widen in surprise even though I reckon I shouldn't be. Not when it comes to her.

"You probably let her pay for everythin', huh?"

My lips flatten. "That's kinda the point behind the Sadie Hawkins dance. The girls ask the guys and pay for everythin'." My tone is dull, and I'm not sure why I even offer up the information.

She steps even closer, and the stench of her breath—staleness intermixed with whatever liquor she's gotten into—makes my stomach roil. "Bet you gave her somethin' in return, huh?"

I clench my teeth so hard it's a wonder my molars don't crack. Instead of responding, I chug the water and set the glass on a coaster on the table for later.

As soon as I set it down, she grabs it with more quickness than I'd expect from someone who's been drinking. With the glass in her hand, she holds it chest level before letting go, and it shatters to the floor at our feet.

I stay stock-still, frozen to the spot. I swear she's getting worse and more unstable with her moods. I'm never sure what'll set her off.

I mean, obviously, *I'm* always a factor, but she's never gone this far before.

I watch cautiously as she bends down, swaying slightly, and grabs one of the larger pieces of broken glass. Part of me screams internally to move away, but my feet won't budge.

She holds up the shard of glass between us, unaware she's cut herself, and blood trickles down her index finger. Her face is a mottled red, angry, and sneering. "You think you're good enough for her?" She raises the glass higher, closer to my neck. "You're wrong. You'll never be good enough for 'em. You'll always be the poor Barnes boy."

Hatred fills each word that falls from her lips, and I despise how they hit that insecure part of me that's buried deep.

I force the words out as calmly as I can while her glassy eyes hold mine. "I get it. I'm not good enough. I'm trash. But"—I lean in closer, daring her to make a move—"what does that make you?"

Our eyes clash in their own silent war. I'll never understand why she hates me. How a mother could hate her own son without any justified reason. Why I don't measure up in her eyes. The hatred she has for me causes me to steer clear of her, but at times like this, when she seeks me out, I'm helpless to do much. Especially without Dad here as a buffer.

I get decent grades. I don't get into trouble. I have a job. I'm not a slob, and I help out around the house. I've done nothing to deserve this kind of treatment, let alone her venom-filled words.

After what's probably less than a minute but feels like eons, I break eye contact and turn to leave the kitchen. To get as far away from her as possible.

It happens so fast, the pain doesn't immediately register when she does it. The wetness, however, does.

I stare down in shock at where she's sliced my forearm, exposed by my rolled-up sleeves.

What the fuck?!

My eyes cut to hers. Without even a trace of emotion on her face, her fingers release the glass, and she turns and staggers out of sight. Dazed, I grab some paper towels to blot my arm, then pick up and toss the larger pieces of glass in the trash. I'll need to sweep the floor to get up the small pieces. Dad doesn't need to deal with this when he gets home.

He's been pulling extra hours lately. A part of me wonders if he's avoiding Mom. He keeps shoving a little bit of money at me when she's not around, quietly saying, "Put it aside for the work you're plannin' on doin' for your truck."

I manage to toss most of the glass in the trash quickly enough before it's time to blot at my arm again. *Dammit.* I take a closer look after applying pressure to it. The cut doesn't look deep enough to need stitches, but I definitely need to clean and bandage it.

My phone vibrates in my back pocket, and I pray it's not Kelsey. I dropped her off at her house, barely escaping with my pants still fastened. Talk about being a little too free with her body. That girl's like a freaking succubus.

Carefully letting go of the wad of paper towels I'm holding against my arm, I slide my phone from my pocket and look at the screen.

Shit.

Magnolia: Can I meet you in the treehouse?

I hesitate, wincing, and press the button. Lowering my voice to a hushed whisper, I leave a voice text.

"I can't. Had a little accident in the kitchen and have to do some first aid on my arm." I lift my thumb from the record button and press *Send*.

I feel like asking why she's texting me when she should be with Dallas. Most everyone else is probably still making out tonight—if not more.

I was doing exactly that earlier before I realized I was just going through the motions. Kelsey might be a sure thing, and all the guys will assume I scored with her, but they don't know that I'm still a virgin.

Maybe it's stupid and cheesy as hell, but I don't want my first time to be hurried on the girl's couch with someone who treats sex like a fast-food drive-through operation. I want it to be at least a *little* special.

Hell, maybe hanging around Magnolia's made me some sort of pansy cheeseball.

Magnolia: I'm coming over. Is your front door unlocked?

I press the record button again as I quietly walk toward the door. "It is now. I'll be in the bathroom." Normally, when my mom gets like this, she hides away in her room afterward, but I'll stay alert, just in case. The last thing I want is for Magnolia to get caught in the cross fire.

Magnolia: On my way.

I swear my best friend moves at the speed of light because I'm setting the peroxide, antibiotic ointment, and bandages on the small vanity when the faint sound of her footsteps trails down the hall. The blood has clotted, but I know the peroxide will upset things again. I'm not looking forward to that *or* the sting.

Magnolia comes into view, concern written all over her face. She steps inside the postage stamp-sized bathroom and closes the door behind her, locking it. Her eyes shift to my forearm before flicking up to meet my gaze.

"Let me help," she says softly.

I merely nod and take a seat on the closed toilet lid with my arm draped over the small lip of the sink so the peroxide will run off my arm and down the drain. I bite back a hiss when the liquid hits my open wound, maintaining my stare on the scuffed baseboard a few inches from my feet.

"Are you gonna tell your dad?" Her eyes dart to mine, and I shake my head.

"He's got enough to worry about with the extra shifts."

Her lips press together in a firm line, and I know she's disappointed with my answer, but this is something I won't budge on. Mom's always been like this. Sure, she crossed a line tonight, but I'm sixteen. I can handle it. No, I didn't handle things well tonight, but she caught me off guard. At least now I know what she's capable of.

Quickly enough, Magnolia has me bandaged and replaces the supplies beneath the sink. She turns to face me, and the weight of her gaze is so heavy, it nearly suffocates me. I avoid her eyes. What guy wants to share a story like this with a girl, let alone a girl who happens to be his best friend? The girl he's been reminded time and again he's not good enough for?

"Are you okay, aside from this?" Out of my periphery, I see her wave, gesturing to my bandaged arm.

I nod slowly.

"Do you need to...clean anythin' else?"

I blow out a long breath before I rise, still avoiding meeting her eyes like it's my job. "I need to sweep the kitchen floor. I didn't get a chance to before..."

She presses a palm against my chest when I move forward, intent on escaping the bathroom. "I'll do it, Hollis."

I give a terse shake of my head. "No. It's my mess. I'll clean it up."

Her sigh is loud. Then she catches me by surprise by reaching up to frame my face with her hands, forcing me to meet her eyes. The blue color seems darker, stormy almost, with both worry and a fierceness that's all Magnolia.

"Hollis, let me help you." She softens her voice. "Please."

I press my lips thin before I finally answer with, "Okay." My voice sounds small, like a child's, and I hate it.

Seeming relieved by my answer, she carefully raises my bandaged arm to press a featherlight kiss to it. A wistful smile tugs at the edges of her mouth. "Just kissin' it to make it better."

I'm speechless. My throat has an enormous boulder wedged in it. How does this girl know just what I need even when *I'm* not sure?

What's worse is, I can't recall a time when my own mother ever kissed my scrapes or cuts. When I needed stitches in my eyebrow, Dad was the one who stayed by my side, distracting me with laughter and the most random stories.

It hits me that someday, Magnolia will be someone's mom. And she'll be a great one. She won't hesitate to kiss hurts and make them better with love.

It's crazy, but right now, the cut on my arm stings a little less because of her kiss.

She releases me and turns to the door. When her palm rests on the doorknob, I stop her with a hand at the base of her spine. With a quick flick of the light switch, we're cloaked in darkness.

"Thanks, Shortcake." I hope she knows just how much I appreciate her right now. How I'd be lost right now without her here to anchor me.

She doesn't turn around, but I hear the affection in her voice when she unlocks the door and tugs it open.

"Anytime."

Once Magnolia helps me clean the kitchen free of any traces of what happened earlier, we grab the small space heater from Dad's shed and bring it with us in the treehouse and plug it in. She pulls out the rolled-up thermal sleeping bags from the corner shelf and lays them out atop the cushions on the floor.

Wordlessly, we remove our shoes and slide inside the sleeping bags. She turns on her side to face me. With my bandaged arm at my side opposite of her, I slide my other hand beneath my head to stare up at the wooden ceiling.

She slides closer, settling her head on my chest, draping an arm over my middle. "You can always talk to me." Her whispered words seem to echo around us.

I want to tell her, but I'm ashamed. I'm also afraid if I tell her what Mom said, she'll agree and confess she's realized she deserves a better best friend than me.

Instead, I turn the tables on her.

"Why'd you come home so early?" I murmur, trying to keep any edge from my tone. "Thought you'd be makin' out with Dallas for most of the night."

When she doesn't answer me, my entire body tenses, muscles going stiffer than a board. *Dammit*, I hate the idea of him touching her. It sucked just watching him hold her hand on the way to the dance. The sight of that alone had me nearly puking in the back seat.

"I did for a little bit," she finally answers.

Bile rises in my throat, and I work hard to calm the urge to be sick. I don't say anything; just wait her out.

Because I know Magnolia, and there's more.

"I just didn't wanna do too much, you know? I wanted to end the night on a good note. So, we kissed for a while, and that was it."

I bite the inside of my cheek as I mull over her words. Finally, I ask, "Are you goin' to see him again?"

It wouldn't be the end of the world. I mean, Dallas is a million times more decent than Ashton, after all.

No one will ever be good enough for my Magnolia, though. I've come to realize that. She's too special. Too incredible and kind.

"I think so." She shifts to peer at me, and I look down. Our faces are so close and I wish I could see more, but without the small light on and only the moonlight gleaming through the tiny window, she's more shadows than anything.

"He was a gentleman tonight?" There's a steely undertone in my voice, but I don't care if she notices. There'll be hell to pay if he was anything less than respectful.

The smile is obvious in her voice. "Yes, Hollis."

"Good."

She shifts back, her cheek against my chest, and we lie in comfortable silence for a while. I let my eyes fall closed as her nearness comforts me and helps me shrug off the painful scene from earlier.

"You should set your alarm, Shortcake."

"I did." Her voice is sleepy, and her words have a faint slur to them. "Just wanna lie with you a little while longer."

I release a long, slow exhale. When I whisper, I think it's more for myself than her. "When you start datin' and get a boyfriend, you know we won't be able to do this anymore."

She doesn't respond, and I assume she's fallen asleep.

Until a few long moments pass, and I hear, "Love you, Hollis."

The combined warmth of the sleeping bag, space heater, and Magnolia curled up against me have lulled me into a relaxed, sleepy state. My lips curve up slightly, and I whisper back, "But not like that."

10

MAGNOLIA

JUST SHY OF EIGHTEEN
SENIOR YEAR OF HIGH SCHOOL

"But—"

My mother cuts me off with a sharp, dismissive wave of her hand. "Magnolia Mae, we've been over this." Her eyes narrow and her mouth purses. "No."

It's unlike me to rock the boat, but this? This is unacceptable.

Which is why I persist.

"But Hollis is my best *friend*," I plead. "There'll be others from my class, so why is it such a big deal?"

She turns her head to stare up at the ceiling as though asking for divine intervention and mutters, "You're about to make me lose my religion, young lady." When her eyes land on me, anger radiates from her perfect-from-a-spa-day pores. "He doesn't belong here with us."

Us. Meaning people with money. It's ridiculous that he lives directly behind us, yet an invisible line separates the wealthier homes from ones like his. An invisible line that seems to dictate who's allowed to be friends, too, according to my mother.

I'd stupidly thought she'd get over this. That she'd finally realize Hollis isn't just a boy who lives in a house on the other side of that "line," but that he's a good person and that's what should matter. She's claimed, time and again, that she's "allowed" me to keep up the "mismatched friendship" because Roy had suggested it could be seen as an act of charity by others.

Since Dallas is in the picture, it seems she's had her fill of this sort of "charity."

"You shouldn't even bother with him anyhow." She turns away and busies herself with organizing her purse contents. She's about to leave to go to a Women's League tea.

"You have Dallas now." She slides her purse straps over her arm and straightens. "He's a nice young man. Comes from a good family."

Translation: His family has money.

Don't get me wrong, I like Dallas. A lot. We're good together. He supported me when I ran for Class President and celebrated my victory, and I did the same for him when he was elected Vice President. We've manned a bunch of successful fundraisers for our school. And yes, she's right about him being a nice young man, but sometimes...I'm not sure he's what *I* want.

Heck, there are times I'm not the least bit sure what I want.

But on the nights when a text message comes through and Hollis shows up to help me out of my window, and we sneak away to the treehouse to talk about anything and everything, I know I want *that*.

I've come to terms that Hollis doesn't see me as a potential girlfriend, especially since I've kept him in the "friend zone" for so long. I'm not sure I could ever be brave enough to try for more. Not only that, but I never want to risk ruining our friendship on a whim that we could have more.

But when we're together, just the two of us, I know that's what I want with a guy. The easiness. The way we can talk about anything that comes up. The lack of judgment. The understanding. The camaraderie.

I want all of it. I just wish Dallas could be the one to give it to me.

"I need to go. Tell Roy I'll be home later." Before I can form a response, she's already out the door, pulling it shut behind her.

My shoulders slump, and a tiny voice in the recesses of my mind lectures, *No slouchin', young lady. Shoulders back, spine straight, chin up. Balance that invisible book atop your head.*

Someday, I hope to permanently get rid of that voice. I amble down the hallway to my room and drape myself across the bed with an inward groan. I stare up at the smooth white ceiling and exhale slowly.

Blindly, I reach for my cell phone that's lying near the edge of the mattress. I scroll through my text messages, pausing over Dallas'.

Dallas: I can't wait to give you your present this weekend.

Dallas: Looks like we may finish up earlier than I thought. Good thing since word is they're backed up just before the back nine. Care to go on a date with your boyfriend tonight?

Dallas is participating in the local golf tournament with his dad. It's a big deal around here since it's played on the LPGA course at the country club, and they raise money for a designated charity. Although, to be honest, the bulk of the people I know who take part do it to see and be seen rather than for the good cause.

My thumb hovers over the keys, and I hesitate to type a response. Instead, I back out of those texts and look at Hollis'.

Hollis: A little birdie reminded me someone's birthday's coming up soon.

I can't help the slow-forming smile that spreads.

Me: Talking to birds these days, Barnes? Weird.

Hollis: LOL.

Me: Still working?

Hollis is a caddy for one of the bigshots who frequents the country club where he works. After he finishes caddying, he'll pull a long shift and assist with the clean-up once the tournament ends. I can't imagine how exhausted he'll be after being out on the golf course, hauling heavy clubs around in the heat and humidity with the sun beating down on him. Speaking of sunshine...

Hollis: Yes, ma'am. They're backed up on the first hole on the back nine.

Me: You'd better be reapplying sunscreen.

Hollis: Worried about me, Shortcake?

Me: Always.

Hollis: Promise I'm reapplying.

Hollis: Gotta run. We're finally moving.

Me: Hydrate and make sure you don't get sunburnt. Love you.

Hollis: But not like that. ;)

I stare down at his final text and wish he were here so I could talk to him. I know he'd never be upset with me because of my mother's idiotic beliefs about him, but it would still hurt him. I wish there was a way to get around it somehow.

I jerk upright as soon as I hear Roy come through the front door and call my name. "Magnolia? Come here, please."

My feet carry me to the bedroom door in a flash, and I tug it open, rushing down the hall to meet him. "Yes, sir?"

He shuffles through the Saturday mail, not paying me attention, and merely tips his head to the side. "That came for you."

It takes me a moment to realize what he's gesturing to. A plain brown cardboard box sits on the entryway table. It's probably about two feet wide and rectangular. I step over to it and peer at it curiously. It's addressed to me, but it doesn't have a return address.

"Thanks, Roy." I heft it in my arms, surprised by how light-weight it is. I start in the direction of my room again but stop and turn back slowly. "Um, I have a question for you."

He raises his head, his dark eyes meeting mine, concern suddenly washing over his features. "Is somethin' wrong?"

"Well," I hedge, "I wanted to see if it would be okay if Hollis came to my birthday party this weekend."

His brows slant together. "Your mother told you no already, didn't she?"

I wince. "I'm sorry. I just thought—"

"Magnolia Mae," he reprimands, "you should know better than to try to play your mother and me against one another."

"I know, and I'm sorry," I rush on, my words hurried. "But it's important to me. He's my best friend, and he's not a bad person like Mother wants to believe."

His expression tenses in thought. "You're still with the Hampstead boy, right?"

I barely refrain from rolling my eyes. He always calls him the Hampstead boy instead of Dallas. While it *is* annoying, it's never condescending. Mainly because Dallas' dad has been a campaign contributor, and Roy doesn't want to rock the boat and risk not having that cushion of support.

Instead of giving in to the urge to roll my eyes, I straighten. "Yes, sir. Dallas is my boyfriend." Silently tacked on is something like, *So there's no reason for anyone to worry about Hollis.*

Roy runs a hand over his thinning hair—it has to be stressful being in the public eye and responsible for decisions that affect voters—and regards me much like a detective might study a suspect taken into custody for a bank robbery. I school my expression and hope it appears calm and innocent.

He appears to mull over the idea. "I suppose it would look good to have him here," he muses, more to himself than me. "Another act of goodwill to those less fortunate."

Finally, he nods with an, "Okay, fine." As soon as my lips part to thank him, he cuts me off with a stern, "But you'd better not make me regret this."

I nod, hugging the box to my chest. "Yes, sir." Then I add a quick, "Thank you."

He copies my nod, and then he's off, down the hall toward his office to...do more work. That always puzzles me. Why come home from work only to do more work? Why not stay and get as much of it done before calling it a night?

That's your future, an inner voice taunts. One that sounds suspiciously similar to my mother's. I shove it aside.

Then I go back to my room, set the box on my bed, and quickly send two texts.

Me: Don't forget about my party on Sunday, mister. Best friends are required to attend.

Then for the second, I type:

Me: I'd love to.

My boyfriend's response is quick.

Dallas: I'll pick you up at seven. Can't wait to see you.

I text an emoticon of a kissing face and set my phone down. Grabbing a pair of scissors sitting in the never-used mug on my dresser that holds a few pens and a Sharpie, I slice open the box.

Pressing the flaps aside, I find a large plain white paper folded in half with my name on it. I immediately recognize the handwriting and unfold it.

Happy Birthday, Shortcake!

I wasn't sure if I'd get to see you on your birthday since I know your mom has strict rules about the guest list and because I'm sure Dallas has planned something cool for y'all to do to celebrate. So, I wanted to make sure you'd get my present safe, sound, and covertly (and I planned it around your mom's schedule).

I laugh softly, recalling Hollis asking me all sorts of questions. I'd remarked how weird it was that he was suddenly so interested in my mother's whereabouts.

I continue reading.

I know we're probably getting too old for model car kits and all, but it made me think of you and Dallas.

Hope you enjoy.

Love,

Hollis

P.S. I know, I know. But not like that.

I sit for a moment, rereading the note and cherishing every word while simultaneously feeling shame wash over me. He knew my mother wouldn't let him come to my party on Sunday. He knew, yet he still planned ahead to make sure he wouldn't miss out on giving me this present.

I trace the pad of my index finger over the firm, masculine slashes of ink on the paper. My heart actually hurts to think about him sitting down to write this. I know he's a guy and all, but I know without a doubt that I'd be hurting if I were in his position and his parents refused to let me attend his birthday party.

I draw in a deep breath before setting the note aside carefully and reaching in the box to withdraw an odd-shaped object wrapped in paper printed with repeated, "Happy Birthday!" and balloons.

When I set the gift on my lap, I don't tear into it. Instead, I peer at it, wanting to savor this moment.

As seniors in high school, there's no telling what will happen once we graduate and head off to college. Things will inevitably change even though that's the last thing I want in some ways, but in others, what I want most.

I wrinkle my brow, trying to guess what he's given me, and come up with absolutely no guesses. Finally, I pluck at an edge of the paper and rip it slowly with equal parts trepidation and excitement. When I reveal about a two-inch portion of the gift, my breath lodges in my throat.

He remembered.

PAST
EIGHT YEARS OLD

"Now, y'all kiss and live happy ever after," Hollis mutters, sounding grossed out.

"It's *happily* ever after, Hollis," I correct.

He gives me a good dose of side-eye—I'd be grounded for at least a week if I did even a smidge of that with my mother—and waves a hand. "And y'all drive off into the sunset with tin cans hangin' from the back of your pink convertible with a *Just Married* sign."

There's no excitement in his voice, which is just disappointing. What good is a best friend if they can't play pretend wedding with you, and do it *well*?

Hollis must notice my disappointment because he nudges my shoulder with his. "I'm kiddin'. You'll make the prettiest bride anyone's ever seen."

I press my lips together, doubtful. "Not with this I won't." I point at the gap between my front teeth. My shoulders slump and the only reason I let them is because we're inside the tree-house. If my mother caught me, I'd get another lecture on "bein' a lady with perfect posture."

"Magnolia." Hollis' serious voice has me lifting my eyes to his. "It's the truth."

I cock my head to the side. A half-smile threatens to break free. "You reckon so?"

He nods, his eyes crinkling at the corners. "Sure do."

I sit and stare at the pink convertible—the same one he'd given me as a present all those years ago and helped me build. The very one Mother had thought nothing of tossing away.

When Miranda had said she'd salvaged many of my belongings, this had still been missing. I hadn't asked our housekeeper about it because Lord knew she'd done me a huge favor as it was in rescuing what she had. But my heart had cracked, knowing it was gone.

Now, though, I see that he repaired it. Tears prick at my eyes as I peer closer and notice the fine cracks and where it must have been glued back together and repainted. The tedious work it must have been so hard to do...

Seated in the convertible are small plastic dolls—upper halves only—that appear secured in place by glue. The female has blond hair, long like mine, and there's a bit of a garish smile painted on her mouth. A dark line bisects her front teeth, much like my own former gap. The male doll in the driver's seat has blond hair, like Dallas, and a wide toothy grin.

From the back bumper of the car, what are supposed to be tin cans dangle from thin fishing line. *Just Married* is written on the back bumper. My eyes pore over every inch of it, amazed that he's gone to such trouble. When I notice the small note carefully taped to the glove box, I can't possibly imagine what else he's thought of.

When I open the note, only two words are written there: **Look underneath.**

As soon as I raise the car to look at what's beneath it, my best friend's name spills from my lips in a ragged whisper.

Because taped to the bottom of the car is a package of Pop Rocks.

Cherry, of course.

11

HOLLIS

SENIOR YEAR OF HIGH SCHOOL
NOVEMBER

"YOU SURE DALLAS IS OKAY WITH THIS?"

I'm not normally a jealous guy, but I'd sure as hell want to spend time with my girl after winning a rivalry game.

Our schedule had to be modified, and we're playing later in the season than usual since a nasty tropical storm hit weeks earlier and postponed a few games.

Magnolia waves me off. "I told him this was our tradition." She grins her perfect smile at me. No gap in sight these days. I still get a sharp twinge in my chest at the absence of it. "Plus, we're runnin' out of time to do this."

Her eyes betray that smile, though. She's scared about heading off to college. I can't lie; it's intimidating as hell. The only thing slightly comforting is that we put in early decision applications to Auburn University, so we're due to hear something soon. Our school counselor and the rep from Auburn made it sound like it's a done deal, but I'm not banking on anything until I have confirmation.

With the number of students on campus, there's a good chance Magnolia and I may never cross paths, but just knowing she'll be around is comforting somehow.

"Only one more game before the end of the season." Her sigh has a hint of sadness.

I wink. "But we're movin' on to bigger and better things."

She smooths down her shirt—it's a newer one she made to include my number and Dallas'.

I'd be lying if I said it didn't bother me a little to share shirt space with the guy. It's dumb as hell, but I've gotten used to having her as my number-one fan and solo cheerleader. Then again, I really can't complain. If I have to share any part of Magnolia with someone, I'm glad it's with a guy like Dallas.

Magnolia's still avoiding my gaze. "So..." She finally flicks her eyes up to mine. "What's goin' on with you and Sarah Jane?"

Sarah Jane and I dated for a few months and only recently decided to cool things off. She's sweet, and her family doesn't care about what kind of house I live in or how much money we have. Her parents are both teachers at schools just across the bay in Mobile.

I toy with the sugar packets in the small dish on our table. "We agreed it's probably not smart to start college when we're in a high school relationship, so we ended things.

"She's fixin' to go to art school up in New York." I lift a shoulder in a half-shrug. "I mean, we'll be overwhelmed by a lot of things changin', so it doesn't make sense to let things get more serious." Another shrug. "We were never head over heels or anythin'. She's awesome, but it's never been more than that." I hesitate before asking, "What about y'all?"

She wrinkles her nose and glances around before leaning in closer. With her voice lowered, she confesses, "Actually, he, uh, said he wants to stay together."

She seems shocked by my lack of surprise. I can't help but chuckle. "Shortcake, you must've seen that comin'."

Her eyes widen. "Not at all."

I shake my head. "He's been head over heels for you from the start."

She cocks her head to the side. "You really think so?"

Something in her tone has me frowning and leaning forward to rest my forearms on the table. "You don't?"

She looks away, focusing on something through the window. "I don't know." When she turns back, her blue eyes lock with mine, and they're troubled. "It's probably dumb, but I want to be with a guy who looks at me like..."

"Like...?" I prompt.

Her gaze suddenly shifts to something over my shoulder, her lips parting slightly.

"What's wrong?" I shift, about to crane my neck to see what's caught her eye, but she grabs my arm. Clenching it tight, she hisses, "Don't turn around!"

I stiffen. What the hell?

Blue eyes meet mine, and the sadness in the depths acts like a fist clenching the center of my chest. "What is it?" I demand.

"Dallas walked in, and he's talkin' with Kendall and the new girl."

"O-kay," I draw out the word slowly. I'm not sure why this is such big news. I mean, sure, our classmate Kendall and the new girl—Charlotte, I think?—are both pretty, but I feel like I'm missing something here.

Her troubled eyes act like tractor beams to mine. I can't look away. "Right now, Dallas is lookin' at her like that."

I'm lost. "At who? Like what?"

She heaves out a breath, and her eyes flick back over my shoulder. "At Kendall. Like..." She swallows hard, releasing my arm, and leans back in the booth. Her shoulders slump. "Like he's lookin' at the most amazin' girl he's ever met." Our eyes lock. "He's never looked at me like that."

I turn slowly to see for myself. Surely, she's just exaggerating. I mean, she's never been one to do that before, but this is her first real boyfriend, so she—

As soon as my gaze finds them, my stomach twists. Because she's right. Dallas' expression is different.

Kendall waves to someone a few feet away and leaves Dallas and Charlotte. He must feel the weight of my eyes on him because he turns his head slightly and catches sight of me. He nods with an easy smile, his eyes quickly finding Magnolia, and that smile widens affectionately. And I realize something.

He's clueless.

I turn back to face Magnolia, who appears queasy.

"Hey." I slide a hand across the table, palm upturned, and she limply places hers in it. "Dallas adores you. That's what I do know." After a moment, I admit softly, "But I see it, too." I give her hand a quick squeeze before releasing it.

She twists her lips and nods. "I shouldn't be upset because I don't feel that with him. But seein' it with my own eyes?" She shakes her head, a sad uptick of her mouth. "It stings a little."

"I can tell you one thing for certain."

Her eyes flick past me, and she straightens so I know Dallas is approaching our booth. "What's that?"

"Dallas doesn't realize it."

I barely finish before her boyfriend sidles up at the end of our table. With an easiness only a guy who's been dating a girl can have, he dips his head to press a light kiss to her lips. Then he straightens and gestures to the girl a few steps away.

"This is Charlotte. She just transferred here from Birmingham."

The new girl smiles shyly and steps forward, waving at Magnolia and me. "Hi." Magnolia and I introduce ourselves.

"I used to go to Collier." I offer up my old elementary school in Birmingham. God knows, it sucks being the new kid, and I can't stomach the idea of her feeling more uncomfortable.

Her smile is a bright reward. "I went there for a while, too."

I suddenly realize I'm being rude and shove over in the booth seat, gesturing for her to join me. She hesitates visibly, her eyes darting over to Magnolia. Just then, my best friend slides over, and Dallas drops down beside her.

Charlotte gingerly slips into the spot next to me, and it's only now that I realize how intimate this is. How my larger, more muscular frame takes up more than my allotted space compared to her petite one.

Dallas and Magnolia are caught up in their own conversation, so I take advantage of it to study Charlotte. The light brown color of her hair reminds me of caramel, and her eyes nearly match it. Her smile is shy, and she practically radiates sweetness.

"How are you likin' it here so far?"

She winces. "We've moved around some for my dad's job, and it can be hard, but here...it's different." She lifts a shoulder in a half-shrug. "Just hard to adjust sometimes."

Her eyes survey me, before she leans in closer to whisper conspiratorially, "I feel like this place is like *The Hunger Games*, but between the kids with money and those without."

She catches me by surprise, and I tip my head back on a laugh. Her mouth spreads into a wide grin, brown eyes sparkling with amusement.

I lower my voice. "You're in good company then. Because I'm basically the male version of Katniss."

"That so?" The corners of her eyes crinkle even more when her smile widens.

Damn, she's cute. "Yes, ma'am."

"You don't mind if I steal her away, do you?"

Dallas' voice interrupts, drawing my attention from Charlotte. He slides out from the booth. His eyes flick to Magnolia before returning to me. "I know this is y'all's night, but—"

"No worries," I interrupt. "Have fun."

Magnolia looks like she wants to protest, hesitating so slightly I doubt anyone else notices but me. Finally, she accepts his outstretched hand and slides out.

"Bye." Magnolia waves before Dallas tugs their joined hands, and they make their way out of the diner.

"So," Charlotte starts.

"So," I parrot back with a grin.

"You and Magnolia are...?"

"Best friends."

She seems to mull that over for a beat. "Huh." Then she tips her head to the side. "Nothing more?"

I shake my head while I'm simultaneously bombarded with the taunting echoed voices of Mrs. Barton and my own mom. *You're not good enough for her! You're trash!*

I inwardly shake them off.

"No, ma'am."

She props her chin in her hand and eyes me. "Girlfriend?"

Another shake of my head. "Not anymore."

One eyebrow arches in surprise. "Bad breakup?"

"No," I say with a little laugh. "We were never serious. Decided it's better to cool things off since we're headed in opposite directions after graduation."

"What're your plans?"

I lean back against part of the booth and window to angle myself to see her better. "I put in an early decision application with Auburn."

"Auburn's one of my first choices."

"Cool." We watch each other in silent appraisal. "So, tell me about Charlotte. What's she like?"

She ducks her chin slightly as if embarrassed and shrugs.

"Not much to tell. My family doesn't come from money, I'm not super girly, and I love cars."

A surprised half-laugh rushes out of me. "I think I just fell in love with you."

Charlotte snickers, and a faint blush spreads across her cheeks. "Whatever."

I stretch my long leg and nudge her flip-flop with mine. "You love cars, huh?"

She perks up, and the light in her eyes shows me that this is a passion of hers. "My dad restores cars in his spare time. He taught me everything I know."

I cock my head in interest. "So if I told you I just finished replacin' the carburetor and am workin' on replacin' the bumpers on my truck, you'd say…"

Unmistakable interest flashes in her eyes. "I'd ask if you'd be so kind as to let me look at it."

I turn in my seat and point out the window toward the parking lot. "See that third light post? There on the left? The blue truck parked underneath is mine."

Her face lights up while her eyes survey my truck. "A Chevy Silverado, huh?" Her gaze flicks to me. "V8? Four-wheel drive?"

"Yes, ma'am."

Her attention moves back to my truck. "Hard to tell for sure from here, but the body looks good."

"Wanna see under the hood?"

The way her eyes light up, you'd think I just told her she held the winning lottery ticket. "Could I?"

I nod and pull out my wallet, leaving enough cash to cover both Magnolia's and my food along with the tip. Even though she's dating Dallas, I still insist on paying when she's with me. It's tough to change a habit like that.

Charlotte slides out and stands, waiting for me. When I guide her out of the diner with my hand hovering at the base of her spine yet not touching, deep down it feels like I'm embarking on something new. Important. Exciting and a little intimidating.

Still, there's a small part of me that wishes Magnolia were here by my side.

12

HOLLIS

SENIOR YEAR OF HIGH SCHOOL
February

"Tell me again why you dragged me here?"

I slump into one of the cushy chairs arranged in a small semicircle a few feet away from the dressing rooms.

"Because I know you'll be honest with me. If I end up lookin' like an old hag, you'll let me know." Magnolia's voice carries from one of the changing rooms where she's trying on her prom dress now that the seamstress adjusted a few things.

I admit, I thought about the fact that my mom does that kind of work, but... Yeah. That wasn't happening. Not in a million years.

I stretch out my legs and cross them at the ankle. The young girl working here at the dress shop catches my eye and flashes me a flirty smile. I offer a polite one because even though I'm not interested, I'm not trying to be an ass.

Charlotte Benson and I have been... Well, I don't actually know what we've been doing. We decided not to label it right now, trying to be realistic with each of us heading off to college. But the past few months have been great.

She's smart, funny, doesn't get jealous of the fact that Magnolia's my best friend, is never demanding when it comes to my time and my job at the country club, and comes over and helps me work on the truck. She even had me bring it over to her place and got her dad to look at it.

He showed me the Chevelle he'd restored and went over the body work he'd done. Mr. Benson gave me a few tips, and then he and his wife insisted I stay for dinner. It was one of the best nights I'd had in a while, especially with my dad working so much and me trying to stay out of my mom's hair. Not to mention, it was the first time anyone had invited me over for dinner without it being a pity offer—like the time Mrs. Barton invited me over a few years back.

The Bensons are a good bunch, down to earth, and welcoming. It's probably from moving around for Mr. Benson's job as a high-level business consultant of some sort and trying to fit in every time.

Charlotte told me he has to wear a suit to work, but you'd never know it when he's at home. Every time I've been over, he's been in a pair of khakis, a polo shirt, and a nice pair of flip-flops. Totally laid-back.

They invited me over for Thanksgiving and Christmas—after Dad and I had our own low-key meal, of course. Mom's even more distant, and I'm pretty certain Dad's sleeping on the couch these days.

I discovered that when Charlotte and I got a little carried away with our make-out session one night. I came home well after curfew, and Dad was already snoring up a storm. I crept past him sprawled on the couch beneath the throw blanket.

After that, I started paying attention to the blanket normally folded and draped over the back of the couch. Every morning, I'd get up for school, and that thing was in a different spot.

When he began leaving his bed pillow on one end of the couch, that confirmed my suspicions. I wish I could help him somehow, but I've never understood their relationship or how a man could put up with someone like her.

It makes me even more grateful for Charlotte and her family. They've shown me what it could be like to be around welcoming and kind people. Even though Charlotte and I haven't mentioned the "L" word or anything, I've had random thoughts about what it would be like if we stayed together through college and got married. About holidays with the four of us together. How awesome that would be.

A jaw-breaking yawn hits me the instant Magnolia walks out of the dressing room in her prom dress, and I try to stifle it. I pulled a shift after school at the country club and headed straight over to spend the rest of my Friday night with Charlotte.

"What'd y'all do last night? Late night movie marathon or somethin'?" she asks, catching me mid-yawn.

I snap my mouth shut because Charlotte and I were definitely not paying attention to the movie playing on TV last night. A satisfied smirk tugs at my lips as a flashback hits me.

We'd been more daring than usual, but only because Mr. Benson went out of town for work and Mrs. Benson sleeps like the dead. Charlotte and I had experimented, showing each other what feels good, and I learned a lot about how to make a girl orgasm.

"Oh." Magnolia's single response, spoken with an odd heaviness, jerks me from my inner thoughts. She clears her throat and can't seem to look me in the eye. "Well, what do you think?"

I internally shake off my train of thought and blink, focusing on my best friend. "Whoa." My eyes go wide. "You look..." I trail off because I'm not sure what to say.

She glances down at herself, and it's plain to see the uncertainty written on her face. I shoot to my feet and draw to a stop when I'm only a few feet away.

"You're beautiful, Shortcake."

It's the God's honest truth. Dallas will be knocked stupid when he sees her in this dress. It's blue, strapless, has lace above the waist, and the rest of it has satiny folds. The color matches her eyes, and she looks like a princess.

Blue eyes meet mine with hesitation. "Really?"

I nod slowly. "Yes, ma'am."

With a weak smile, she glances down at herself, and I hate the doubt I see. I take her by the shoulders and gently turn her to face the mirrored wall. Standing at her back, my palms rest on her bare shoulders, and I lower my head to her ear and speak softly.

"You look beautiful, and Dallas won't know what hit him."

The tension in her features eases a little. "You sure it doesn't make me look—"

I cut her a sharp look. "Don't even mention that," I practically growl.

Her mother's been on a kick about Magnolia's weight, and it pisses me the hell off. She wants Magnolia to be the spitting image of herself, and it's never going to happen.

Magnolia clearly got most of her genes from her dad, and she's grown a little curvier lately. Not fat or unhealthy, but even so, her mom's response to it has been to lecture Magnolia about her eating and tell her she should cut back.

"You sure?" Her expression reflects uncertainty, and I hate it.

"As sure as I know there'll always be a redneck with a gun rack and the Confederate flag flyin' from the back of his truck."

This gets a little laugh out of her, and the tenseness eases a fraction.

"Remember what Shakespeare wrote, Shortcake." I silently

will her to believe my words. "About beauty bein' in the imperfections."

She slowly nods before whispering back, "Thanks, Hollis."

"Anytime." I move to drop my hands from her shoulders, but she stops me, placing hers over mine. Our eyes lock in the mirror, mine silently questioning.

"Will you save a dance for me?" Her question is so faint that I have to strain to hear her.

"Of course."

She smiles back as her hands release mine, and I step away.

While I wait for her to change back into her clothes, a text comes in from Charlotte.

Charlotte: Hey, handsome. Last night was amazing. Hope you're not too tired today. Let me know if you want me to bring you food for your lunch break later. Mom's making red beans and rice and her famous cornbread.

My stomach growls in response to her text. Good Lord, Mrs. Benson's cornbread is so good I could easily eat my weight in it. Just as I start to text back a *yes, please*, she sends another text.

Charlotte: P.S. I'm still smiling like a weirdo today. And tingling. Because of you last night.

Shit. Every molecule of my body ignites, thinking about last night. *Damn*. This girl's addictive.

"Everythin' okay?"

I jump in surprise at Magnolia's question, lose my grip on my phone, and end up juggling it to keep it from crashing to the floor. I finally manage to clutch at it clumsily.

My best friend eyes me like I'm one of the odd folks who jump the barricades during a Mardi Gras parade and risk getting run over by the floats just to nab beads or a moon pie. Then her eyes narrow on me.

"You look guilty." Her gaze darts to the phone in my hand. "What's goin' on?"

I do my best to act nonchalant. "Nothin'. Just a text from Charlotte." I shove the phone in my back pocket and hurriedly say, "All set?"

She nods quickly, raising one hand that holds the hanger of the garment bag. "All set."

Once we're in my truck and heading back to her house, she says, "Y'all seem to be doin' well." Her overly casual tone makes me uneasy for some reason.

"We're good. Just takin' it day by day." *Aside from last night, that is.* One edge of my lips tugs upward at the reminder.

"Are you still a virgin?"

If I hadn't already slowed to a stop at the four-way intersection, I'd have slammed on the brakes hard enough to give us whiplash. Making sure there aren't any cars behind me, I whip my head around to stare at her.

"*What?*"

She's as cool as a cucumber, sitting in the passenger seat like she didn't just blurt out a question like that.

"Are you still a virgin?"

Magnolia and I talk about anything and everything—that much is true—but ever since Dallas came into the picture and then Charlotte, things have shifted a bit. Which is why I'm caught off guard by her sudden interest in my sexual status.

I study her for a moment before I answer quietly. "Yes." My voice seems to echo within the truck cab. When she doesn't react or respond, I stare. "Are you askin' for a reason?"

"No." Her tone is defensive. "I just wondered."

I force a laugh, trying to inflect humor to detract from the awkwardness I'm feeling. "You're suddenly wonderin' whether I've had sex or not?"

She lets out an exasperated sound. "I was just askin'. Don't be gettin' a bee in your bonnet, Hollis Barnes."

I grin, shaking my head at her, and continue driving. When

she makes no move to say more, I prompt, "Well, go on. You can't just ask me if I'm a virgin and not offer up your own status."

She lets out a loud sigh. "Of course, I am."

I screw up my face in disbelief. "How is that an of course? You've been datin' Dallas for what? Almost two years?" I toss her a look of disbelief. "I honestly thought y'all would've done it by now."

I swear I can practically feel her prickle with defensiveness. Her voice takes on a prim and proper tone. "Just because people date in high school for a while doesn't mean they're fixin' to just...drop their drawers and knock boots."

God, she sounds like she belongs back in Scarlett O'Hara's day right now. So self-righteous, her Southern accent growing thicker.

"Well, then I reckon I should tell you we dropped our drawers last night, but no boots were a knockin'." I attempt a joke before realizing in horror what I've just confessed to.

Shit.

The silence is now deafening.

Finally, when Magnolia speaks, her voice sounds hollowed out and small. "I reckon that was a little more information than I needed."

I scrub a hand down my face, frantically scrambling for a way to salvage this conversation, but I come up empty. I pull in her driveway, then shift to put the truck in park. I always get out and open the door for her—her and Charlotte both, for that matter—but I stop with my fingers resting on the door handle, not yet pushing it open, and turn to blurt out, "I'm sorry, Shortca—"

"No worries! I've gotta go. Thanks for goin' with me." Then she bounds from the truck with a speed that rivals the time she ran the bases during her best hit at a baseball game one summer.

Leaving me sitting here with my hand still on the door handle.

I watch her go because that's all I can do. I'm not welcome in her house, even if I wanted to chase after her and apologize.

She disappears inside, and I back out of the drive to head around the corner and turn onto my street, making an immediate turn into my driveway.

As soon as I turn off the ignition, I let my head fall back against the headrest with a soft thump.

What a colossal mess.

13

MAGNOLIA

SENIOR YEAR OF HIGH SCHOOL
APRIL

IT TOOK A FEW DAYS FOR HOLLIS AND I TO GET BACK ON TRACK after that awkward conversation on the way home from the dress shop. I'm pretty darn certain every molecule in my body sighed in relief at getting my best friend back one hundred percent again.

Next month, we graduate. My mother's making me endure a final summer etiquette camp before I head off to college. I admit, I'm dreading it more than usual and not just because Lora Ann will be there, fresh with insults to sling at me like always. It's really because I don't want to miss out on this last summer with Hollis before everything changes. It sounds dramatic even to myself, but I feel it in my bones that once we head to Auburn, our friendship will shift. And that worries me.

I walk over to my bookshelf, my bare feet soundless on the plush carpeting. Reaching behind a large stack of books—collector's editions by Shakespeare and Hawthorne and other classics that my mother approves of—I withdraw what's tucked behind them and hold it in my hands like a priceless treasure.

In a way, it is.

The model car Hollis repaired for me is one of the sweetest gifts I'd ever received. All the expensive gifts in the world pale in comparison to this. Because not only did he give me something meaningful, but he also committed time in making it for me.

With a wistful smile, I replace it where it stays hidden and safe. Just as I back away and move to check my reflection in the floor-length mirror, my phone vibrates from where I left it on my bedside table. I hurry over to it, expecting a text from Dallas telling me he's on his way. He should be here soon since we're all meeting here to catch the limo to the dance.

Instead of Dallas' name, though, it's Hollis.

Hollis: Psst! Open your bedroom window.

I frown, wondering what the heck he's up to. When I raise the blinds and see Hollis standing outside my window in his tux, all breath lodges in my chest.

His easy grin makes me smile. When he holds out his arms and does a slow turn for me, like he's modeling, I roll my eyes with a little laugh before quietly unlatching and sliding open my window.

"What are you doin'?" I hiss quietly.

He moves closer and gestures for me to step aside. His hands grip my windowsill, and far too flawlessly, he swings his tall body into my bedroom. As soon as he plants his shiny black shoes on my carpet, he smooths down his tux.

"How do I look?"

Handsome as all get-out. That's my initial thought. It's funny how you can practically spend every day with someone yet not really see them. Every so often, I'm jarred by the fact that with each day, Hollis becomes less of a boy and more like a man.

His shoulders are broader, his muscles thicker, but not in a bodybuilder kind of way, and he's grown even cuter. Dark scruff that would make most guys look messy and unkempt sprinkles his jawline, but it actually makes Hollis more attractive.

"You look handsome."

His eyes sparkle before he surveys me from head to toe. Something indecipherable flickers in his gaze before he twists his lips in a disappointed frown.

"What?" I glance down at myself, wondering what could possibly be wrong.

"Somethin's just not right." He shakes his head. "You can't go to prom like this."

Alarm spreads through me. "Wh—" My response is cut short at the sight of what he pulls from his pants pocket.

A packet of cherry Pop Rocks.

I deflate in relief and swat at his chest playfully. "Hollis Barnes!"

His wide toothy grin is infectious, and he snakes an arm around my waist to tug me in for a hug. He ducks his head and dusts a little kiss to my temple. "You look beautiful as always, Shortcake."

I close my eyes, relishing in the comfort of my best friend. "Thank you."

"All right, now. Open up." I back away and watch as he tears open the candy. I open my mouth, and he shakes some Pop Rocks onto my tongue, and instantly, the crackling starts.

He shakes some into his mouth, and then, crackling candy in our mouths, we grin at one another as though we're sharing the world's biggest secret. Once we're finished with the candy, he glances around, as if looking for something.

"What'd you need?" I ask.

"Where's the purse you're bringin' tonight?"

My brows slant together as I wonder why on earth he's asking that. But it's Hollis, so I grab the small wristlet purse hanging from its strap on the handle of my closet door. I hold it up to show him, and he waves me over, holding out his hand for it.

Suspiciously, I place it in his large palm. He flicks the clasp to open it and reaches in his pants pocket, withdrawing another packet of Pop Rocks. He drops the packet inside my purse, closes it, and hands it back.

His lips part as if to say something more, but his phone chimes once, and he reaches in his back pocket. He reads a text message and then responds quickly. With an apologetic expression, he leans in and drops a kiss to my forehead. "Gotta run and pick up Charlotte. See you in a few."

"Okay."

When he's halfway out my window, I rush over and whisper-hiss, "Love you, Hollis."

He pauses, head turning back to me, and his expression sends a rush of warmth through my veins. "But not like that," he finishes with a sweet smile. Then he's gone, striding quickly through the backyard without a backward glance.

I close and latch my window and right my blinds. Afterward, I gingerly sit on the edge of my bed and open my purse to stare down at what he placed in it, and I think back to Grandpa Joe's recent sermon on unexpected blessings.

That summer when I was eight, I never expected I'd get my own version of a guardian angel and best friend.

With a small sigh, I close my purse and set it aside. Time to touch up my makeup before Dallas gets here. My mother and Roy want to take pictures before the limo drives us to the convention center, where our dance will be held.

As I add a little more lip gloss, I try to give myself a pep talk about later tonight. Dallas and I have talked about taking things further, and I think I'm finally ready. I mean, I love being with him, and even though he's headed to the University of Alabama and I'm going to Auburn, I feel like maybe we can actually keep the relationship going. It's not like we don't have email and Face-Time and everything.

I stare back at my reflection in the bathroom mirror. "Tonight, you won't be a virgin anymore," I whisper.

I'd be lying if I said a mix of trepidation and excitement wasn't plaguing me right now.

Tonight has been magical. Dallas has been so sweet, and we've slow danced to practically every song the DJ has played. He's kissed me dozens of times, and they've been little tender ones that make me want more.

Charlotte is a blast to be around, and we're dancing like crazy people and singing at the top of our lungs to Taylor Swift's "Picture To Burn." The guys are chatting off to the side of the dance floor, their amusement evident as we dance like madwomen and laugh at each other's antics.

When it ends and fades to the DJ's voice who says, "We've got a slow one, now, dedicated to Shortcake." I jerk, my eyes immediately finding Hollis, whose mouth tips up, and he winks at me. "Shortcake, wherever you are, this one's for you."

Coldplay's song "Everglow" begins playing, and suddenly, it's like something surreal happens. The edges of my vision grow hazy when I focus on an approaching Hollis. I tip my head to peer up at him as he takes my hand in his and places his other at my hip. We settle into an easy slow-paced sway, our bodies moving as one.

I stare up at him in wonder. "You remembered." After that day in the dress shop, I hadn't brought up how I'd asked him to promise to save me a dance.

With a slightly confused look, a faint smile touches his lips. "Of course I remembered."

For whatever reason, I release his hand to bring it up and rest my palm on his firm chest under the guise of first smoothing down his shirt. He's since discarded his jacket, like Dallas has. His body heat radiates through the fabric. The hard muscles of his pecs beneath my hand make me wonder how it would feel without the barrier between us.

That wayward thought has me sucking in a sharp breath, and I avoid his eyes. He drops his head to bring his lips to my ear. "He behavin' himself?" He leans back, waiting for me to meet his concerned gaze. When I merely nod, relief is evident in his features. Then he ducks his head again. "Remember to be safe tonight."

I nod as heat floods my face. Hollis always acts like a big brother, but when the song nears the end, and he covers the palm I have on his chest with his own, I become transfixed by the sight of our hands together.

Unable to look away, I swallow hard as a foreign sense of awareness spreads through me. Hollis' callused fingertips, slightly stained with grease even though I know he scrubs himself clean after working on his truck, have me riveted to such an extent that I don't realize when the song has ended and bled into another until the large hand at my back breaks through the haze.

Hollis backs away with a quick wink before slipping his arms around Charlotte. Dallas steps in front of me, blocking my view, snapping me from the odd trance.

Hollis is my best friend, and my lingering sadness over so much change occurring soon is clearly messing with my mind.

That must be it.

14

HOLLIS

PROM NIGHT

"YOU'RE KILLIN' ME." MY WHISPERED GROAN FILLS THE SILENCE OF the bedroom.

Charlotte's on my bed beneath me, the fabric of her prom dress hiked up to her waist, baring her tiny panties. She clutches my ass, urging me to grind against her. My dick feels like it's about to burst free from my pants.

"But what a way to go." She watches me with a half-lidded gaze.

I place an openmouthed kiss on her collarbone, then nip at it before running my tongue over her skin. She rocks her hips against me, grinding against my dick, and I barely stifle a hoarse groan.

"I want you, Hollis." The way she says this catches my attention, her words working their way through the haze of lust clogging my brain.

I rise up to peer down at her. We've talked about it, but I've never pressed the issue. Especially since she basically told me her first time was shitty. I've always left the ball in her court. I respect Charlotte too much.

"Are you sure?" I rest my weight on one forearm. With my other hand, I trace her jawline with my thumb. "You know I'm not—"

She presses a finger to my lips, stopping me. "I know you're not trying to pressure me." Her eyes soften. She drops her arm before raising her head to dust a kiss on my mouth. One edge of her lips quirks upward. "And tonight's been perfect."

It really has. I place a kiss to the tip of her nose before drawing back. "If you wanna stop at any point, just say so."

She nods before tugging me back down, and soon, our mouths seal over one another, kisses turning more heated, wetter, deeper. She guides me in unzipping her dress, and when we carefully pull it from her, I struggle to draw air into my lungs.

She's so damn sexy in her lace bra and panties. I quickly strip off my own clothes down to my boxer briefs, and I try to take things slow, try to ease into it, but she wants no part of it. She unhooks her bra and shoves off her panties, dislodging me from on top of her in the process.

I flick an amused look her way. "In a hurry?" I reach over to check the time on my phone. "Still a few hours before curfew for you."

Her fingers slip inside the waistband of my boxers, and she starts sliding them down. My dick juts out, and she draws in a sharp breath.

I slip off the bed, slide my boxers the rest of the way off, and kick them to my bedroom floor. Before I can take my spot on the bed again, she reaches out and takes me in her hand.

"*Fuck*," I breathe out.

Her smile is full of mischief as she sits up and runs her tongue along the tip, darting along the top to lap up the moisture there. I thread my fingers in her hair and my grip tightens when she fits her lips around my length and glides her hot mouth up and down in agonizing strokes.

Shit, there's no way I'll last if she keeps this up. I'll be a one pump chump, and I can't have that embarrassment hanging over me. Especially not for my first time.

I tug her gently, steering her back from me. Looking down at her lips, wet and slightly reddened from my kisses, I say exactly that.

She lies back and tells me to hurry up and get a condom. When she spreads her legs, baring what I've become well acquainted with these past few months, I can't help but lower my face between her thighs.

With my lips fastened around her clit, I gently flick my tongue against it, just enough to drive her crazy. Her hips rock, and I slide a finger inside her, groaning when her wet heat clenches me tight. She clutches my shoulders.

"Hollis, please." Her breathless whispers sound pained. "I need you now."

I slide on the condom and press inside, inch by inch, trying to ensure I don't hurt her too badly, but she just groans. "Hurry up and do it already."

I hesitate, but the look she gives me tells me she's serious. I thrust deeper and freeze, panicked at her expression when her eyes pinch shut. "Shit, I'm sorry, Char—"

Her eyes flash open, and she tugs my head down to whisper against my lips, "Don't apologize. It's just... I need to get used to you inside me."

Shifting slightly as if she's testing how things feel, it makes me sink even deeper, and she bites her bottom lip with a tiny moan.

"You feel so good," I whisper against her lips. Fitting my mouth to hers in a hungry kiss, I drive in and out of her.

I barely hold myself off, but when I reach between us to

work her clit, and she hits her orgasm, I let go. Afterward, we lie in my bed, heaving like we've just run a marathon, and gaze at one another with a knowing smirk.

A long while later, after I sneak out of my room to grab a snack for us—and simultaneously pray I won't encounter my mom—Charlotte insists on going at it again, citing scientific research purposes.

I'm hesitant since I heard girls can be tender down there afterward, especially since this was like her first time all over again—and I tell her this—but she persists. "We need to make sure the first time wasn't a fluke." Her smile is full of naughtiness.

Of course, I have no choice but to prove her wrong.

And I think I succeed, if the way her inner muscles clench around me during her orgasm is any indication.

The second time with Charlotte is slow, gentler because whether she wants to admit it or not, I caught the little wince when I pushed inside her. I try to take my time and make it good for her.

Once I drop her off at home and sneak back into my house, I strip off my clothes and slide into bed. The sheets still smell like us, and a satisfied smile tugs at my lips. Tonight was pretty damn awesome.

Just as I drift off to sleep, a niggling thought sprouts at the back of my subconscious that I did something I shouldn't have.

Or maybe that I did something with the person I shouldn't have.

$\sim$

A FEW WEEKS LATER...

When I pull onto my street on my way home from school, my first thought is how glad I am that only a few weeks of school are left.

The second: How relieved I am not to have a shift at the country club tonight after having worked later than usual last night.

As soon as I realize my usual spot in the driveway is taken, I slow, my tired brain wondering who the vehicle could belong to.

Until it dawns on me.

I rush to park and get out of my truck, moving around to survey the shiny Chevelle that's obviously been the recipient of some serious TLC.

The front door opens, and before I turn around, a familiar male voice booms, "Better not be puttin' your grimy paws on my lady!"

I laugh and raise my hands in mock defense. "Yes, sir!" Slowly, I turn around, and my uncle Johnny, my dad's brother, strides over and pulls me in for a quick hug before backing away to survey me.

"Boy, you just keep growin' taller every time I see you."

I laugh. "It's been a while since you've seen me."

He grimaces with an apologetic expression. "Yeah, I know." He shakes his head, gazing at the car. "Once things took off, it seems like I've hardly had time to breathe."

My uncle started a custom body shop outside Atlanta. I don't think anyone expected his business to achieve success as fast as it did, but after he toyed with his own '68 Corvette and revamped the entire look, making it sleeker with all the custom work, word of mouth spread about Custom Motorwerks. He travels to overseas car shows to show and, often, sell his "projects," as he calls them.

We both study the Chevelle for a beat. "Jay told me you did

some work on your truck." He turns his attention to it, and I suddenly feel embarrassed.

"I, uh, haven't done any major work on it."

He steps up and runs a hand over the front fender, then surveys the rest of the modifications on the body work before his gaze flicks to me. "You do all this yourself?"

I run a hand over my hair nervously. "Yes, sir." Then I rush to tack on, "But I had some help from my girlfriend's dad."

His eyes trace over the vehicle. "Nice." He straightens. "You know, you could always shadow me in my shop if you want some hands-on experience. Apprenticeships are hard to come by, but judgin' from this,"—he tips his head to my truck—"you've got potential."

I nod in thanks. "I appreciate it, but I'm headin' to Auburn."

He studies me for a moment, and I wonder if he knows just how much I wish I knew what I wanted to do with my life.

Dad suggested I major in business, but I think he wants me to be the first college graduate of the family more than anything. I can't fault him for wanting more for me. It just sucks not having a real clue about things.

"Well, if you change your mind, you know how to reach out." He winks. His eyes crinkle at the corners, so similar to my dad when he smiles.

Which is more rare these days, unfortunately.

Uncle Johnny claps a hand on my shoulder. "Now, tell me all about this girlfriend of yours. Your dad said sh—"

"Hollis! You'll never believe this!" Magnolia rushes around from the backyard to my driveway. "I found—" When she notices that I'm not alone, she comes to such a comically abrupt stop that I can't restrain a laugh.

Her mouth forms an O. Immediately, I watch the transformation from my Magnolia into the prim and proper one her mother had a hand in creating.

She straightens and smooths down her simple sundress. "I'm so sorry, sir. I didn't mean to interrupt like that."

Before she can excuse herself, my uncle pipes up with, "You must be the girl I've heard all about."

My head whips around, and I part my lips to correct him, to tell him she's not my girlfriend, but Magnolia beats me to it. She approaches us, coming to a stop a few steps away on the driveway.

"Oh, no, I'm sure that's not correct."

Phew. That was close.

She smiles sweetly. "Unless you've heard only delightful things about me, of course."

Shit, shit, shit.

"Well," my uncle starts, eating right out of her sweet, Southern hand, "I heard his girlfriend was a pretty little thing who spent nearly all her time helpin' him with this truck of his."

The instant it dawns on Magnolia, it's so obvious it'd be hilarious if this were any other situation. But I don't want to embarrass her any more than she is. I jump in with, "This is Magnolia, Uncle Johnny. She lives in the house behind us."

"Magnolia," he repeats, clearly having been told about her by Dad. "Yes, I've heard about y'all bein' joined at the hip."

She relaxes minimally, but her polite smile looks a little brittle around the edges. "Yes, sir. Hollis and I have been best friends since we were eight."

"When you forced me into it," I mutter good-naturedly with a smug grin.

"Oh, you!" She swats at me, and I laugh before telling my uncle how she'd introduced herself that day.

He chuckles. "Sounds like you're a force to be reckoned with, young lady." Then he turns to me. "You're one lucky guy with two lovely ladies in your life."

It catches me off guard only because I've never actually

thought about it, but he's right. I gaze down at Magnolia and nod.

"I reckon I am."

15

MAGNOLIA

AUBURN UNIVERSITY
AUBURN, ALABAMA
FRESHMAN YEAR

DALLAS BROKE UP WITH ME WITHIN THE FIRST WEEK OF CLASSES, and I was surprised how easily I got over it. Sometimes, I miss him a little, but I reckon what I really miss most is having an actual boyfriend my parents approve of. It's probably for the best that my courage fizzled out on me on prom night and I didn't lose my virginity to him.

College life is a brand of insanity all its own. It's a combination of overwhelming, fun, and stressful.

I lucked out when it came to dorms, though. My dorm is coed by floor, and Hollis is on the second while I'm on the third. Although our class schedules don't coincide, I sometimes get to see Hollis in passing on the stairs. Once or twice, I've run into him at the library when I'd been studying for an exam.

He and Charlotte have continued dating, and he's invited me to join them several times, whether it's to a bar or a club, some campus event, or a football game, but I've declined. I've distanced myself a bit, letting them have their time together, because the last thing I want is to be a third wheel.

The worst part about declining their invitations to hang out is, it means I haven't seen or had much time with my best friend in a while. And, *boy*, do I miss him. At least we still text.

It's Friday, and I'm being held captive—along with my other classmates—by Professor Jenner in my American Foreign Policy class. He's notorious for going off on tangents and droning on with stories from his experience working in DC. They never have anything anyone can glean from them and have nothing to do with the exams, so I find myself zoning out, wondering what's on the menu in the dining hall since I'll escape this class by one.

My phone lights up where I'd slid it partially beneath my binder. Carefully, even though Professor Jenner doesn't notice since he's so enthralled by his own storytelling, I slide it out to read the text.

Hollis: Whatever you do, do NOT eat the meatloaf for lunch.

Then he attaches a GIF from the movie *Wedding Crashers* with Will Ferrell hollering to his mother about meatloaf. A split second later, he sends another GIF with the famous basketball player Shaq, saying, "NO, NO, NO, DON'T DO IT!!!"

I quickly type a response, telling him to stop making me laugh since I'm in class.

Hollis: Are you coming to Azalea's tonight? It's Friday, after all. Need some downtime.

I'm already preparing to type no even though I've heard that bar is a fun place to go. Apparently, they have a bunch of rooms, some with pool tables, a karaoke room, one designated for live bands, and a large sports bar.

Hollis: If you give me some lame excuse one more time, I swear I'll convince your roommate to let me in, and I'll drag you out myself.

Hollis: Not kidding.

I worry my bottom lip and type.

Me: I just want you and Charlotte to have time together, that's all.

There. That's safe, right? Not rude or petulant sounding.

I hope.

Hollis starts typing, those three little dots dancing, and I flick my eyes up to my professor to make sure he hasn't switched gears. Sure enough, he's now reminiscing about how he met the Clintons. When I focus back on my phone, I nearly jerk in my seat. Shock reverberates through me.

Hollis: We broke up.

Hollis: I thought you knew.

Whoa. Sweet mother of all that's holy, I had no idea.

I start typing but then erase. Crap. I don't know what to say. Is he heartbroken? Angry?

Hollis: It's cool, Shortcake. Mutual agreement.

I snicker under my breath.

Me: Get out of my head. Mind reading is freaky.

He sends a GIF of someone laughing maniacally.

Hollis: Now, are you coming out with me or not?

I sigh inwardly. I guess it might be okay. One thing's certain; it'll be nice to hang out with him again.

Me: Okay.

Hollis: I'll come scoop you up at seven.

It's October, and our football team doesn't have a game this weekend, so things aren't quite as hectic around campus with hardcore tailgaters. The more subdued atmosphere of our dorm is indicative of that.

Inside my room, though, I'm a hot mess. All because I cannot, for the life of me figure out what I should wear tonight.

"You have a hot date tonight or something?" Stephanie, my roommate, asks in her usual bored tone. I don't take it personally, though. She has the same tone when she aces an exam after stress-eating peanut M&M's from the Sam's Club monster-sized bag.

My parents argued with me over this roommate arrangement. They'd insisted they could pay extra and get me a private suite, but I wanted the entire college experience—complete stranger of a roommate and everything.

Stephanie is my complete opposite. From Michigan, she's totally comfortable in her own skin, doesn't seem to care what others think of her, and she marches to her own drum. From her penchant for dying her hair colors only found in a rainbow and painting each of her nails a different color, she's bold and so beautiful in the way she carries herself. I admire her, and well, I also envy her.

She's also far more experienced when it comes to frequenting bars around campus. I admit, I told my parents I wanted the full college experience, but the truth is, I haven't been brave enough to chase it.

"Not a date. Just goin' out with a friend." I continue surveying the contents of my small dorm closet. "Tryin' to decide what's appropriate to wear to Azalea's tonight." Then I quickly add, "I've never been there before."

Silence greets my answer so I assume she's done with our conversation. It isn't until she suddenly appears at my side, startling me, that I realize she's still listening.

"Okay, first of all, you have friends?" Her eyebrows nearly hit her forehead in shock. "Because I've never once seen you go out with anyone."

I press my lips thin and squint at her. "Must you be so rude?"

As soon as the words spill out, I cringe because I sound exactly like my mother.

She just takes it in stride. "All right...now, take the stick out of your ass and say that like a normal nineteen-year-old would."

A laugh escapes me because she's just so...different from anything or anyone I've ever met. "You don't have to be rude about it."

She weighs my response before grimacing. "Meh, I'll let that sad attempt slide. Better, but it needs work. Now"—she levels me a serious look—"let's talk about the fact that you've never been to Azalea's before. How is this even possible?"

My tone is dry when I say, "I'm guessin' you've been there before."

The disbelief plastered on her face tells me the answer before she even answers. "I thought everyone had. It's kind of a rite-of-passage thing." She shrugs. "Everyone knows they serve alcohol as long as you're at least nineteen and have a college ID." With a dry laugh, she adds, "Guess they figure they've got to have *some* standards and all."

I'm terrible at this whole college thing. Everyone says these are the best years of our lives, but I still feel like I'm a random leaf that's landed atop a river flowing aimlessly downstream.

Guess it's better than being plopped somewhere in the murky waters of Mobile Bay.

"Okay," Stephanie starts. "You obviously need assistance so"—she reaches a hand into the extremely cramped array of hanging clothes to retrieve a hanger with my favorite pair of designer jeans draped over the rung—"wear these and"—she plucks another hanger with a cute silky blue top with a silver pattern and hardly any back to speak of that I'd purchased on a whim the day before I moved into the dorm—"this."

Like a statue, I stand here holding the two hangers. "But the top has hardly any back to it."

At her raised eyebrows silently saying, *And your point is?* I add, "It's chilly tonight." And it goes without saying that I don't want to take a jacket to a bar and keep track of it the entire night.

As though I'm a child who needs guidance, Stephanie explains patiently, "When you go to a bar, hordes of people are there, so it's warm—hot, even—and you won't need a jacket. Plus"—one edge of her mouth tips up in a hint of a smirk —"when guys see skin, it activates their inner caveman buried under the whole frat boy façade." She slows down her speech. "This is a good thing."

I stare down at the hangers in my hand. "I don't know about this."

She lets out an exasperated sound. "We're getting you laid tonight, girl. Just put it on."

I sputter. "But I'm not tryin' to get..." I trail off because...well, that word sounds so crass.

My roommate's lips quiver as she obviously tries to fight a smile. "Go ahead," she drags out the words. Slowing her speech more, she says, "*Laaaaid*. Say it with me. Laaaaid."

"Laid," I manage to force out.

She lets out a huff so powerful it tousles her bangs. "That was weaksauce. Now, put on the clothes, wear those cute silver flip-flops, and put on that darker lipstick you have but never wear."

I stare at her. "How do you know I have—"

She gives me a droll look. "Seriously? We're roommates. You're telling me you've never snooped through my stuff while I was gone?"

I rear back, mortified. "Absolutely not." I shake my head. "I would never—"

She barks out a laugh and pats my cheek. "You're just too precious. Now, get dressed. Wear the lipstick. Get laid." Her features morph, resembling that of a stern teacher, and I tense.

"But don't bring him back here because I've got to study for this damn Intro to Religious Studies exam, and you know I can't study in public."

She told me about this when we first became roommates. Apparently, she does better on exams when she studies in her room versus at the library or a coffee shop and doesn't feel like chancing that anytime soon.

Wide-eyed, I nod. "I promise not to bring anyone back."

"Sweet. Good talk." Then she returns to her side of the room and slides back into her desk chair to resume her studying.

By the time seven o'clock rolls around, I'm dressed in the Stephanie-approved outfit and wearing the darker lipstick she suggested. She gives me a quick thumbs-up in approval before turning back to her study material. The knock on the door is right on time.

I open the door to Hollis dressed in a pair of khakis and an untucked polo shirt. The shirt's hem reaches the waistband of his pants, and on his feet are the nice pair of leather flip-flops I bought him for Christmas. When I drag my eyes back up his form, our gazes clash, and his eyes sparkle with amusement.

"Do I pass muster?"

I tip my head to the side with a smile. "Yes, sir."

"Ready?"

I nod and turn to grab my little wristlet. As soon as I do, I hear a choked sound from behind me.

"Shortcake? Where in God's creation is the rest of your shirt?"

"Whoa, dude. Hollis Barnes?" Stephanie calls out, leaning back in her desk chair. She narrows her eyes on him and throws up a hand. "Hold up. *You're* the friend she's going out with tonight?"

"Yes, ma'am."

She mutters something that sounds like, "All the ma'ams and

sirs kill my damn soul," before asking, "Are you prepared for the exam on Monday in Holt's class?"

My eyes volley back and forth between the two of them. I had no idea they knew one another, let alone had a class together.

He gives her that quick wink that's become so familiar. He's probably the one guy on this earth who can pull off a wink and not have it come off as arrogant or sleazy. "I'm as prepared as I'll ever be."

She makes a sound of disgust. "I despise people who are naturally great test takers."

"You'll do fine," he tells her. "Just don't overdo it, or your brain will revolt."

She mutters something and turns back. Hollis' gaze flicks to me, his brows slanting together, a crease forming between them. "It's a little chilly out there. Might want to change."

Before I can part my lips to respond, Stephanie pipes up without even turning around. "She's perfect as is, Barnes."

He frowns. "I wasn't tryin' to imply—"

She exhales loudly and spins around. "Dude. She's beautiful. You saying that she should change when she looks hot as hell is a little insulting." Then she pins me with a look. "Don't you dare change. You look so freaking perfect it makes me throw up a little in my mouth." She spins back to her desk. "Now, please go so I can get some studying done."

I press my lips thin, warring with indecision until I finally force myself to walk to the door. Saying goodbye to my room-mate, Hollis and I walk down the stairs, talking like we normally would.

Conversation is easy, and I realize how much I've missed this. I shouldn't have stayed away from him simply because of his relationship with Charlotte. Because of that, I've missed out on spending time with my best friend.

As we stroll on the sidewalk, I'm grateful Azalea's isn't but a block and a half away since there's a slight chill in the air. I hesitate before finally asking, "What happened?"

I don't look at him. Can't, if I'm being honest. And it's for the worst reason. Because I don't want him to see how torn I am over his breakup with Charlotte. How a part of me is almost happy because I can have my best friend back again. How another part of me hates that, because I genuinely like Charlotte and thought they were good together.

Lord have mercy, I'm an absolute hot mess. Someone needs to bless *my* heart already.

"She met someone."

I jerk, so surprised that I misstep. Hollis grabs my upper arm to steady me. "Whoa. You okay?"

I nod quickly. "Yes."

He releases me, and the warmth from his hand lingers. As I let his answer sink in, anger churns inside me, like an impending thunderstorm in the South, ready to unleash the loudest thunder, the fiercest lightning, and the harshest downpour of rain.

The sign comes into view for Azalea's, and I focus on walking and not falling prey to any uneven sections of the sidewalk again.

"I can't believe she'd choose someone over you." My words come out sounding almost petulant, but I can't help it. This is Hollis Barnes we're talking about. Who in their right mind would choose another guy over him?

Someone who's clearly delusional, that's who.

An easy laugh rumbles from him. "Shortcake, it's all good. I told you. It was mutual."

Wait. Mutual as in he met someone else too? If so, where is she? Oh, holy hell in a handbasket, *please* tell me he's not bringing me out to meet her.

We stop in the line draping the front of Azalea's. I'm fairly sure it's ridiculous to have them check IDs, but they're going through the motions.

"I can practically smell the fire, you're thinkin' so hard." His warm breath flutters against my temple, sending a rash of shivers down the length of my spine. He backs away to peer at me, and I finally manage to brave a look at him.

"So..." I trail off, unsure about asking simply because I don't know if I want to know the answer.

"So..." he parrots, a faint smile tugging at his lips.

"It was mutual, meanin'...?"

He appears to think it over. "Meanin', we both realized we made sense in high school, but we want different things now."

I frown. "But I thought you loved her."

His expression softens, and he traces an index finger between my brows. "I realized there are different kinds of love. Sometimes, though"—his eyes take on a faraway look—"you realize that you're better off friends instead."

I'm about to ask him if he met someone else, too, but he reaches for his back pocket and withdraws his cell phone. He types quickly with a little smirk before repocketing it.

"My roommate's here." His eyes lift to mine and he slings an arm around my shoulders as we move with the line of people, getting closer to the entrance. "You'll like him. Seems like a good guy." He leans in, lowering his voice. "Plus, he's the Lacoste-polo-and-khaki-wearin' kind who comes from a wealthy family."

I roll my eyes. "You know I don't care about that."

"I know." His gently spoken response silently adds, *But your parents do.*

"What's his name?" We step up and offer our IDs to the bouncer. He checks them with a flashlight and stamps our hands, waving us inside. Hollis guides me in front of him.

"Preston Dodge."

I stop so abruptly, Hollis is barely able to stop himself from barreling into me. My head whips around. "Preston Dodge, as in the Dodge family who has a middle school named after them and a statue of a grandfather in downtown Mobile? The guy whose father is the attorney general of Alabama?"

He nods. "Yes, ma'am."

Oh my stars. The Dodge family is famous as far as local standards go.

Dazed, I allow him to lead me to the bar. "Want a beer or water? Or somethin' else?"

"What are you gettin'?"

"Beer."

My eyes widen. "Really?"

He laughs. "Come on, Shortcake. It's college. One beer won't hurt."

"Okay," I hedge. "I guess I'll have whatever you're havin'."

A moment later, Hollis hands me my first beer in a plastic cup. It's cold, and I stare at the contents dubiously. It looks an awful lot like urine. The smell isn't much better.

I follow him, careful not to bump into anyone and spill my beer. Once we get to an open barstool at the counter against a wall, he reaches to take my cup and waits for me to slide onto the seat. He sets my beer on the counter and points at it, a stern expression taking place of his usual easygoing one. "Don't let this out of your sight for even a second."

I nod. I've heard enough stories about that sort of thing. "I won't."

He glances around, flicking his eyes through the crowd until they stop. He grins and lifts his chin in greeting. I follow his line of sight and discover a guy weaving through the throngs of people and heading our way.

Wow. There isn't a doubt in my mind that this is his roommate, the infamous Preston Dodge. I recall seeing a photograph of him and his family on some political commercial but never paid it much attention.

A tiny laugh bubbles up, threatening to break free, because he's dressed exactly as Hollis described him. His Lacoste polo shirt is smooth and free of wrinkles, tucked into a pair of khaki pants, a leather belt cinching a narrow waist. On his feet are an expensive pair of leather flip-flops I recognize since Roy only wears the OluKai brand that's normally shy of two hundred dollars.

Even in the dim lighting of the bar, his light blue eyes are clear and crisp in color, reminding me of the prettiest afternoon sky in the summer. His nose is straight, and with high cheekbones and an angular jawline, he could probably model if he wanted to. He's gorgeous.

Hollis was right. Preston is exactly the kind of guy my parents would love. Heck, the fact that he's the son of the Alabama State Attorney General would be enough to have them trying to arrange our marriage. However, most of the guys my parents choose for me tend to tip the scales as far as being pretentious as all get-out, so I'm interested to see where Preston falls on that scale.

"Barnes!" He exchanges an easy handshake-back-slap hug with my best friend before turning his attention to me.

"And how did this roughneck manage to get you to tag along tonight?" His eyes sparkle with humor. "He bribed you, didn't he?"

Hollis shoves at Preston's shoulder playfully. "I told you I was bringin' Magnolia."

Preston steps closer and extends a hand for me to shake. When I place my palm in his, he says, "Nice to meet you, Magnolia." Instead of shaking my hand, he swivels his wrist and dips his head to place a light kiss on the back of it.

"That's enough, Casanova." Hollis laughs and tugs my hand from Preston's.

Someone calls out Hollis' name, and he waves before turning to me. "You okay for a moment? I didn't realize our resident advisor's lendin' a hand at the bar tonight."

Preston waves him off. "I'll make sure nothin' happens to her."

Hollis holds my gaze, waiting for me to answer. I nod. "I'll be fine."

The crowd swallows him, and I pick up my untouched beer, anxious for something to do with my hands. I bring it to my lips to take a sip, and as soon as the liquid hits my taste buds, I turn my head to the side to try to casually spit it back into my cup.

Lord have mercy, that's positively *putrid*.

Then I realize Preston just witnessed this. With an inward wince, I dart a cautious look at him.

He's grinning like a fool. "I reckon you're not a fan of beer, huh?"

I cover my mouth and laugh. "Sorry about that."

"No worries." He takes a sip of his own half-full cup of beer, amusement sparkling in his eyes as he watches me grimace at his action. After swallowing, he laughs. "I promise it's an acquired taste."

I twist my lips. "Well, let's just say I won't lose sleep over it if it doesn't happen."

He laughs again and slides his phone from his pocket. "Let me text Hollis to grab you a bottle of water while he's over at the bar." He types quickly and pockets it.

When his eyes rest on me again, the interest in them is palpable. He takes another sip of his beer, eyeing me over the rim, before asking, "Well, Miss Magnolia, I know your feelin's on beer. What I'd really like to know is"—he tips his head to the side—"whether you're datin' anyone."

I shake my head, unable to break eye contact. "No."

His mouth spreads into a wide, satisfied grin. "Well, then. I reckon I know what my goal is now."

I furrow my brow in a mixture of curiosity and confusion. "What's that?"

He steps closer to where I sit on the barstool and settles his free hand on the counter. His eyes are intent, and determination is evident in his tone when he answers.

"To change your answer."

16

MAGNOLIA

AUBURN UNIVERSITY
FRESHMAN YEAR
POST-SPRING BREAK
MARCH

I'D PREFER NOT TO ADMIT THE NUMBER OF TIMES I OVERHEARD other girls in my dorm talk about how everything changed when they met a guy—when they met *the* guy. I always inwardly scoffed at them.

Then Preston Dodge entered my life. He's shown me time and again that he's more than a gorgeous face. More than a son whose family has wealth and notoriety that hails from pre-Civil War days. His easy charm wooed me initially, but then we bonded over stories of being forced to attend etiquette classes and cotillion. Over families who stress the importance of appearances and conducting oneself in public.

He always does his best to make time for me. We have study dates and get together with Hollis and a few other guys and head to Azalea's for beers—or, in my case, water—and play pool or darts. Preston and I are, dare I say, nearly perfect for one another.

Of course, my parents adore him and have accepted him into the fold like they've known him for years. I'd considered inviting him home with me for spring break, but he and his friends had already made plans to head to Cabo before we met.

I admit, I was a bit envious of Preston being able to relax and soak up the sun at a resort while I spent my break at home, pacifying my mother by letting her parade me around to her little gatherings and women's tea. It was torturous. The only good part of it was when I had time with Hollis in the treehouse. Of course, he was working shifts at the country club for extra money, so I didn't get as much time with him either.

The week back at school after the break starts off stilted and awkward between Preston and me. I chalk it up to the struggle of post-vacation exhaustion. I mean, I'm not an idiot; it's expected drinking would be involved. They're college guys, after all.

"Going out with Prepston again, huh?"

I roll my eyes at Stephanie's nickname for him, smoothing down my dress while I internally war with myself over my choice of heels. Preston's due to pick me up for dinner before we attend a party at the fraternity he's considering "rushing."

Prepston. The moniker stuck as soon as the two met. She zeroed in on his collared shirt and pressed khaki pants, the expensive watch on his wrist, and began to call him Prepston to his face. He took it in stride, being the sweet, easygoing guy he is. That's one of the things I appreciate, and I think I can learn a lot from the way he doesn't let others' opinions or comments get to him.

Plenty of people have opinions on Roy and his decisions and work in the community, and sometimes they aren't the kindest or politically correct. I've been lucky enough not to become the center of attention by default because he's shielded me as much as possible, but with his aspirations to run for governor of Alabama, I know my reprieve will be short-lived.

Preston hasn't had the same experience. He's told me how his father pressures him to keep up a perfect façade when all he really wants is to be allowed to be a normal college kid.

"I mean, duh, of course the infamous Prepston's wining and dining you," Stephanie continues. She lies on her bed, scrolling through whatever social media thing on her phone.

I'm the rare person without any social media accounts. My mother continues pressuring me to promote myself on social media, like I'm some sort of a show dog, but it's one thing I've dug in my heels on. I just can't stomach the idea of playing a part in the fakeness.

Mother has more followers than our local mayor, and she's proud of it. Apparently, selfies of her having tea with the ladies at Women's Club and photos of her fundraising dinners are something to fawn over.

"Yes, ma'am." I lean toward the floor-length mirror affixed to the closet door and double-check my lipstick.

"The power couple of Auburn. Attorney general's son and a state senator's daughter," she muses, still scrolling on her phone. "I can just see the headlines no—"

I turn, curious as to why she cut off her sentence only to find her staring at her phone with a horrified expression.

"What's the matter?"

Her head jerks up, and when her eyes meet mine, a sense of dread washes over me. "What is it?" I say slowly.

She worries her bottom lip, glancing down at the screen of her phone, a tormented expression on her face. "Shit," she breathes out. With a wince, she holds out the phone for me.

I step closer and accept it, peering down at whatever it is

that's rendered her speechless— *Oh, sweet mother of all that's holy in this world.*

The Instagram photo acts like a pair of invisible fists clenching my lungs, rendering me unable to breathe.

"I'm sorry," she whispers raggedly. "But *shit*, Magnolia." She buries her face in her hands. "I'd sure as hell want to know if it were my boyfriend."

My lips part, then snap closed before I finally compose myself. "Don't apologize." I toss the phone onto the edge of her mattress, and she lifts her head to look at me. "It's not like you twisted his arm and made him have a spring break that resembles the male version of *Girls Gone Wild* with photos to prove it."

I draw in a deep breath, trying to calm myself. "I'm sure his father is on the phone with him now tryin' to do damage control and get that taken down."

She snorts derisively. "Yeah, good luck with that. We live in the age of screenshots."

My phone buzzes on my desk with an incoming text message. When I walk over to read the text, I can't say I'm surprised in the least.

Preston: Hey, Sugar. Dad called, so I'm running behind. Should be done in ten minutes or so.

That little nickname—Sugar—now makes my skin crawl.

Runnin' behind, huh? I bet.

Stephanie turns over, flopping onto her back. "And, really. What kind of moronic friends think it's okay to post this pic and tag him in it? I mean, *come on*, people."

We fall silent for a moment while I mull over how to handle this new development. Instantly, I dredge up all the lessons drummed into my head as far back as I can recall.

Chin up.

Posture straight.

Smile with confidence.

Act with graciousness, kindness, and poise.

"Guys are douchebags." I've never heard her speak in such a gentle tone before, and I bristle because I know why she's doing it. "It's not a reflection of you."

She pities me. That, and she doesn't know that the scene in that photo might have been warranted. Because things work differently in college, and everyone—even clueless little me—knows it.

I haven't slept with Preston yet. And, judging from that photo, the effects of that abstinence had been plaguing him.

Breathe in, breathe out. I can practically hear the clinking of my battle armor sliding into place.

I have a date tonight with my boyfriend—no, that's not right. I have a dinner date with a guy who claimed to be my boyfriend but ended up sucking face—and had roving hands on her, too—with some girl in Cabo.

"Oh, I know that look." Stephanie backs away. "Just remember, you always say orange washes you out, so prison won't be a good choice."

"Are you feelin' all right?" Preston asks me. Again. For what must be the tenth time tonight.

"Right as rain." I smile prettily while contemplating his dismemberment.

Someone hollers his name, and it booms over the loud music in the large frat house, drawing Preston's attention. He lifts his chin at the guy and smiles before turning back to me.

His features sober, and concern is etched on his face. "Just stressed about your research paper?" He tips his head to the side, and his lips turn down, a frown marring his face. "You need to eat. I should've insisted we have dinner anyway."

Every single part of my vertebrae stiffens at his words and the pure male chauvinism that colors them. I adopt a casual smile and shrug, glancing past him to survey the crowd of party-goers. I haven't missed the looks and hushed voices when others spot us. The looks of pity or snide laughter. Like Stephanie said earlier, you can delete a post, but the screenshot can live forever.

This appears to be the case for the photo Preston was tagged in. When I focus on his face, I'd be lying if I said his attractiveness hasn't dulled considerably.

"Guess what?" I inject cheerfulness in my tone and rush on before he can respond. "I've just started an Instagram page and wanted to see if you'd be okay with me postin' a photo of us and taggin' you."

He stills for a split second, and I probably wouldn't have noticed had I not been paying close attention. His smile is a little tight around the edges now. "Sure."

"Great!" I pull out my phone and go into my photos. I select it and turn my phone, a wide smile pasted on my face. "What do you think of this one?"

The instant his eyes lock on the screenshot I had Stephanie forward to me, he pales beneath his tan. When those blue eyes rise to meet mine, I could easily drown in the guilt visible in the depths.

His lips part, and the muscles in my face begin to ache with the force I'm using to hold my smile in place. I put my phone inside my small wristlet, averting my eyes. He wraps a hand around my upper arm, steering me off to the side and into a corner, away from prying eyes.

"Magnolia, I can explain."

A cynical laugh breaks free. "My *word*! I *know* you're not about to use that clichéd intro to your excuse on me."

He sputters, and the desperation drips from his every word.

"I was drunk, and it didn't mean anythin'. I swear!" If this isn't egregious enough, he quickly tacks on, "Plus, I used protection."

Bless his little heart because he just hammered the final nail in his own coffin.

I grab his beer and chug every disgusting drop of the heinous liquid before thrusting the red Solo cup at his chest, suppressing my gag reflex and praying my poor stomach will forgive me for making it suffer through that wretched beverage.

"Well, I reckon I'm done here." I slip around him with a "See you 'round," and don't look back as I rush through the throngs of partygoers.

My heart thumps so erratically, I fear it might beat right out of my chest. It seems to take a century before I finally make it to the front door, all the while ignoring the male voice calling my name.

Fool me once. That's all it takes for Magnolia Mae Barton. Except I have a bone to pick with that old saying because, in this case, the shame is on both of us. Him for doing what he did and, in the process, bringing shame to me, if the looks and hushed whispers from the others are any indication.

Once I cross the threshold and step outside, the humid air is a welcoming change from the stifling air-conditioning inside.

Well, that *and* the cheating ex-boyfriend.

Spotting a gap in the group of partygoers enjoying the warm night along with those outside to smoke, I squeeze through only to stumble into a hard wall of muscle. I mutter an apology and move to step around him, only to be stopped by his voice.

"Shortcake?"

My head jerks up at my nickname, and my eyes collide with a familiar pair of brown ones. Hollis peers down at me curiously.

"You okay?"

I give a short shake of my head. "I need to get out of here." Good grief, the desperation in my voice fuels my anger.

Without a second thought, his palm falls to the base of my spine, and he guides me away from the large house. We barely make it more than ten steps when I hear, "*Please,* Magnolia! You've gotta listen to me!"

My body instantly tenses at Preston's voice, and without looking up at Hollis, I utter a hushed plea. "Please keep walkin' with me."

The hand at my back becomes more supportive, and we continue until we make it to the sidewalk. Every footfall that sounds from behind us, growing closer, has my breath quickening in desperation for something to stop him. To prevent him from reaching us.

As soon as the soles of my sandals make contact with the sidewalk, Preston reaches for my arm, tugging me around to face him. "Magnolia, wait—"

Hollis whirls around on him, and I swear his broad chest and shoulders appear to dwarf Preston. His features are severe, tense, and anger radiates off him in waves. "Back. The. Fuck. Off."

His eyes dart back and forth between Hollis and me, before settling on me and a myriad of emotions flickers across his face. "Look, if we can just talk... I *swear,* she didn't mean anythin' to me."

I turn back around. "I said I'm done." I start walking, focusing so intently on not tripping on the uneven parts of the sidewalk that I barely miss the muffled, "*Fuck!*"

The sound of flip-flops slapping along the concrete walk signals to me that Hollis is catching up. I don't slow my pace that, quite honestly, resembles that of someone aiming for a gold medal in the power-walking Olympics.

My best friend falls into step beside me, and we don't talk.

He doesn't pry for information and doesn't try to make small talk. And I realize just how well he knows me.

Only someone who's known you for a little over a decade, someone who can pick up on the nuances of your personality, knows how to navigate a situation like this. And for me, that someone is Hollis Barnes.

Still ensnared in my own thoughts, I don't pay attention to the way he types out a quick text. To the way he steers me up the stairs and guides me to his floor. He unlocks the door and ushers me inside with a "Don't worry. He won't be comin' back here tonight."

I nod, wrapping my arms around myself, suddenly feeling vulnerable. When he pulls me toward him, tugging on my arms and placing them around his waist, I settle my cheek against his chest with a sigh.

He smooths his hand along my back in soothing strokes, lightly pressing a kiss to my hair. He couldn't possibly understand how much I appreciate this—how much I appreciate *him* right now. He makes the humiliation a little less suffocating and my molten hot anger less oppressing.

"I really thought he was different. That he wouldn't do this sort of thing." My breath hitches, and I hate how fragile my voice sounds. "I should've known better than to think he wouldn't go and sleep with some random girl on spring break." At my words, his firm chest feels like it tenses even more beneath me.

"You know what the worst part is?" I whisper, my cheek against the smooth fabric of his simple cotton T-shirt with Auburn University printed on one short sleeve and Aubie, our tiger mascot, pictured on the other sleeve. He smells like safety and comfort. And like a best friend should, he knows that my question was rhetorical and remains silent, waiting for me to continue. "I swear I had an inklin'. I mean, I thought about sleepin' with him, but it just never seemed like the right time."

The hand at my back stutters a split second before resuming its soothing pattern of strokes. A long beat of silence passes before he speaks, his voice low and tender. "If it didn't feel right, then you did the right thing." Then he speaks against my hair in the barest of a whisper. "He doesn't deserve you."

I swallow hard and close my eyes, attempting to muster bravery for my confession. "Does it make me a horrible person that I'm more upset that he made me look stupid? And not because I'm heartbroken?"

He eases us apart, and I fix my eyes on the center of his chest, vulnerability surrounding me. With his index finger under my chin, he nudges up, forcing me to meet his deep brown eyes. In a gentle tone, he says, "Hey."

"Hey," I whisper back.

Raising both hands, he cradles my face. His deep brown eyes flick over my face, and affection lines his features. "You're not a horrible person. I don't reckon you could ever be anythin' less than perfect."

I twist my lips derisively, and when I shift a fraction, I catch sight of his slight wince and narrow my eyes. Out of the corner of my eye, I notice his right hand.

I gasp. "Hollis, your hand!"

My eyes dart up to his, and he shrugs off my concern. "It's nothin'."

I take hold of his wrist in my hands to get a better look. His knuckles are beat up from here to kingdom come. In a flash, it dawns on me. He punched Preston. On my behalf.

I pinch my eyes closed, still cradling his hand in mine. "Hollis." His name spills from my lips in a breathy wisp.

"I'd do it again in a heartbeat." His deep voice, the threaded steeliness in his tone indicative of his remaining anger toward Preston, wraps around me like a safeguard. I open my eyes and find him staring down at me. "I'm sorry, Shortcake." Remorse etches his face. "I thought he was a good one."

He feels bad for introducing us. "It's not your fault." I hold his gaze for a long beat until he finally gives a curt nod. Then I switch gears. "Now, we need to get this"—I tip my head, gesturing to his hand—"cleaned up."

"It'll be fine."

I squint at him sternly. "Do you have a first-aid kit?"

A huff of a laugh breaks free, and he shakes his head. "I think there's one stuffed in the back of my closet."

I point at him. "Sit and I'll get it."

His eyes crinkle at the corners. "Yes, ma'am."

By the time I finally uncover the first-aid kit, I've disrupted Hollis' closet a bit and a few well-worn cotton shirts have slid off the hangers. I replace them on the hangers aside from one.

"For heaven's sake, this shirt is the softest thing I've ever felt." I emerge from his closet grasping the kit in one hand and the shirt in the other.

He wrinkles his brow. "It's older than sin."

A thought hits me. "Do you wear it a lot?"

At my hopeful expression, he laughs. "You can have it as payment for this." He holds up his battered hand.

A few minutes later, I've cleaned his wounds and applied some antibiotic ointment. Ignoring his grumbling, I insist on wrapping his knuckles with nonstick gauze, and something flickers in my memory.

I realize the last time I bandaged up my best friend was that night long ago. My eyes drift from his hand up to his forearm and I run my fingertip over the area that now shows no evidence of the cut from his mom. His other hand snags my wrist and my eyes dart up to find him watching me curiously. I place a quick, light kiss to his bandaged knuckles and gather up the first-aid kit.

Replacing the kit and ensuring his closet isn't a god-awful mess, I turn to find him lying on his side on his bed that's flush against the wall, his head on the pillow, and a watchful expression on his face.

I gingerly lower myself on the mattress, face-to-face with him. He rests his bandaged hand on my hip and, as though this simple contact comforts him, his eyes fall closed even though it's clear to see the self-recrimination in the crease between his brows and slight tic in his jaw.

I take advantage of this moment to study him. A small smile tugs at the edges of my mouth as my eyes trace over his features. He's changed from the young boy who made a little girl—a girl who never fit into the world that stressed perfect appearances—feel true acceptance.

The boyish curves of his face have given way to sharper, more distinctive lines of a young man. His lanky build has grown into lean, honed muscles that slink together with inherently smooth movement. His dark hair is longer on top and shorter along the sides, and I know without touching it that it'll be as soft as it was years ago.

Regardless of the changes in Hollis' appearance, some things remain the same. He still has the biggest heart and the kindest soul of anyone I've ever known. I reach out a fingertip to trace that troublesome crease between his brows before veering off to run the pad of my finger over that scar bisecting his eyebrow.

His eyes flash open, locking with mine, and my breath catches in my throat at the intensity in his gaze. I pull back, but he catches my wrist gently and draws my hand close to press a light kiss to the center of my palm.

My lungs seize, and I swear my heart skips a beat at the

sensation of that tender kiss. As quick as it happens, he startles me with his sudden question.

"You know what we need to do?"

"Nooo," I draw out the word slowly. "What's that?"

"We need to get outta here. I mean, after all, you're all dressed up with nowhere to go." His eyes spark with excitement. "And I know just the place."

"This is...not *quite* what I was expectin'."

I stare—gawk, if I'm being honest—at the most dilapidated bar front I've ever seen. The Pink Elephant—or ink Elhat, according to their sad excuse for a sign with multiple letters missing—looks as though it's a front for something much seedier than just serving alcohol.

Hollis chuckles. "Ye of little faith." With a wink, he adds, "Trust me?"

I stare at him with wide-eyed apprehension. "Right now, I'm not so sure."

His grin is wide and makes him even more endearing. Even if he is trying to coerce me into entering the seediest bar around. "Come on, now. What's the worst that could happen?"

I flick my eyes to the darkened windows of the bar. Good Lord, the tint is so dark, you can't even see if the lights are on inside. "The worst that could happen?" I give him a skeptical look. "I reckon I could get an STD just by—"

He dips his head closer and levels me with a look. "Never thought you to be judgmental and close-minded like your mama."

Ouch. Well, that just flat-out stung, but now that I think about it, Hollis has a point. Just because I've never been inside a place that looked like this one shouldn't necessarily mean anything bad.

"You're right. I'm sorry." I dart another curious glance at the door of the bar. "How'd you find out about this place?"

His expression softens, and his lips quirk slightly. "I was at the junkyard lookin' for a part for the truck and came across this gentleman. Got to talkin'. He told me about this place.

"Turns out he owns a garage where he does body work and offered to let me use his equipment after hours." He shoves his hands in his pockets and lowers his gaze to his shoes. "Said I reminded him of his son."

"Aww, that's sweet." I pause at his somber expression. "Does his son live far away?"

As soon as I ask, his lips turn down, and I instantly know I won't like his answer.

"He died overseas. Army."

I reach out and lay my hand on his arm. "Oh no! Poor thing."

"You'll like Mr. Ted." His eyes brighten when they rise to meet mine. "He's a straight shooter."

"I can't wait to meet him." With a bit more pep in my step, I start for the door, but Hollis' hand on my wrist draws me to a stop. I toss him a questioning look.

"Anytime you want to leave, you say the word, 'kay?" His eyes hold mine with such intensity, my breath hitches. "You've had a rough night, but I wanted to try to get your mind off things..." Hollis darts a quick glance at the door before returning to me as if he's second-guessing bringing me here.

"And I'm grateful for this." My soft voice seems to echo in the night air. The blaring of Lynyrd Skynyrd's "Sweet Home Alabama" ekes out even from behind the closed door of the bar.

A corner of his mouth tips up. He holds out a large palm and waits for me to place mine in it. When I do, he doesn't immediately start for the door. I look at him. His eyes crinkle at the corners. "To turnin' this night around."

I smile up at him, allowing my eyes to trace his features. The way he always looks at me as if I'm something precious. The way he smiles at me, not just with his lips but eyes, too. The comfort of his hand holding mine.

"Let's do it."

17

HOLLIS

"THIS IS THE BEST NIGHT *EVER*!"

Magnolia swings her arms out in childlike glee like only a person with low—wait, who am I kidding? More like zero—tolerance can. She nearly knocks over Mr. Ted's beer.

I've been watching over her the entire time. She's had a total of two screwdrivers which she happily announced didn't "look like urine, unlike beer."

She even made friends with the scary biker sitting at the far end of the bar giving off serious loner vibes. She managed to get him to dance to Toby Keith's "I Love This Bar," to everyone's amazement.

Mr. Ted and I exchange an amused look above her head. She sits on the barstool between us, leaning forward to rest her elbows on the worn bar.

"Young lady, I reckon it's time for you to start headin' home before you end up howlin' with the coon dogs later on."

Mr. Ted's right. I need to get her out of here and back in her bed. Otherwise, she'll be hating life in the morning.

She sways slightly in her seat. With a bright and carefree smile, her expression is an extreme contrast from earlier. "Mr.

Ted?" Her expression sobers, and she leans closer to the older man, lowering her voice. "Isn't Hollis just the best?"

I look away and take a long drink from my bottle of water because even though I know she's tipsy, I don't do compliments well.

"He's a good one, all right," the older man agrees.

"He's my best friend," she continues as if I'm not right beside her, listening to every word. "Do you know he was my first kiss?"

My entire body freezes. We've never brought it up since that day long ago. I can't help it. I turn my head to the side to watch her. She doesn't pay me any attention, but her eyes take on a faraway look.

"I wasn't his first, mind you, but he was mine. And it was one of the sweetest things anyone's ever done for me. I thought I was fixin' to be like that girl in that movie..." She snaps her fingers a few times, brow furrowed in thought, and I swear she's the cutest thing I've seen. Suddenly, her entire face lights up. "*Never Been Kissed*! That's it!" She grins and props her chin on her hand with a loud sigh. "But Hollis saved me."

Mr. Ted eyes me over her head, and it's easy to detect the humor in his voice. "Good thing he was around."

"That's the God's honest truth." She lets out another sigh before she straightens abruptly. "Hey, Mr. Ted?"

"Yes, Magnolia?" he says with the practiced patience of someone who's dealt with countless inebriated folks.

I take another drink of water just as she says, "You reckon he'd help me get rid of my virginity, too?"

I choke and sputter so much the guy beside me thumps my back. Finally, I get myself under control and use one of the bar napkins to wipe my mouth. I draw in a deep breath, trying to ready myself to face her after that.

"Time to head out, Shortcake."

I need to get her out of here. Especially if she plans to keep spouting off questions like that last one.

Relief floods me when she nods with an "Okay," before turning back to her new friend. "Now, Mr. Ted. Don't you forget about me, ya hear? Because if I play my cards right, Hollis'll bring me back."

I gently take hold of her arm and guide her off the stool and a few steps toward the door. She continues talking to him.

"And don't forget to add a little sugar to your collard greens next time you make 'em," she calls out while I walk her, step by step, until we're at the exit.

Because, of course, Magnolia would be the one to trade recipe secrets in a bar.

"It'll take out the bitter bite of the collards!" she finishes a split second before I lift her by her waist, carry her outside, and plant her on the sidewalk.

As soon as her feet touch the concrete, she stamps her hands on her hips. Her stern features match her scolding tone. "Hollis Barnes, that wasn't very polite."

"Yes, ma'am, I know. But I've gotta get you home before you regret tonight and hate me in the mornin'."

Her expression softens. "Don't you know I could never hate you?"

I sling an arm over her shoulders, allowing her to lean her weight on me, and guide her along the sidewalk. She slides an arm around my waist. "I sure hope you feel that way tomorrow."

Her head rests against me. "Always," she says, just shy of a whisper, and I hold her tighter.

A few girls pass by us, arms linked, the one in the middle a little unsteady on her feet. When her eyes lock on us, she calls out as her two friends help her past, "Aww! I love love tooooo!"

A small laugh escapes me, and Magnolia's arm at my waist tightens. I glance over at her. "You okay?"

"Mmhmm," is all I get in return.

I frown. "If you feel sick, just let me—"

"I'm fine, Hollis," she mumbles in a weary voice. "Just tired."

Less than a minute later, we're stepping up to the dorm. I think she's sobered up a little on the walk back, but I wish I could keep an eye on her through the night just the same. But, well...I reckon she wouldn't want me hovering over her tonight of all nights and—

"Can I spend the night with you?"

I jerk my head to stare at her in surprise. She lowers her gaze as if she suddenly feels shy and quickly rushes on with, "Never mind. You've helped me enough." She tries to draw away from me, but I hold tight to her. "I'll be fine." She tries to inject firmness to her words, but I can hear the vulnerability clear as day.

"Shortcake." I wait for her to raise her eyes to mine. "I told him not to come back tonight, and after what went down, I know he won't. So..." I tip my head to the side and try to offer her a comforting smile. "You're welcome to stay with me."

She holds my gaze for a long beat before nodding slowly. "Thank you."

A moment later, we're inside my dorm room, the entire building so quiet you could hear a pin drop since the designated quiet hours are enforced.

I don't know what has me feeling antsy, but I scramble to pull out clothes for her to change into. After she disappears into our Jack-and-Jill-style bathroom we share with the guys next door, she returns with her hair pulled back in a ponytail. The scent of mint lingers as she gets closer. She must've used toothpaste on her finger to rid herself of the taste of liquor.

She appears almost shy, her clothes clenched in her hands in front of her, dressed in my T-shirt and a pair of my boxers. I'm not sure what to make of it, but deep down, something about seeing her in my clothes is strangely satisfying.

"Can I set these somewhere out of the way?"

I tip my head to the area near my desk. Then I quickly head to the bathroom to brush my teeth and change into a pair of pajama pants and an old T-shirt. Once finished, I pull the door closed behind me.

"You can take my bed. I'll grab a blanket and sleep on top of his bed."

"Could you"—she hesitates with a wince—"lie with me for a bit?"

"Okay." My voice is low and huskier than usual. I walk over to her and peel back the covers. She slides between the sheets, shifting to her side to allow me some room on the twin mattress. She frowns and shakes her head, sitting up.

"Can you lie on your back, and I'll just curl up along your side? That way, you'll be more comfortable, right?"

I shift to my back. As soon as she curls up with her head on my chest, an arm draped over my chest and a leg over one of my thighs, I let out a slow exhale and close my eyes. Damn, it's been a hell of a night.

"This is nice," she whispers.

My mouth curves up slightly, and I whisper back, "It is."

Silence fills the room and just when I think she's drifted off, she whispers again. "Can I ask you a question?"

"Mmhmm." *Shit*, I'm tired.

"What's an orgasm feel like?"

My eyes flash open, and everything stills. I'm afraid to speak, let alone move. Thank God she doesn't look up at me. Even with the bit of light from outside shining in through the blinds, I'm not sure I could handle her staring me in the eyes, waiting on my answer.

I clench and unclench my jaw, wondering how the hell to handle this. Finally, I just think, *The hell with it.*

"Shortcake, you mean to tell me those guys never gave you a damn orgasm?" *Fucking asshats.*

And goddamn Preston. I grind my molars wishing I could hit him again. *What kind of guy would date her for so long without giving her an orgasm?*

She shakes her head against me. "No."

Something in the way she says that one word sends prickles of unease through me. "Wait. You mean, never with a partner, right?"

Her voice sounds tiny, and I can practically feel the embarrassment radiating off her. "I know I sound stupid, but I've just never felt comfortable tryin' to...you know. With myself."

I stare at the dark ceiling. Lord help me. This is a conversation I never thought I'd have with her.

Ever.

"I mean, I've googled it." Her index finger starts tracing a random pattern on my chest, and my abs contract instinctively. The reaction down below is jarring because my dick begins to harden.

Not okay. Especially when part of her arm rests just a few inches above it. Not to mention, just because she's asking me a question about masturbating doesn't mean she wants to sleep with me.

Even if my buddy down there is delusional enough to think so.

"The diagrams are so confusin'."

Diagrams? What the hell is she talkin' about?

"I mean, you'd think that with all the info on the internet that guys would be able to zero in on the clit. But *noooo.*" She drags out the last word, then releases a long, disappointed sigh. "Then again, it's not like I've been able to work my magic on it, either."

A choked sound escapes me. "Uh, Shortcake? I'm not sure this is a conversation you should be havin' with me."

She shifts to prop her chin on my chest, and a shaft of dim light illuminates part of her face. "You're the only person I *can* have this conversation with."

I part my lips to protest, but she interrupts with, "Hollis, just listen for a minute." A split second of a pause hangs between us before she tacks on, "Please."

When I stay silent, waiting her out, she continues. "You were my first kiss. You're my best friend and..." She trails off before starting again, her voice hushed. "I just know that I can tell you anythin', and you won't laugh at me or make me feel stupid."

I drag a hand over my face slowly with a silent groan. *Shit.* Of all the things she could bring up.

"Are you good at, um, you know...findin' a girl's clit?"

My hand stops at my jaw, and I run it along the slight scruff, trying to buy time.

"I swear, Hollis, I won't breathe a word to a soul." Her hushed pleading tone has me wavering. "I just don't want to be clueless forever."

Dammit. As idiotic as it sounds, I know if our roles were reversed, she'd suck it up and talk to me about it. Which is why, even though my tone is resigned, I grit out an answer.

"Yes."

She practically vibrates with curiosity. Even her voice perks up. "Yes, you know how to find it?"

I toss an arm over my eyes and grunt an, "Mmhmm."

If I could drown in awkwardness, *this* would be the moment.

"So, you've made a girl, um...orgasm that way?"

"*Magnolia*..." My tone is exasperated as hell. And for good reason.

"I'm just askin' because—"

"Yes."

There's a millisecond of a pause before she softens her tone to a hesitant, "And you're sure of this?"

I fling my arm off my eyes and speak through clenched teeth. "Yes."

"How can you be so su—"

"Because she came all over my goddamn tongue!"

Fuck. I didn't mean to say it so loud. Or be that crude.

I rush to apologize. "I'm sorry, Shortca—"

"Did you like it?" Her voice has a hint of breathlessness to it.

I pinch my eyes closed and murmur quietly, "Yeah. I liked it a whole hell of a lot."

My damn dick is getting harder to the point where pretty soon, she'll notice. But it's not because I'm thinking about the times I went down on Charlotte. It's that my mind has replaced her with Magnolia, and now I'm thinking about *her* riding my face. Thinking about the little sounds she might make. How she might taste.

How I'd damn sure find her clit and make her come. How she wouldn't wonder about much of anything after I finished.

Fuck.

Her voice sounds small when she finally says, "He never wanted to do that." Then in a derisive tone, she adds, "Always said it wasn't his thing."

If I could go back and punch Preston harder, I'd do it just for that alone. What a selfish little shit.

I lower my eyes to her partially illuminated face and run a finger down her cheek. "He's a clueless asshole."

Magnolia falls silent for so long, I think she's done with the conversation. I relax, my muscles losing the rigid tension, and close my eyes.

"Could you show me?"

My eyes snap open, and I stare at her, my lips parting in shock. "*What?*"

She shrugs. "It would be the same as the kiss you gave me. You just show me how it's done right so I know from here on out."

I huff out a laugh filled with exasperation and disbelief. "Not quite how it works, Shortcake."

"What about dry humpin'? I've never done that before."

"You are not. Askin' me. To dry hump you," I grit out.

"I am." She nods.

I don't respond because I'm not sure I can. Or what the hell to say.

"I just"—she drops her voice, her tone gentler—"need to know if *I'm* the problem."

I don't know what the hell I did, but it must've been a hell of a doozy to piss off the big man upstairs and get tortured like this.

"This is so fuckin' awkward," I mutter under my breath.

She shifts, rising up to straddle me before lowering herself down. Right over my dick that's clearly jonesing for action since he hasn't seen any since Charlotte and I broke things off. And it's not for a lack of offers. Guess I'm old-fashioned, but I want to be with someone I actually care about and like. Someone I want to spend time with.

It doesn't mean it makes my dick happy, but that's too damn bad.

"Ohhh..."

Yep. She's realized exactly what I'm packing. These pants don't disguise much, and the boxers she has on aren't much of a barrier either.

She rocks her hips experimentally, ripping a pained sound from my throat, and she immediately stops. I mash my lips together and close my eyes.

"Did I hurt you?"

I shake my head.

"Can I...do it again? Because it feels good"—her palms

flatten against the hard wall of my chest, her voice catching slightly when she grinds against me—"when I do that."

Shit, shit, *shit*. Without thinking, I find my hands gripping her hips. I keep my eyes closed, and it's dumb, but a part of me rationalizes that if I keep them closed, this isn't real.

That I'm not doing anything wrong. That we're not crossing some line.

When I tighten my hold on her, guiding her to work herself against me while I give a shallow thrust upward, that little hitch in her breathing sends a surge of heat flicking through my veins. "Make sure you're gettin' your clit."

There's no mistaking the breathlessness in her tone now. "I am."

My voice is low, gravelly. "One sign you're doin' it right is when you're wet."

Now, she's moving on her own, to her own rhythm, without my guidance. I slip my fingertips beneath the waistband of the boxers she rolled down a few times and graze my thumbs against her hip bones. God, her skin is so damn soft.

"I'm—" She breaks off, her breathing choppy. "I'm really wet."

Hearing her say it makes my cock leak at the tip, wetting my pants to combine with the slight dampness from her. I wish there were more light so I could see those cotton boxers. Wish I could see the spot of wetness from her pussy.

Fuck. I roll my hips, pressing my cock harder against her, and she gasps. Her movements are more frantic now, and I know what she's chasing.

"It's…"

"I know." My whisper is ragged. "Keep goin'. Make yourself come hard."

Shit. My balls tighten, a pressure building as a tingling spreads through me.

"*Oh, Hollis.*" The way she whimpers my name has me gritting my teeth to hold back. No way in hell will I get off before her.

Without thinking, I slide one hand up beneath the front of her shirt. When I find her braless, I can't resist running the pad of my thumb over her hard nipple. She instantly arches into my touch, continuing to work herself over me.

Her nipple feels perfectly puckered, and I'm dying to get my mouth on it. To suck on it while she rides me hard.

Magnolia suddenly shifts. My eyes squint open—I'm equal parts scared shitless that this is only a dream and also that it's not. That I'm doing the worst thing I could possibly take part in. That I'm betraying my best friend by taking advantage of her.

She sheds her shirt, letting it drop to the floor, and *fuck me.* The faint light on her body... She's just *perfect.*

I jerk upright, bending at the waist. Cupping the weight of one breast in my hand, I latch onto her nipple, sucking it deep into my mouth. When I flick my tongue against the hardened tip, her faint cry of my name urges me on. One of her hands clenches my shoulder in a near death grip while the other cups the back of my head, as if to prevent me from stopping.

No way in hell anyone could make me stop. She tastes so fucking good.

I move to her other nipple while I palm her firm ass cheek, urging her on. The front of my pants is damp, and I'm dying to tear everything away and have her sink down on me. To bury myself deep inside her.

"*Fuck*, Magnolia." I groan the words against her skin, then flick the tip of her nipple again with my tongue. Her tortured-sounding moan urges me on. "I need you to come, baby girl. I don't wanna come without you."

The clench of her hand on my shoulder tightens, and her breathing turns even more ragged, telling me she's close.

"What do you need?" I toy with her nipple, laving it before circling the areola and repeating. "Tell me, and I'll do it."

"I..." She falters, and I sense the hesitation even through the thick fog of arousal hanging over me.

"Tell me."

When she answers, her voice is so faint, I strain to hear her. "A kis—"

She doesn't finish because I grip her ponytail in my fist and fit my mouth to hers, mindless to being gentle. The kiss is hungry. Explosive. Desperate. Wet. My tongue darts inside to toy with hers, and her ragged moan gets lost in the mix. I can't seem to get enough.

Finally, I retreat slightly to catch her bottom lip between my teeth and gently tug on it. I can't help myself. My voice is hoarse, heavy with lust. "You taste so fuckin' good."

That's the instant she explodes.

"*Hollis.*" My name comes out as a shaky whimper, laced with a sense of both wonder and surprise. She fastens her lips to mine, her scream muted by mouth as she comes.

The damp heat from her body has me mindless to anything but the feel of her beneath my palms and the weight of her on top of me. The way she moans while I kiss her and work her over my hard cock.

One more deep thrust against her is all it takes before every muscle in my body goes rigid and I jerk, my cock pulsing and shooting in hot spurts. "*Fuuuck.*"

She breaks the kiss, breathing ragged like my own, and slumps against me. I lean back to lie flat with her sprawled out on top of me. Smoothing back stray strands of her hair from her face, I lightly trace slow circles over her bare back. My heart thunders in my chest, taking its damn time to slow down.

Our breathing is the only sound in the quiet room. With her

cheek pressed to my chest, she moves, and it's almost like she's nuzzling me.

"Hollis?" Her barely audible whisper causes every muscle in my body to tense. I'm honestly not ready to let reality intrude just yet.

I draw in a slow breath and close my eyes to concentrate on everything at this moment. I may only be a college freshman, but I know enough to realize that what just happened wasn't something casual.

At least not for me.

"Gotta get cleaned up." I slide off the bed and rush to grab another pair of pajama pants before darting into the bathroom to clean up and change.

The entire time, I'm internally laying into myself.

Dammit. What have I done?

Magnolia Barton is and has been my best friend for years, but there's something between us that hints at more being possible. We have a spark.

No, that's not right. It's more like a lit match to kerosene. Hot as hell.

But maybe she doesn't feel it. Not only that, but just because this happened doesn't mean she feels anything for me aside from just needing a body tonight. She's never once implied she feels something for me—something more than friends. Plus, she's been drinking tonight.

Tonight's opened up the biggest fucking Pandora's box for me—the one I held in secret. The one I shoved away in some dark part of my mind because I knew—*know* with painful certainty—that I have no chance in hell of her reciprocating my true feelings.

I head back to the bed and hope like hell she's already asleep. When I slide back into bed, she instantly curls up at my side, taking the same position from a moment ago.

Shit. What if I've just fucked up the best friendship I've ever had and took advantage of—

"Hush."

I stiffen in alarm. Is she talking to me? Or did she already nod off, and she's talking in her sleep?

When she raises her head to peer at me in the darkened room, I try to gauge her reaction and come up empty.

"Hush?" I repeat, unsure.

Her lips flatten. "You're freakin' out."

I stare at her in disbelief. "And you're *not*?" I grind the heels of my palms to my eyes with a groan. "I just took advantage of my best friend." *God, I'm so fucked.*

"Well, you're in good company since I did the same thing," comes her quick reply.

I drop my hands from my face to stare at her. How can she be calm about this?

"Magn—"

I'm stopped by the kiss she dusts on my lips. She offers a satisfied, sleepy smile before curling up at my side and resting an arm over my chest. Instinctively, I curl an arm around her, holding her tight to me, and drop a light kiss to the top of her hair.

Her voice slurs as if she's already half asleep, and she whispers, "Love you, Hollis."

The arm I have around her tightens a fraction, and I realize for the first time the words won't come.

The sound of her steady, even breathing is a welcome relief, letting me off the hook.

Because no way in hell can I say, "But not like that." Not this time.

I'm not sure I'll ever be able to say it again.

18

MAGNOLIA

I WAKE UP IN BED HOW I NORMALLY DO: BURROWED BENEATH THE covers, from head to toe. My mother used to panic when I was little, telling me I'd suffocate.

Clearly, that never happened.

Awareness settles in, bit by bit, and I realize I'm curled up, half-lying on top of a hard, warm, *very* male body.

And then it hits me.

I made out with Hollis Barnes last night!

Wait, no. That's not quite right. I dry humped him, and he showed me the world of orgasms and how magical they can be.

My cheeks heat, and a mischievous smile threatens to form until I realize the full extent of what I did last night.

I crawled on top of my best friend and rubbed myself against him. Granted, he seemed to enjoy it, but what guy wouldn't? It doesn't mean anything. Plus, he's always done whatever it took to make me happy.

I admit, I let the alcohol take hold and free my inhibitions last night, but I wasn't completely drunk. Just a little tipsy.

Then I took advantage of my best friend. The same one who saved me from a jackwagon of an ex-boyfriend. The one who's lying here while I snuggle against his hard body, my leg thrown over his.

I groan and bury my face against his chest as mortification fills me.

What if I've ruined our friendship?

No. Absolutely not. I won't allow it. I'll set things right somehow.

"You done suffocatin' yourself under there?" His husky voice teases me from above the covers.

"Mmm, not quite," I murmur, the remnants of sleep still evident in my voice.

Silence hangs between us for a long moment before I finally work up the courage to speak.

"I'm sorry." My voice is tiny and not the least bit confident. I'm a coward of epic proportions, because I'm still hiding beneath the covers.

His body goes rigid before he tentatively asks, "For what?"

"For...takin' adva—"

I'm interrupted by the sound of a key turning in the lock seconds before I hear it swing open. I tense, but Hollis goes impossibly rigid.

"Hey, I'm just grabbin' some stuff and headin' back out." Preston's voice is tentative, almost like he's asking Hollis for permission. He's probably heading back to the frat house.

A part of me wonders if he hooked up after I left. Oddly enough, that idea doesn't bother me. I just hate that I wasted so much time with him.

"Oh, whoa. Sorry. I didn't realize you had someone over." My ex-boyfriend's voice is hurried and nervous. Guess he noticed the large lump beneath the covers next to Hollis.

Boy, am I glad he gathered up my clothes and put them in his closet. Although my sandals are by the door—ones I've worn plenty of times while Preston and I dated—but clearly, he's not one for noticing details.

The sound of items being shoved in what I assume is some sort of backpack or duffle bag hits my ears before he tells Hollis, "I'm out of your hair till Monday."

Hollis finally responds with a simple, "Got it."

I don't realize I'm holding my breath until the door closes and leaves us in complete silence. Only now do I let it out with a slow whoosh.

"That was close." His low voice sounds different. He's probably panicked about getting caught with me here. "No doubt that would've been rough."

I need to try to salvage this before I make my escape as dignified as one can when not wearing a shirt—I'd never put it back on last night. Quickly, I toss back the covers and scramble over him and off the bed. Without making eye contact, I grab my clothes from the closet and head for the bathroom, tossing over my shoulder, "I'll be right back."

As soon as I click the door shut and lock it, I exhale slowly. The person staring back at me in the mirror looks different. Mussed hair, a faint tinge of redness around my mouth from his scruff when we kissed. Even my eyes appear a little dazed, with mascara flaking beneath them. All in all, I look like I was thoroughly ravished last night.

Can you imagine what it would've been like if he'd done more? If we'd gone all the way? It feels as though I have a devil perched on my shoulder whispering this.

I force myself to snap out of it and shove away those errant thoughts before I quickly dress in last night's outfit. I've never done the walk of shame, and I certainly never expected to do one after a night with Hollis Barnes.

Once I've tidied my appearance as much as I can with limited resources, I emerge to find Hollis sitting on the bed, bare feet planted on the floor, elbows resting on his knees. He appears lost in thought with his gaze on his feet until he hears me approach. His brown eyes rise, and when they lock with mine, I can barely suppress the cringe at the uncertainty and nervousness in the depths.

He regrets last night.

Being faced with his obvious regret feels like someone's just stabbed me in the chest. I force a smile and reach for my wristlet.

"I should get out of your hair. I want to—"

"Magnolia, I—"

We both speak at the same time, but Hollis' cell phone interrupts us. He grimaces, looking like he resents the intrusion, but the moment he glances at the caller ID, an odd expression crosses his face.

"Hello?" His face is impassive now, his tone polite but curt. "Yes, ma'am. She's right here." With a shuttered expression, his eyes flick to mine, and he hands me his phone. "It's for you."

Cautiously, I accept it from him and glance at the screen only to have every fiber inside me tense in alarm.

Does she have some odd sort of radar? And why is my mother callin' Hollis? I didn't even realize she had his number.

"Hello?" I say warily.

"Magnolia Mae Barton! Young lady, are you tryin' to send me to an early grave? I've been tryin' to get a hold of you for hours and hours now. Why, I was about to call the local police and file a missin' person's report."

Always dramatic, that's my mother.

"I'm sorry, Mother." I wince, realizing I put my phone on silent in case Preston tried to call me. I'd never bothered to check it, not wanting to deal with everything last night.

I unzip my wristlet and withdraw my phone, horrified to see just shy of one hundred missed calls. A fraction of that horrified feeling breaks off into fury when I see how many of them are from Preston.

It's only exacerbated by my mother's next words.

"Preston was worried sick about you and called to let us know y'all had a little spat. He said you ran off." When she tacks on, "With *that Hollis boy,*" her nasty snarl is unmistakable.

"My *word*, Magnolia! You really must find a way to break ties with him. He's comin' between you and Preston, and that just won't do." She sighs, and her tone turns into something that sounds almost dreamy. "Preston is such a nice young man. And he comes from a wonderful family."

"Do you know what he did over spring break?" I challenge.

She sighs. "Now, Magnolia." Her condescending tone is much like the one she used when I was a small child. "You know how men can sometimes be when they get together and there's alcohol involved."

At her at-the-ready excuse for him—for all men who cheat, really—my lips flatten in anger. "So, if it were Roy, it would be acceptable?" My question comes out far sharper than I intended, but I can't help it.

"You watch your tone with me, young lady," she warns. But she doesn't answer my question.

"Now, you listen here." She barely takes a breath before starting in again. "Roy and I have discussed this, and you and Preston will mend the relationship. There's too much at stake right now. Stop being so selfish and get over this little hissy fit."

Too much at stake? My eyes fall closed as the realization hits me. Without opening my eyes, I reach up to pinch the bridge of my nose, the sign of an impending headache already beginning to throb at my temples.

"Too much is at stake, meanin' Preston's father and Roy have some sort of agreement," I state dully.

I don't bother to phrase it as a question. I should've known.

Heck, I should know by now how things work. Nothing in my life is truly mine.

I was the idiot who introduced him to them. This is my fault.

"Preston's ready to make amends. He feels just *awful* about the way everythin' played out. He was on his way to you this mornin' to apologize."

Right. And how much of the apology was based on him actually wanting to and not these adults playing puppet master?

"I need to go." I hate how defeated I sound, but I've been backed into a corner.

"Do the right thing, Magnolia."

My mother's final words aren't *I love you* or *I miss you, sweetie.* I may no longer be a child, but even though I know I'll never have one of those mothers who hugs you like she never wants to let go, wants to know about exciting things that happen in your life and celebrate them, and who doesn't try to stifle who you are but helps you shine even if you have countless imperfections and idiosyncrasies, I still yearn for it.

She doesn't wait for me to respond before she ends the call. Wearily, I open my eyes and hand the phone back to Hollis.

"Sorry about that."

"No need to apologize." He studies me carefully. "You okay?"

I take a step back and force myself to look him in the eyes. "I owe you an apology for last night." When he starts to protest, I hold up a hand to stop him. "That was inappropriate on so many levels. You mean the world to me, Hollis." My voice cracks on the first syllable of his name, and I press my lips thin to battle against my turbulent emotions. "I can't bear the idea of ruinin' our friendship, and I promise to never put you in that position again."

His stare is heavy, expression indecipherable. "What'd your mom say?"

I swallow hard past the lump in my throat and let out a derisive laugh. "Apparently, they have an agreement with Preston's father and have coordinated us gettin' back together."

Jaw clenched, his nostrils flare before he turns his gaze to the ceiling and grips the back of his neck with his hand. I reckon he doesn't want me to get involved with Preston again. Especially after what went on last night.

Lord knows I feel the same way.

I force myself to ask, "Are we okay?" *Please say we are, please say we are*, I internally beg.

Hollis drops his hand and studies me for a moment before giving a quick nod. He must notice the mix of frustration and anguish on my face because his features soften, and he stands and opens his arms for me.

As soon as I step into his embrace, I'm engulfed by a sense of comfort, setting me at ease the way only he can. I know it's a brief reprieve, but I accept it wholeheartedly.

"We're always okay, Shortcake." His voice contains a tinge of huskiness, and he presses a light kiss to the top of my head.

In the recesses of my mind, I can't help but wonder if we really are.

19

HOLLIS

FINALS WEEK
May

I'm confident about how I've done so far on my final exams, even if my heart wasn't really in it.

Dad wants me to be the first college grad in the family, but I feel like I'm wasting the partial scholarship and racking up student loan debt for nothing. I still don't have a clue what I want to major in, let alone do with my life. I picked business because of his suggestion, but I can't say I've ever had wet dreams about opening up my own place or anything.

With just one more exam left to take in an hour, it's hard to believe I'll soon have one full year of college in the books.

Mr. Ted offered me a summer job, helping him in his shop, doing some of the body work. He said he knew of a cheap place for rent, but I haven't made up my mind. I miss Dad, but with the long hours he works, it would mean being around Mom more, and I'm not sure the country club can give me enough hours to get me out of the house. Regardless, I still want to head home and spend some time with him.

I've packed up the bulk of my stuff from the dorm and stowed it in my truck. I plan to hightail it home right after my last final. I toss a few last-minute things into my large plastic laundry bin I'm now using as a catch-all just as my phone vibrates on my desk next to my wallet and keys. I wonder if it's Magnolia wishing me luck on my last final.

I reach to grab it, only to see it's from home. I'd normally dismiss it, since Dad always calls when he's at work and away from Mom, but something urges me to answer this time.

"Hello?"

As soon as her familiar voice explains the reason for the call, my knees give out, and I drop to the floor so hard the impact rattles from my ass all the way up my spine. The phone clatters to the floor beside me. It feels as though a herd of elephants are stomping on my chest, making me gasp for breath.

I finally manage to shake off a fraction of the shock, and I drag myself upright, clutching my phone in my hand. Quickly, I scoop up my wallet, keys, and the laundry basket with my things tossed inside, and rush for the door. It opens seconds before I reach it, and Preston enters.

"Hey, man, I—" He stops, his eyes going wide. "What happened?"

I grit my teeth as I push past him. "My dad died."

20

MAGNOLIA

ONCE I FINISH MY LAST FINAL, I FEEL LIKE I'VE BEEN SUCKED DRY of any remaining brain power.

I try calling Hollis after I finish, but he doesn't answer. I sent him a text earlier to wish him good luck with his finals, and it still says *Unread*, which is unusual for him. Normally, he sends a quick response.

An uneasy feeling churns in the pit of my stomach, so I decide to stop by his room on my way back from the PolySci building before I grab the rest of my things and drive home for the summer.

I step up to the door and knock, and Preston answers with a hopeful-sounding, "Hey."

I get the feeling he expects me to pop up out of the blue and confess that I want him back and forgive him. That's never happening—not even with the pressure from my parents and his father.

After everything happened in March, I told Preston I'd be civil toward him for appearances, to tide my parents over and get them at least *somewhat* off my back, but made it clear the chances of us getting back together were as good as the chances of another hurricane *never* hitting the Gulf Coast.

In other words, *zero* chance. My mother might think it's fine for me to turn a blind eye to a cheating boyfriend, but this is one area I refuse to budge on.

"Hi." I dart a glance past him, looking for my best friend. "Is Hollis around?"

His brows knit together. "I thought you'd gone with him." He must see the confusion written on my face because he pales and appears almost nervous. "Uh, he rushed out of here about an hour or so ago."

Wait a second... That means he missed his final exam.

Now, I'm really confused. "What are you talkin' about?"

Preston runs a hand over his hair in obvious agitation. "When I asked where he was goin', he said his dad...died."

The hallway sways, and he instantly reaches out and grasps my upper arm to steady me. Vaguely, I recognize that I'm allowing him to touch me only because shock has taken hold. In any other instance, I'd shrug him off.

Oh, dear Lord. Hollis has always been so close with his father. And to me, Mr. Jay has been so much more than just a neighbor, more than just my best friend's dad.

My heart aches deep within my chest, and I press my hand to my lips to restrain the sob threatening to break free. I turn, my vision hazy at the edges, but the desperation to rush to my room and grab my things is urgent. "I need to go."

My feet somehow carry me down the hall, and I don't register Preston's voice calling out to me. Hollis needs me. I have to be there for him. My chest feels like a cavernous hole has been hollowed out at the grief he must be experiencing.

Everything passes in a blur. I absently recall Stephanie snagging our residential advisor so I could scribble my signature on the final checkout sheet. Then my roommate helped me pack my car with the rest of my belongings.

Thankfully, the sun high in the May sky with no rain clouds in sight means clear roads for the drive home. It takes me about three and a half hours, which is a blessing since, at other times, I've gotten stuck in what seems to be never-ending construction traffic on both I-85 and I-65.

When I take the exit off I-10, it dawns on me that I never called my parents to let them know I was driving back tonight. They're not expecting me until Saturday since I told them I wanted to take my time to pack up, have some last-minute girl time with Stephanie, and not be so rushed. Turning into our neighborhood, I automatically make the right turn into Hollis' driveway and park behind his truck.

As soon as I turn off the ignition, everything hits me at once. Mr. Jay's gone forever. Hollis and I have never dealt with a death in the family, and I know everyone grieves differently. What if he doesn't want me here? What if he just wants to be alone?

The humidity is already growing thick inside my car now that the air's not running, so I palm my keys and slide out, slipping my phone in my back pocket. Standing in the driveway, I decide to check the treehouse first before I brave ringing the doorbell and risk facing Mrs. Barnes.

I stride through the backyard, quickly climb the ladder, and hesitantly push open the door before poking my head inside. As soon as I lay eyes on him, relief settles through me a split second before anxiousness takes its place. I hover, unsure if I should climb the rest of the way inside.

In a pair of khakis and a dark cotton T-shirt, he's sprawled on the air mattress he stores inside, a fresh blanket draped over it, and his flip-flops are kicked off in a corner. Two bed pillows prop him up, his dark hair contrasting with the pale blue pillowcases.

He takes a swig of whiskey straight from the bottle before clumsily setting it on the floor. The bottle's just shy of a quarter of the way empty, and he doesn't even glance my way. Instead, his dull gaze is trained on the ceiling like it holds the secrets of the world. It's startling when he finally speaks in a flat monotone, making it clear he's aware of my presence.

"Either get in or out."

It's not rude, the way he says it. Just...matter of fact. There's no emotion, no heat in his words. It's like he's an empty shell.

Anguish assaults me, much like the way the waves batter against the Gulf shoreline during the fiercest of storms, at seeing Hollis like this.

I quickly climb the rest of the way inside and kick off my flip-flops. Slipping my phone from the back pocket of my shorts, I set it and my keys on the shelf. Silence hangs heavily between us, the only sound the low din of the old window unit air conditioner.

Moving to stand beside him, I gentle my tone. "Can I just... lie with you?"

His eyes fall closed, his expression tortured, and I sink my top teeth into my lower lip anxiously. Maybe it was a bad decision to come here. I'm only bothering him. I spin around, ready to leave him be, when the scratchy rasp of his voice stops me.

"*Please.*" One word. That's all he says. But it holds so much meaning.

Instantly, I lower myself and curl my body around him. He raises his arm, and I rest my cheek against his chest. The tension radiating through him is practically tangible, and I hold him tight, wishing I could comfort him somehow because, *good Lord*, I know this isn't enough.

"I can't believe he's gone." His hushed voice overflows with sadness. I detect the faintest slurring of his words from the effects of the whiskey.

I press my eyes closed at the rush of tears threatening to spill. "Neither can I."

Mr. Jay was an amazing man. Warm, friendly, and with a heart of gold, that man never once judged me because of my family. He never saw the money or politics most others do.

He was the man who taught me how to hold a hammer correctly and the difference between a Phillips head and a flat-head screwdriver. When their old refrigerator died, he'd taught Hollis and me how to use Teflon tape when hooking up the ice maker on the new one and how to lay down a thin piece of toilet paper beneath the connection to check for leaks.

As we got older, he may have had less and less free time due to his work schedule, but I knew, sure as the sun would rise the next day, that he loved with all his heart. He'd taken me in and always treated me as he did Hollis. And I would forever be grateful to him for it.

"I have to meet with the attorney." Hollis' voice is so faint, I strain to hear him. "Apparently, he named me executor of his will."

"When is the—"

"There won't be one." His answer is succinct.

Alarmed, I raise my head to peer down at him, but his eyes are still closed. He mumbles, "He didn't want a funeral or anythin' showy. He told me that, time and again."

I frown but lower my head again. Placing a palm over the center of his chest, I cautiously ask him what I've been wondering all along. "What happened?"

"He went to the ER, thinkin' he was havin' a heart attack. He had an aortic aneurysm." His chest rises and falls with deep breaths, like he's fighting against his riotous emotions. "It ruptured before they could do anythin'."

I tighten my hold on him, and even though I try my best to

be quiet, tears cascade down my cheeks freely, dampening his cotton shirt.

His hoarse voice is heavy with a mixture of anger and hurt. "The worst thing is, Mom can't be bothered with any of it." A rough laugh breaks free, but it's the furthest thing from humorous. "She's upset because he was due to get a bonus once he hit his anniversary mark in two months."

"Oh, Hollis," I whisper raggedly.

Silence hangs heavily between us, for so long that he startles me when he finally speaks again.

"I go downtown to sign some things tomorrow mornin'." He lets out a long sigh. "I plan on finishin' that bottle over there tonight." The grief in his voice makes it sound huskier than normal. "You might wanna head home."

I tense. "Are you spendin' the night out here?"

"Mmhmm."

I hesitate before asking, "Can I—" I break off nervously, before forging on. "Stay here with you?" Then I rush to add on hurriedly, "Just to make sure you're okay since you plan on drinkin' and everythin'."

"You don't have to watch over me, Shortcake." A hint of a smile graces his voice. He presses a light kiss to the top of my head.

"I know," I say softly. "But if it's okay, I'd like to stay here with you."

Hollis exhales a long, slow breath, and when he doesn't immediately answer, I worry he'll refuse.

He catches me off guard when he whispers, pressing his lips to my hairline, "You're really the only person I want with me right now." He pauses a beat. "But I'm not sure you should see me like this."

"I'd like to stay," I repeat gently. "I just"—my voice cracks, and I pause before regaining my composure—"don't want you to be alone."

"You're probably hungry after that drive," he murmurs quietly.

"A little." A faint smile tugs at my mouth. Only my best friend would be worried about me and whether I've eaten at a time like this.

"Want pizza?"

I raise my head to peer down at him. "I can order it for us." I'm sure he's forgotten to eat, so maybe I can get some food into him too.

He reaches up to gently cup the side of my face with his palm. "Thank you." His eyes bore into mine with heartfelt urgency. "For bein' here when I need you."

"Of course," I whisper. He closes his eyes, one edge of his lips tipping up faintly, and I gently add, "I'm always here for you."

I dip my head to press a light kiss to his cheek. But at the last second, he shifts, and my lips land on the left side of his mouth instead.

We both freeze in place. The softness of his lips, the sensations that bombard me instantly cause my breath to lodge in my throat, and my eyes widen in shock.

His eyes open slowly, and when I start to back away, about to offer a hasty apology, his palm moves to my nape, drawing me to a stop. With an intense gaze centered on me, he guides me to meet his mouth again. It's achingly slow, as though he's giving me time to turn away. But the heat in the depths of his dark eyes drags me under, and I can't bear to do anything but place my lips on his again.

Little coaxing kisses lull me into a fog of lust. The playful nip of his teeth to my bottom lip has me gasping, and he takes full advantage of it. He deepens the kiss, his tongue diving inside to toy with mine, and soon, it's hard to decipher who's really kissing who.

Grief. Everyone processes it differently, and I know that maybe I'm allowing him to use me as an escape, but I don't care. Because right now, with Hollis' body against mine, it feels right. Perfect. Like the precise moment the scorching summer sun beats down on your skin in midday, warming you through to your center. The comforting heat settles deep and soothes you so thoroughly to your bones.

That's how this feels.

I can't get enough of him. He tastes like whiskey and those breath mints he often carries with him. More than that, though, he tastes familiar. Even though the last time he kissed me was nearly two months ago, my body recognizes him instantly. Every single part of me is on full alert.

Our kiss turns frantic, devouring, and I end up beneath him, with his hard body braced above me. Fingers of his other hand tangle in my hair, and he works his mouth on mine. I fist my hands in the soft fabric of his shirt, dragging the hem upward desperate to touch him. When my fingers graze his hot, muscled flesh, a deep growl reverberates in his chest.

I spread my thighs wider, eager for him to press against where I ache for him most. His khakis don't do much to mask his arousal prodding insistently against the front of the fabric, and he rocks against me in a way that rips a little moan from my throat. The sound of it seems to urge him on because the kiss gets wetter, a little wilder, and he rocks his hardness against the spot where the ache grows more and more urgent.

When he eases away slightly, a dark lock of hair slides over his forehead, and I smooth it back. His eyes study me as if he's trying to decipher my thoughts.

"Magnolia." Urgency and torment are interlaced in his tone.

"I don't wanna fuck up our friendship any more than I did that night."

Even though it became more of a silent agreement that we'd never bring up what happened the night things imploded between Preston and me and swept everything under the carpet, he's bringing it out in the open now.

21

HOLLIS

HER BLUE EYES HOLD MINE, HER BREATH WHISPERING AGAINST MY lips when she speaks.

"This feels right to me. But"—a crease forms between her brows—"if you don't want this..." She swallows hard, and it practically echoes throughout the treehouse. Gaze dropping to focus on my chest, when she whispers, the uncertainty and vulnerability are unmistakable. "I've just...never felt this with anyone else."

I rest my forehead against hers, closing my eyes. The whiskey may have dulled my pain slightly, but I haven't drank enough to not know what the hell I'm doing—and what I'm fucking *craving* to do.

"You can show me what I've been missin'." Her words hang between us, and for a split second, I'm too scared to respond.

I clear my throat, attempting to rein in some composure, before I raise my head. "You want me to show you...?" My shocked disbelief is obvious.

She traces a fingertip along my bottom lip in such a light caress that it sends a shudder down my spine. Her eyes blaze with something that borders between uncertainty and intent. "Everythin' I've been missin'."

I can't help the playful smirk that forms as I lean back, resting on my knees. My eyes drift over her eager yet still nervous expression. "I'm about to show you what those assholes have been missin' out on."

Tugging off my T-shirt, I let it drop to the floor and don't miss the way her eyes drift over my body in appreciation. With her hips cradled in my hands, I gently graze my thumbs over the silky skin just beneath the hem of her shirt. Her breath catches, eyes darkening, her gaze searing me with heat. When her tongue darts out to wet her bottom lip, I can't restrain my groan.

I unfasten her shorts and ease them down her long legs and toss them aside. Taking in the sight of her with the sunlight pouring in through the small window, I smooth my palms up her thighs and settle on her pale yellow cotton panties. My dick jerks at the sight of the damp spot, and I flick my eyes back and forth between it and her eyes that study me with a mixture of anticipation and blatant want.

I skim my thumbs along the elastic edges of her underwear, then carefully slip beneath it, watching her closely for any sign she wants me to stop.

"Is this okay?" My voice is gravelly and thick. I swear my dick is about to wear a hole through my khakis, it's pressing so hard against the zipper.

She nods with a breathless, "Yes."

Her body arches when my thumb glides along where she's already so wet, and my guttural, "*Fuck*," practically echoes between us.

"Touch me. Please." She whispers this with a hint of hesitance as though she's not sure I want to. As if she doesn't realize how badly I'm dying to rip off these panties and taste her on my fucking tongue.

The instant I spread her thighs wider, her scent engulfs me, and my dick hardens even more. Beneath her panties, I graze her opening with the pad of my thumb. When she immediately stiffens, I freeze. My eyes lift to hers cautiously.

"It's just your calluses—" she says in the faintest whisper.

"Sorry." I lift my palms away. "So many rough spots from—"

"Don't stop." Her tongue darts along her bottom lip again, and it brings all sorts of X-rated ideas to mind. "They're rough." Hurriedly, she tacks on, "In a good way."

With a gentle grip of her thighs, I bracket her entrance with my palms, holding her panties aside to bare her.

Shit. She's glistening and pink and so. Fucking. Perfect.

I gently trace the pad of my thumb along her slick lips, and her sharp intake of breath morphs into a moan when I sink just the tip of it inside her. She's so goddamn wet. I'm torn between wanting to fuck her with my tongue and make her scream and the urge to push inside right now and be her first.

Her hands suddenly reach down to shove her underwear off, and I move back to help her. Once they're tossed aside, she's hit with sudden shyness and tries to close her thighs, but I stop her with my hands.

"Don't hide from me." My voice comes out more gruff sounding than I intended. I swear she's nearly sending me over the edge before I've even tasted her. I soften my tone. "You're perfect. So goddamn wet," I say on a half groan.

Her pussy glistens, and I lean forward to spread her apart with my thumbs. My eyes dart to hers as my mouth hovers over her. Her scent drives me fucking wild. "Please tell me I can taste you."

Her hands move to latch onto my wrists, her features lined with nervousness. "I, um…"

Pressing my lips together, I force myself to regain some control before I speak. I need to put her at ease. Holding her gaze, I promise, "If I do anythin' you don't like, you tell me. Okay?"

She nods, her top teeth sinking into her bottom lip, and it makes me want to give her a much better reason to do that.

I lower my focus to where no man has ever put his mouth. The fact that I'm her first, that she's letting me, sends a fierce sense of pride rushing through me.

But along with it comes the understanding that I have to make sure I don't fuck this up. That I manage to shove aside the lingering haze from the whiskey and pay attention to any cues that she doesn't like—or wants—something.

I dip my head close and draw her clit into my mouth, sucking briefly before releasing it and repeating the action. Her hips arch instinctively, and her body's response urges me on.

Internally, I chant, *Go slow, go slow, go slow,* because every urge drives me to fit my mouth to her. To devour her like she's my last meal and I'm an inmate on death row. To completely disregard the fact that she's a virgin. That none of the assholes she'd dated bothered to take the time to make her feel good like this.

With the tip of my tongue, I toy with her clit, intermittently sucking gently. Her fingers thread through my hair, gripping me as if she's afraid I'll stop. My mouth glides lower, and I work her clit in slow circles while placing wet openmouthed kisses to her pussy.

When I get to her opening, I drive my tongue deep inside her, and her taste—*God, her taste*—has my dick harder than it's ever been before. I suck at her lips, then run my tongue over her entrance before thrusting it inside again. I'm a madman, desperate for more of her taste. Again and again, my tongue surges inside her, as deep as I can, while I stroke her clit.

She works herself over my tongue, riding my face. I add more pressure to her clit and continue driving my tongue deep inside her. Her thighs tense on either side of me, and I know she's close.

"*Hollis*." This time, the way she says my name on a whimper-like moan has me pressing my dick against the mattress to try to stave off the urge to come in my fucking pants.

I increase my efforts on her clit while I feast on her. A moment later, she goes rigid before her inner muscles spasm around my tongue, her thighs closing tight against my head while she rides out her orgasm.

Once her shudders subside, I draw away. It just about kills me because she tastes so damn good.

I move her legs aside now that they're relaxed and not trying to cinch me in place, and their limpness sends a surge of male pride through me because *I've* done this. That I was the first guy to go down on her and make her come all over my face.

Rising up to rest my weight on one forearm, I drag my other hand over my mouth to clean off her wetness. She probably won't want to kiss me if I taste like—

"Hollis?"

The gentle affection in her voice, even with the lingering breathlessness, has my mouth curving upward. "Shortcake?"

"Will you..." She trails off for so long I don't think she'll finish. Finally, she adds with a barely audible whisper, "Kiss me?"

I don't bother answering her. I shift so I'm nearly nose to nose with her.

"You want me to kiss you again?" I tease her softly.

She nods slowly. "I want to...see how I taste on you."

22

MAGNOLIA

HE GOES IMPOSSIBLY STILL, AND I WONDER IF I'VE MISSPOKEN. Maybe that's not what guys want to hear.

Good *grief*, I'm so terrible at this. I wince, closing my eyes with an inaudible groan. "I'm sorry. That's probably—"

"The hottest damn thing I've ever heard?" His gravelly voice skitters along my body, leaving a trail of arousal in its wake. He drops tiny kisses along my jawline, and *oh, sweet Lord*, who knew that could feel so good?

Lips dance along my skin, his teeth gently nipping at me, and I don't ever want him to stop. His hot breath washes over me, sending delicious shivers traveling down the length of my spine when he brings his lips to mine. "You taste so fuckin' good."

He captures my mouth, his tongue seeking out my own. Experiencing my own flavor intermixed with Hollis is more intoxicating than anything I've ever experienced.

I tug him closer, needing to feel him pressed between us. Hard. Heavy. Thick. When I reach for the waistband of his pants, his fingers latch onto my wrist, stopping me. I know the confusion is etched on my face, but he simply gives a little shake of his head.

"I'm not done with you yet." His murmured words are gentle, but there's a hint of mischief in his eyes.

"What do you mean?" I ask slowly, confused. I glance down between us at his obvious arousal. "Don't you want—?"

His lips dust over mine, cutting off my words. He leans back slightly. "Doesn't matter what I want." After another soft kiss, his lips curve against mine in a smile. "I'm not done with you, baby girl."

His mouth leaves a trail of kisses along my jaw, and when his lips find a sensitive spot near where my neck and jawline meet, I shiver. My nipples instantly harden in response. One large palm rests on my bare hip, and with aching slowness, it skims up my side beneath my shirt before pausing beneath the underwire of my bra. His thumb brushes the fabric, barely grazing over top my nipple, and I arch into his touch.

"Is this okay?" His hot breath against my neck causes a rise of goose bumps on my skin.

I nod before bravely offering, "You can take it off."

The thumb caressing my bra-covered nipple stutters briefly before resuming its torture. He draws my earlobe into his mouth and gently sucks before releasing it.

"If I do that, I'll want to get pretty well acquainted with these." He cups a breast for emphasis.

My eyes fall closed as he rakes his teeth over my earlobe. "How well acquainted?" I whisper.

He nips at my earlobe again, sending shivers shimmying through me. His voice dips lower, heavy with arousal. "You want to know all the dirty things I want to do to you?"

All I can manage is a simple, breathless, "*Yes.*"

He lets out a small groan before propping himself above me,

peering down with those deep brown eyes. Leaning his weight on one arm with our eyes still locked, he slowly lifts the hem of my shirt. But not once does his attention veer to my breasts. He holds my gaze as though he's making sure I'm okay with this, with this progression.

Hollis Barnes has always had a heart of gold. I've known this from the start. But now, with the way he watches me for any sign that I've changed my mind, I realize he's so much more.

The young boy I once knew who took it upon himself to protect me from anyone who hurt my feelings has turned into a man who's still hyper aware and always looking out for me. Always protecting me.

Even if it's from himself.

This sets him apart from guys his age who only focus on getting lucky with girls and partying.

His tongue darts out to wet his upper lip, his tone low and seductive. "I want to suck on your nipples like I did that night."

A rush of breath escapes my lips. "I want that, too."

His eyes flick to my mouth. "But I'll want more if I do that."

Arousal floods my bloodstream, making me ache with want. With need. "What else?"

His heated gaze practically incinerates me on the spot. "I'll want to feel what it's like to have your pussy grip me tight." His Adam's apple bobs when he swallows hard. "Not sayin' it to pressure you..." Somber eyes plead with me to believe him. "Because I'd never force you to do—"

I place my finger over his mouth to stop him and whisper, "I know." I trace his full lips and his eyes fall closed, as though he's memorizing my touch. Once I drop my finger from his mouth, his eyes open, and in a gentle, hushed tone, I say, "Tell me what else you want."

His thumb rakes over top of my bra where my nipples prod

against the fabric. "I'll want you to ride me while I suck on these."

A whimper escapes me, and my lips part on a panting breath. "What if I want that, too?"

His eyes flash, his tone hoarse. "Which part?"

"All of it."

I barely get the last word out before his mouth captures mine in a kiss that's frantic and needy and wet. Devouring. Our tongues tangle and I clutch at him, desperately trying to draw him closer.

He removes my shirt, and his fingers snake beneath me to unfasten the clasp of my bra, quickly tossing it aside. The contact of our heated flesh, without any barrier between our upper bodies, makes me frantic with the need for more.

His fingers tunnel into my hair, steering my head as he takes control, his mouth on mine, branding me with its scorching heat. The sensation of the hard angles of his body against my softer curves has me gasping against his lips. I can't get enough of his kiss, of his touch. I might not be experienced, but no other guy has made me feel like this when they kissed me.

Desired.

Sexy.

Beautiful.

Loved.

Deep down, I know this could blow up in our faces, but I love Hollis, and he's the only guy I truly trust. I know he won't do me wrong, and he'll always respect me.

I skim my palms along the sleek muscles of his back before dipping beneath the waistband of his khakis. My fingertips graze the tops of his firm glutes, and he groans against my lips, drawing away slightly. His mouth is swollen from our kisses, and we're both slightly out of breath.

He closes his eyes on a wince. "God, your hands on me..." He trails off with another groan when I sweep my fingertips along his sides, and he arches into my touch.

"I want to touch you." I wait for his eyes to open and find mine. "Will you let me?"

His jaw tightens, and for the briefest moment, I wonder if he'll say no. Finally, he gives a short nod and rolls onto his back, bringing me with him.

I rise to my knees, straddling him, and smooth my hands down his firm pectorals and lower over his hard abdominals. The muscles flex beneath my touch, his breathing becoming choppier. I unfasten his pants and pull down the zipper, tugging them down his hips and legs. He kicks them off, leaving him in only a pair of dark gray boxers.

The length of his erection presses firmly against the fabric, creating a firm ridge. My fingers tuck beneath the elastic and gently ease it down over his length and off his legs. Then I take a moment to get my fill of him.

The hard curves and indentations of his body are fascinating. I track my eyes down his form, drinking in the sight before my gaze returns to his. He watches me with a hint of amusement, one arm bent, the large bicep thick and on display with a hand tucked beneath his head.

"What do you think?" he asks in a husky voice.

A slight smirk tugs at the edge of my lips, and my eyes are drawn back to where he's impossibly hard. When I lightly trace my index finger along his length, he jerks in response. Startled, I draw back, but he stops me, cinching my wrist in his grip. He guides my hand to him once again.

"Just sensitive," he says gently. "Touch me all you want."

I curl my fingers around him, and he's so thick I wonder how he'd even fit inside me. He's velvety smooth yet hard as steel.

Using the pad of my thumb to gather the moisture lingering in the slit at the very tip, I bring my thumb to my lips, unable to resist my curious desire to taste him. The instant I suck the salty fluid off, he lets out a muttered, "Fuck," as a shudder wracks his body.

The visible effect my touch has on him sends a thrilling surge of power rushing through me. I scoot back, gathering my hair to one side, and press a light kiss to the head.

"Is this okay?" I murmur, dropping another soft kiss to it. "Can I...?" I hesitate before whispering the rest. "Put my mouth on you?"

His hips jerk as though a jolt of electricity shocked him, but what urges me on is the way he says my name on a tortured moan. A muscle in his jaw clenches, and he grits out a simple, "Yes."

I lower my head and wrap my lips around him and suck gently, experimenting to see what he likes. Gliding my tongue along his hard length, I work my mouth up and down. With each of my movements, with each lick and suck and glide of my mouth, I watch him. To gauge his response.

His hungry, heavy-lidded eyes, his flared nostrils, the way his lips part, the rough sounds ripped from his throat, and the way the cords of his neck appear strained send satisfaction coursing through me.

The veiny ridges of his erection fascinate me, and I run my tongue along them before taking him in my mouth as deep as I can. Another shudder rolls through his body, and his hands fly to my hair to fist it tightly, a look of agony on his face.

"*Holy fuck, yes,*" he grits out. His eyes close briefly as if he's fighting to maintain control. When they flare open, his heated gaze locks on me, practically singeing me. "So fuckin' good."

When I suck a little harder, he releases a strangled moan and one hand leaves my hair to fist the blanket in a punishing grip. His hips arch into my touch, and it urges me on.

As I slide my mouth down on another stroke, his sudden grip on my shoulder draws me to a surprised stop. "I want my mouth on you at the same time."

It takes me a moment to realize what he means, and when he tugs, guiding me to straddle his face, my own face heats up with embarrassment.

It quickly fades because he doesn't hold back. He grabs my hips and pulls me down to his mouth. His tongue dives inside me, tasting me deep. I clutch at his firm thighs, delicious shivers racing through my body as he devours me.

"*Hollis.*" His name falls from my lips in a whimper before I force myself to regain focus and slide my mouth down over him. I want to make him lose control like he made me. And by the way he's torturing me, I reckon it's a safe bet he'll make it happen again.

His powerful grip holds me in place while he teases me with his tongue and lips. Whimpers bubble up from my throat while I slide my mouth up and down his rigid length.

Hollis glides a thick finger through my wetness, thrusting in and out, tormenting me and making me ache for more. Fastening his lips around my clit, he gently sucks before grazing the sensitive flesh with his teeth. He gives my wet core a deep, openmouthed kiss and that's all it takes to send me tipping over the edge.

My orgasm rips through me, my breath rushing out hot and fast, and shudders take hold. I can't retrain a whimpered moan, even while my lips are still wrapped around his length.

A low, almost tortured-sounding growl rumbles from him, the subtle vibrations teasing my sensitive flesh. In a haze of euphoria, my hips thrust against his face as I ride out my release.

Once I finally settle from the orgasm-induced high, he carefully shifts me off of him. Pressing me back against the blan-keted mattress, he props himself on his forearms above me.

I frown in confusion, my attention darting between his face and his obvious arousal. His thick erection, still slick from my mouth, brushes against my hot skin, sending shivers skittering down the length of my spine.

His eyes bore into mine, heavy with lust. When he closes them on a brief wince and groans, "*God*, I want inside you," I urge him closer.

Wrapping his long, thick fingers around his length, he guides the tip to my entrance, dragging it through my folds. His eyes track the movements as if he's mesmerized by the act. Suddenly, he stops with a muttered expletive.

I stiffen in alarm. "What's wrong?"

He drops his forehead to my shoulder. "I don't have anythin'."

Without realizing it, the words spill out of my mouth. "I'm on birth control, and...well"—my voice fades, sounding small and hesitant—"you know I've never done this before." The need to have him inside me is all-consuming.

Slowly, he raises his head, affection lining his features. "Shortcake, I'd never do anythin' to put you at risk." His brows slant together severely. "I promise you."

"I know."

"But you know there's always a chance..."

I reach up and palm the side of his face. "Please, Hollis."

He doesn't say a word, studying me carefully as if he's searching for a sign of hesitation. When he doesn't find any, his eyes fall closed, and he presses his face into my palm, like he's basking in my touch.

Those brown eyes open and the hunger in the depths nearly robs me of breath. He lowers his lips to mine, and his kiss... It's a kiss unlike all the others. His lips touch mine with a tender reverence that brings me to tears.

This is what everyone strives for. Kisses that not only affect you on the surface but reach inside to touch your soul. More than that, though, they settle even deeper.

They become imbedded in the depths of your heart.

23

HOLLIS

Something's shifted. My heartbeat thunders so loud within my chest, I swear the whole neighborhood can hear it. Deep down, I think I realized this wouldn't be like any other time. This is just *more* because it's Magnolia.

I fist my cock and guide the tip to her entrance, dragging it along her wet lips. Even knowing I need to be gentle, it's a strain to hold back and resist the urge to drive into her, knowing she'll be as tight as a fucking vise.

My hand's unsteady, affected by a slight tremor filled with both need and the weight of what's about to happen. Because this is more than sex. More than fucking.

I'm about to make love to my best friend. To the girl—to the woman—who's had my heart from the very beginning. She's always been there for me.

I press inside her a fraction, and when she gasps, I freeze, but she urges me on.

"It just caught me off guard." Her voice sounds a little hoarse. "The stretchin'."

"It'll probably hurt." I bite my lip with worry because the last thing I want to do is hurt her in any way. *Fuck*, I'm more nervous now than I was when I lost my virginity with Charlotte. "If you want me to stop, just tell me."

"I will."

I sink in farther, and *goddamn*, she's so damn tight she's nearly strangling my dick already. She's slick and hot, and the way her breath catches, the way her inner muscles clench me tight every time I inch inside farther, has me gritting my teeth, fighting for restraint.

"Hollis." She gasps, her hands clutching at me, thighs tightening at my waist. With her legs cinched around me, she uses them to tug me closer, and that's when I surge forward, burying deeper.

Her entire body goes rigid with discomfort and apologies instantly fall from my lips.

"I'm sorry, baby girl." I sprinkle kisses along her face. "So sorry."

I try to give her time to adjust, continuing to drop kisses along her jaw and gently graze her earlobe with my teeth. All the while, I whisper to her. I tell her how beautiful she is, how honored I am to be her first, and that I love the feel of her heartbeat against mine.

I love you. These words catch in my throat. Intense emotions barrel through me in their wake, but once they settle, I realize it's only truth.

After a long moment passes, she finally releases a slow breath. Her hands move to my head, and her fingers sink into my hair, combing it back.

I raise my head, and blue eyes filled with what looks like wonder lock with mine. "I feel so full." She shifts, and I groan in response, my eyes falling closed on a wince. Then she whispers, "I love the way you feel inside me."

Fuck me. She has no idea what her words do to me. My cock jerks in response, and she lets out a little moan. I roll my hips tentatively, and when she doesn't wince but urges me on, I continue with shallow thrusts.

Her palms move to my ass, and I press deeper, fitting my mouth to hers. I taste her, my tongue toying with hers while I thrust, her pussy gripping me with her searing-hot tightness.

I break the kiss but leave my lips barely on hers. "Time for you to ride me, baby girl."

Without waiting for a response, I roll us over so that she's on top. I can tell as soon as she lets out a little gasp and, "*Oh!*" that she feels how much deeper she sinks down over me.

It's fucking heaven.

I let my palms slide up from her hips to cup the weight of her tits in my hands, and when she arches into my touch, she sinks even deeper. My eyes nearly roll back in my head as lust shoots through my veins, and I struggle to draw in a breath.

She braces her hands on my chest and begins to move, working herself over my cock. Her tits taunt me so much I can't resist pressing a hand to her back and drawing a nipple into my mouth.

I groan at the sensation of added wetness around my cock. I toy with her nipple, raking my teeth over the hardened tip before suckling it. *Shit*, I won't last long if she keeps working her pussy over me like this. While I use my lips, teeth, and tongue on her nipple, my girl starts panting and does something that surprises the hell out of me.

She starts talking.

"Hollis," she says, her breathing choppy. Gripping her hips, I pull her down while simultaneously giving an upward thrust, and she gasps. "You're so deep."

I raise my head to take her mouth again. Then I suck gently on her lower lip before releasing it. "I want you to come all over me." My voice is rough, gravelly with arousal. Her inner muscles clench me in response.

My attention moves to where our bodies are joined. Every time she moves over me, I catch a glimpse of the shiny slickness coating my dick. I raise my eyes to hers.

"Look at us," I command. When her eyes follow my focus, her body shudders, but she doesn't look away. "See how wet you are?" Her eyes flick up to me. "So fuckin' hot."

Tangling a hand in the hair at her nape, I guide her mouth to mine in a feverish kiss. When I begin driving upward on her down thrusts, it sets her off. Her movements become frenzied, and the way she moans against my lips has me hovering on the edge.

I slip a hand between us to thumb her clit in circles, and she straightens, silently encouraging me on. When her inner muscles tighten around me, I lock my jaw, vying against the urge to come.

"Come for me, baby girl." I grit out the words while continuing to work her clit. From her ragged breathing and jerky movements, I can tell that she's close. "That's it," I urge her on, my voice gruff. She feels so fucking good, clenching me tight like a wet, hot fist.

Her head tilts back, and she stiffens on top of me before shudders overtake her. She comes apart and *fuck*. She's so goddamn beautiful. Her hair falls down her back with some strands dangling over one bare shoulder, the ends teasing just above one nipple.

When her pussy clamps down on me in a punishing grip, it has me gritting my teeth. My balls tighten near painfully before she lets out a keening cry. "*Hollis*."

I roll her over on her back, grip her hips, and drive my cock into her with deep thrusts as she rides out her release. It's painful as hell to pull out, but once I do, I wrap a fist around my cock, slick from both of us, and with just two glides of my hand, I explode in hot spurts, painting her skin.

Once I finally manage to get my breathing under control and lift my eyes to her, I find her watching me with a satisfied, smug grin. Hair tousled and her mouth reddened from our kisses, this is a sight I want stored in my memory. The tender way she looks at me makes me feel like I can conquer anything with her by my side.

I reach for my discarded T-shirt and carefully clean her. Darting a worried glance up at her, I ask, "Are you okay?"

"I'm fine." The slight breathlessness in her voice has the edges of my mouth tipping up.

I toss the shirt aside and reach for the rolled-up sleeping bag I'd carelessly dropped aside earlier. Unrolling it, I drape it over her relaxed body before settling in beside her and tugging her close. The way she curls around me, her leg over the top of my thigh, her cheek against my chest, feels natural.

And as shitty as it might be, I can't help but compare it to Charlotte. Not because I'm lusting over her—*hell,* no—but because it never felt like this with her. With Magnolia, it feels like so much more.

I'd never admit it out loud because, hell, even in my head it sounds cheesy, but being with Magnolia like this feels like...*home.*

Her small hand settles over the center of my chest and I know she feels the erratic tempo of my heartbeat. It's slowed a little but still thumps rapidly because—

"Hollis?"

I drop a light kiss to the top of her head. "Ma'am?"

A little laugh escapes her, and she shifts to face me with a curious expression. "Why do you do that?"

"Do what?"

"You always ma'am me," she says with a smile.

I tuck her hair back behind her ear. "You sayin' you don't like it?"

"I like it. I just always wonder why you do it with me. I mean,"—she lifts a shoulder in a half shrug—"I get that it's bein' respectful, but it's not really necessary with me, is it?"

My expression sobers and I cup the side of her face in my hand. "It's more necessary with you than with anyone else."

Because you mean more to me, I add silently.

When she studies me as though trying to decipher my words, I offer, "You're the most important person in my life, and I never want you to think I don't respect you."

"Oh, Hollis," she whispers. "I could never think that." She places a small kiss to each corner of my lips. "You're always a gentleman." She gently sprinkles kisses along my jawline. "And the world needs more Hollises out there."

I grin just before a groan escapes me when her mouth veers off to place openmouthed kisses along my neck. "Can't have that. Because you might get confused and wouldn't be able to tell the difference between all of us."

Her soft laughter against my skin makes me shiver seconds before she straddles me. She reaches for me, where I'm half hard already, and wraps her fingers around me. Her smile is knowing, and *damn*, the way her eyes have that mischievous glint does something to me.

"Look at you, gettin' all bold." I smirk.

She stills and those blue eyes go wide, her expression turning to worry. A little nervous, even. "Is that okay? To touch you again like this?"

"It's more than okay." My eyes flick down to where her hand grips my dick. "Reckon you can tell that."

Her lips form a slow grin and she glides a smooth palm down my length, slowly fisting me in gradual strokes. "Think you're up to showin' me how it's done again?"

Fuck yes. "You've gotta be sore, Shortcake," I protest. Thank God, I've still got a lick of common sense lingering.

She doesn't miss a beat. "If you're gentle, there won't be a problem."

Ah, look who's become a little siren.

I close my eyes on a wince, my nostrils flaring while I fight against the urge to take her at her word. Keeping my eyes pinched closed, I grit out, "I don't want to hurt you," on a slow exhale.

She leans over me, her hair tickling my chest. Her warm breath against my ear has my dick pulsing. "You'll only hurt me if"—her hold on me shifts slightly as she guides me to her entrance—"you don't let me have you again."

When she glides my tip along her slick lips, her wet heat practically singes me. I press upward instinctively, my dick already on board. I grip her hips, clenching them tight. "You're torturin' me," I complain in a hoarse whisper.

"Then let me put you out of your misery."

She sinks down on me with aching slowness, giving her body time to adjust to having me inside her again. Her slick pussy grips me tight and I clench my jaw, doing my best to resist the violent urge to drive upward in a deep thrust. Once she's fully seated, perspiration beads my forehead from the restraint.

Her hands brace on my chest, and I open my eyes to find her watching me with a slightly glazed look. Her lips are parted, her nipples puckered. A sense of wonder crosses her face when she lifts slightly and slides back down. "Is it always like this?" she whispers raggedly.

I move, one arm reaching to cup her nape, threading my fingers in her hair to guide her mouth to mine. Before I claim her lips, I murmur three words that are startling in how much truth they hold.

"Only with you."

24

HOLLIS

I SHOULD'VE TAKEN MAGNOLIA UP ON HER OFFER TO COME WITH me, but she looked so sleepy and happy, I couldn't bring myself to make her get out of bed. Hell, it was hard enough dragging myself away from her this morning.

I told her I'd bring back coffee for us unless she wanted to hit the diner when I got back. She'd kissed me and told me she voted for the coffee option because she didn't want to share me with anyone else just yet.

We'd sneaked inside my house late last night to shower and brush our teeth. I'd never been more thankful for my mom's room being on the other end of the hallway. Afterward, we curled up in the treehouse, sleepy and worn out in the best way possible.

Our final words from last night still linger in my mind, and I wonder if I'm reading too much into it.

"Love you, Shortcake," I murmured while I held her in my arms, sleep quickly dragging us under.

Her drowsy voice had mumbled back, "Love you, too," instead of the usual response of, "But not like that."

I know she was probably worn out and too tired to realize

what she'd said, but it made the possibilities hammer away at me because...*shit*. I've always loved Magnolia Barton. And, sure, it didn't start as more than a friendship kind of love, but without me realizing it, over the years it slowly morphed. She's always been a part of me, ingrained in my soul.

Now, after brushing my teeth, I pull my keys from the pocket of my khakis. I'm dressed in a collared polo, but I'm still wearing my leather flip-flops Magnolia got me last Christmas. I get as far as pulling open the front door of the house when I hear her.

"Finally finished with your little rich whore?" My mother's voice is full of malice.

I don't bother turning around, but my spine stiffens. "You should watch your mouth. I'm not the helpless boy I used to be."

I can practically feel her anger growing like an impending storm. "You'll never be good enough for her. You're crazy if you think they'll accept you. You're just charity for h—"

I slam the door closed behind me, cutting off her outburst, and quickly stride to my truck. Thankful that my mom's car is in the garage, I maneuver and back around Magnolia's car before I pull out of the driveway.

It takes less than ten minutes to find the attorney's office. Herman Yates is an older gentleman in his late fifties. Impeccably dressed, he greets me with a firm handshake and guides me inside his office where we each take a seat on opposite sides of his desk.

He slides a thick file folder to the center of his mahogany desk and opens it. Resting his forearms on the wood, he peers at me with a somber expression.

"I have quite a few items I'll need your signature on, and I'll explain everythin'. Don't hesitate to ask me questions if you need further clarification."

Within minutes, he proceeds to blow my mind.

I stare at him in shock. "I'm sorry, sir. But did you say...?" I falter, unable to finish my question.

A look of understanding passes over his expression. "You inherit the house." He shuffles some papers, his index finger running down the paper before he nods in affirmation.

But that's not what has me so stunned.

"I'm responsible for disbursin' funds to...my mother?" I feel like an idiot for repeating everything, but I'm stunned.

He nods. "Your father emphasized this when we drew up the will. You're responsible for determinin' what funds"—his eyes lower to the paperwork in front of him before they lift to mine—"if any, should be allotted for her livin' expenses." He grimaces as if he's about to deliver worse news. "I hate to say this, son, but your father contacted me about a week and a half before he passed with an odd request."

Odd? I don't say anything, waiting for him to continue.

Mr. Yates withdraws a thick, sealed envelope from the file and hands it to me. "He asked me to make sure you received this. That you were the only person I could deliver it to."

I take the envelope in my hands, my thumb brushing over the way my father scrawled my name on the front. I'm not sure why, but an uneasy feeling settles over me.

Mr. Yates rises from his chair. "If you'll come with me, I can show you to the conference room and leave you to read that in case there's anythin' I might need to help you with."

I rise from my seat and follow him down the hall to a room. There's a small oval table with a handful of comfortable-looking chairs surrounding it.

"Thank you," I manage to get out. He simply nods and closes the door behind him.

I sink down into a leather chair and draw in a deep breath before letting it out slowly. Then I carefully rip open the envelope. When I slide out the stapled, folded papers, I smooth them out, fighting against the way they want to crease and fold back up.

Hollis,

I went back and forth with whether I should write this, but in the end, I knew I couldn't leave you without the truth. I just wish I'd had the courage to tell you myself.

Before I get into that, I need to tell you how proud I am of you. I've always been impressed by the way you handle yourself, even as a young boy. You're a rarity in this world, and I hope you realize that regardless of how much money you have in your pocket, you're an impressive and smart young man. Whatever you come away with after reading this, please know that I've always loved you and admire the man you've become.

When you flip this page over and see what I've included, I hope you're not angry with me—

With trepidation coursing through me, I thumb the top corner of the paper and turn it over to reveal what's stapled behind it.

A check? What the fuck?

All oxygen is ripped from my lungs when I scan the names listed on the check. I'm baffled by what I see and hurriedly turn back to read the rest of my father's letter.

Grace Barton offered me this check to coerce me into convincing you to go to a different university. Pride made me refuse the money even though it was more than enough to cover a full year at another school. She insisted I keep the check, likely thinking I'd change my mind. I reckon not many people refuse the Bartons' money.

Maybe you'll be upset with me, but I knew I couldn't do that to you. I'd already done enough in pushing you to be the family's first college graduate. But I see the potential in you, son. I know you're meant for great things. Whatever career path you set out on, I'll always be supportive of you.

Now, for the hard part.

Christ. The hard part? I internally scoff. How is any of this not hard? I scrub a hand down my face, weariness taking hold, but I know I need to read on. I turn to the next page, where he continues.

Many moons ago, I fell in love with a young girl—your mother. She was full of life, laughter, and more beautiful than anyone I'd ever laid eyes on. Unfortunately, she didn't return the feeling. You see, she was in love with someone else.

He came from a well-to-do family, and your mother's family lived on the outskirts of town. She wore hand-me-downs, or her mother, who had a gift for sewing, made her clothing. She'd sneak away to be with this boy. He never brought her around his parents, but she thought things might change. Then she got pregnant, and she was sure things would change after that.

She was wrong. He rejected her because he knew his parents wouldn't approve. They would disown him, and he was prepared to graduate high school and head to Auburn University like the men in his family before him. They'd been founders of the university. He couldn't throw away everything just for a girl he got pregnant.

I'd been her friend—her best friend—and I knew I had to step in. I told her I'd marry her as soon as we graduated. That she'd be taken care of. I loved her more than anything in this world, and I knew I'd take having her in my life however I could. I thought she might grow to love me.

Instead, your mother grew distant as time passed. It became worse after you were born. Maybe because you resemble him a bit, and she had to face the reminder of the boy who rejected her. I don't know, son, but what I do know is, I loved you the moment I first laid eyes on you. And when I held you in the hospital, I knew I'd do everything in my power to protect you and ensure you had the best I could provide.

I know my job didn't allow us to have many extras, but I hope you know I loved you like you were my own. I never thought of you in any other way. To me, you've always been my son.

But now, maybe you can understand your mother a little more. I'm not telling you this to excuse her behavior but, rather, to give you this information. When my job brought us down here, and she insisted on the house we bought, I knew there was more to it but went along with it because she seemed almost happy. It was brief, of course, and I reckon she thought things would turn out differently.

Forgive me for not telling you before. The last thing I ever want is to cause you pain. I never knew how to say it, and I was afraid. I was scared to lose the one person who taught me about love. The person who inspired me to be a better man.

My son.

You may hate me, but please know I've always tried to do my best by you. I consider you my son, and I need you to know you've made me so proud and always have, regardless of what anyone else says—especially your mother.

If you want to reach out to the man who is your father—God, that hurts just writing it—you don't have far to go. Just be careful, Hollis. I don't know if he realizes who you are or not.

Know that I've always loved you, son. It doesn't matter if you're my blood or not. It never once mattered to me.

Be happy and learn from my mistakes. Never let a day go by when anyone makes you feel subpar. Pave your own way. Know that I'll be watching over you and loving you always.

Love,
Dad

I grind the heels of my palms against my eyes, damp from tears attempting to escape. *Fuck.* I don't even know what to make of this. It's like my entire world has toppled off its axis.

When I flip the page and come to the last thing included in the stapled stack of papers, my breath lodges in my chest.

Staring down, with fresh eyes, at the photograph of the man I've come to know, I now notice the small similarities. The shape and color of his eyes and his square jawline. Although I inherited my mother's dark hair and lips, I can't believe I never noticed this before.

Then again, every interaction I've had with the man hasn't exactly been relaxed or easy. He's always busy grilling me about my friendship with his stepdaughter.

Magnolia.

25

HOLLIS

After I grab the coffee I promised Magnolia, I feel a little less on edge. My mind's been racing since I left Mr. Yates' office and I really need to talk everything over with her.

I slide out of my truck carefully with the coffees, shutting the door with a little shove of my foot. So intent on heading to the treehouse where she's waiting for me, I don't immediately notice the woman standing a few feet away until I nearly collide with her.

Arms crossed over what I know is an expensive silk blouse, her chin raised primly, Mrs. Barton eyes me before her gaze flicks to where Magnolia's car sits in my driveway.

"I've given you more than your fair share of passes." She steps closer and uncrosses her arms. Her upper lip curls slightly with distaste. "You don't seem to pick up on the clues. You may have lost your daddy, but that doesn't mean I'm handin' over my daughter as a token of my sympathy."

One perfectly manicured index finger pokes me in the chest. "You're not welcome in our home and never will be." She punctuates this with another jab of her finger, and I swear it seems to puncture deep to my core. "You're not good enough for her, and *so help me, God*, if you don't leave that poor girl alone once and for all, you'll regret it.

"Y'all have some sort of co-dependent relationship, and it's not healthy. Let her have a life of her own without you always hoverin' on the sides." Her mouth flattens to a severe line. "Now, you're goin' to send my daughter back home, since I refuse to"— she waves a hand dismissively toward the backyard—"even touch that termite haven of yours. And tell her to turn on her phone." Her eyes narrow dangerously. "Are we clear?"

I grit my teeth before I force a calm response. "Yes, ma'am."

Like a switch has flipped, she turns on a smile so fake I'm hit with a wave of nausea. "Good. You have yourself a lovely day, now." She spins around and strides away quickly across the lawn to her house. As if it's a second thought, she tosses over her shoulder, "My deepest sympathies again for your loss."

I stand at the edge of my driveway with a sick churning in my stomach. *What the fuck was I thinking?* Every heavy step I take, crossing through the backyard, seems to emphasize another reminder.

I'm not good enough.

I don't have money or expensive clothes.

I don't even know what I want to do with my life. Hell, I'm still unsure about my damn major.

Of course, what ricochets through my brain, screaming louder than all the other thoughts, is the point Mrs. Barton made.

Y'all have some sort of co-dependent relationship, and it's not healthy.

As much as I despise having that woman in my head, I can't deny she's right. Magnolia and I have never ventured off, separately, before. Not really. We've always had each other as backup of some sort.

Am I preventing her from living her own life?

As I hover at the base of the steps, the thought settles inside me, weighing heavily. Pain lances through me, ricocheting deep in my heart. And, even through the stifling haze of pain and regret, the realization of what road I need to choose becomes clear.

Drawing in a few deep breaths, I set the coffees on top of one another and grip them in my hand while I carefully climb up into the treehouse.

Magnolia's dressed and lies propped up in bed with my cheap edition of Shakespeare's sonnets in her hand. As soon as she sees me, the widest, happiest smile spreads across her face. It only causes a searing pain to radiate through me, knowing what I have to do.

It must be written on my face because her smile wavers. "Hollis?"

I hand her the coffee before I lean against a wall and toy with the coffee sleeve on my cup. "We need to talk."

Her laugh is a little forced. "Even I know when a guy says that, it's never good."

I force myself to be calm, to get everything out. Setting my coffee on the small shelf, I start, "I, uh, sat in the attorney's office for a while after I signed all the paperwork. I have the house, and I'm in charge of givin' my mom an allowance." I make a face. "Which is weird," I continue, "but I realized that this entire year I've been goin' through the motions, not really sure what I want to major in, let alone do with my life."

Magnolia watches me, listening patiently, which urges me to press on.

"I'm plannin' to take my uncle's apprenticeship offer." I shrug. "It's the one thing I've always loved."

Her eyes regard me before she carefully asks, "So, you won't be goin' back to school?"

I shake my head slowly. "No."

"And..." She hesitates, lowering her eyes. "What about us?"

Two invisible fists reach inside me to clench my lungs, ridding me of the ability to breathe. When I don't answer, her eyes lift to mine, and it's an instant punch to the solar plexus. I hate the pain etched on her features—it's fucking torture knowing I'm hurting her—but after her mom's words settled in my brain, I feel like this is the only way.

Hell, both our moms have always said I'm not good enough for her.

I don't realize I've spoken the thought out loud until she sets her coffee down and jumps up from the mattress. "I don't care what they say! I can transfer where you are and—"

"No." I shake my head. "There's no way you can throw away Auburn for another school. That'd be a huge mistake, and we both know it."

She reaches for me. "*Please* don't do this. We can make it work."

"*How?*" I explode so suddenly she rears back in shock. "How can we do that? We've always been together, every step of the way. How do we know we're not better off apart?"

Her mouth flattens in a thin line. She holds my gaze, her chin lifting stubbornly. "Because I love you, Hollis. That's how I know."

My eyes close briefly on a painful wince, her words stabbing me clean through. *Fuck*, how I wish she meant those words. That there wasn't the silent *But not like that* tacked on the end.

I let out a defeated sigh. "I don't know what I want to do with my life, Shortcake. I can't hold on to you while I'm like this. You need to find someone who's...better for you. Who your family approves of." My voice cracks, and I swallow hard past the tightness in my throat. "We both know that'll never be me."

"But, Hollis..." The way her voice wobbles on my name

drives that invisible knife deeper into the center of my chest.
"We can—"

"*No.*" My tone is firm. Final. I refuse to let her throw her life
away for me.

Her brows clash, the fine lines between them more
pronounced. The longest beat of silence hangs between us, the
air vibrating with tension.

Finally, she lets out a shaky breath and I can practically feel
the instant she gives in to defeat. "Are we still friends?" Her voice
catches on the last word, the sheen of tears brimming in her
eyes.

"Always."

I barely get the word out before she launches herself at me,
wrapping her arms around my waist so tight I can barely
breathe. Holding her close, I press my lips to her hair and close
my eyes to savor the moment.

I reckon it may be the last time I get to hold her like this.

"I'm sorry. I literally just got the message about Jay," Uncle
Johnny apologizes.

I immediately called him after Magnolia left to head home.

"My secretary's on maternity leave, and the temp sucks, for
lack of a better way of sayin' it. I'm lookin' up flights as we
speak."

"No, don't bother. Honestly, there's no reason for you to head
here."

Silence greets me on the other end. Finally, my uncle says, "I
don't like the idea of you there with her." His voice is low, and
the concern is obvious.

"Actually, I wasn't plannin' on hangin' around. I wanted to
ask you for a favor."

"Anythin'."

"That apprenticeship you mentioned a while back? I wondered if—"

"It's yours." Then he hesitates, making me nervous. "But I'm in the UK right now, and it would mean travelin'. Things are pretty busy."

I exhale with relief. "I'm good with that."

His tone softens. "You sure?"

I close my eyes and run a hand down the back of my neck, gripping the tense muscles. This is my chance. To prove that I can make something of myself.

"Yes, sir. Never been surer."

26

MAGNOLIA

**SOPHOMORE YEAR
NOVEMBER
AUBURN UNIVERSITY**

"WE ARE *NOT* WATCHING *THE LAKE HOUSE* AGAIN." MY ROOMMATE stamps a hand on her hip, pursing her lips in irritation. "I'm officially staging an intervention."

I roll my eyes. "It's just a movie."

Stephanie stares at me like I've lost my mind. Which I haven't.

The only thing I've lost is my heart.

"You sob every time you watch it. Like it's the *first* time you've ever seen it."

I lie back on my bed. "Fine. I won't watch it when you're around from now on."

"Not the point!" she says with exasperation. Jabbing an index finger in my direction she commands, "Get up. Shower. Dress in something cute. Slap on some makeup." With a stern look, she adds, "*Now*."

I stare at her warily, and with a cautious tone, I ask, "Why?"

"Because we're getting out of here to go and be *social*."

I wrinkle my nose at the word "social." "No, thanks."

Her eyebrows rise, and that look? Oh, boy. The girl's got a bee in her bonnet, for sure. "I didn't ask. I *told* you." She gestures to the bathroom. "Go shower. Now."

I heave out a breath as I drag myself up off the bed. "Fine."

Nearly an hour later, Stephanie's managed to coerce me into wearing a long-sleeved dress I haven't put on in months and pair it with an infinity scarf. The weather's been far cooler than normal, so I pull on a pair of knee-high boots. I manage to apply some light makeup, and it feels odd when I do, considering I've lived in yoga pants and gone sans makeup since the summer.

Since he left.

The pinch in my chest isn't quite as fierce, but it still hurts. Like an ache that seeps all the way to the marrow of your bones.

A part of me wishes he would've just left and never stayed in touch. But the other part—the far larger part—lives for the brief and sporadic text messages with a photo from wherever he's at for work. He never types anything more than, **Greetings from [his current city or town], Shortcake.**

Photos of places I've never seen.

Of a life I don't share with him.

It doesn't escape my notice that those photos never include him. Maybe it's his way of trying to ease my ache of missing him so much.

When I began receiving mail from him, it was bittersweet. He never writes anything aside from my address on the envelope, but inside, he stuffs a postcard from wherever he's traveled to for his uncle's business. But that's not the only thing he sends me.

He always remembers to include a pack of cherry Pop Rocks, too.

"Come on, woman. Hurry it up!" Stephanie demands, tapping the toe of her boot on the floor. I hurriedly brush my hair and leave it in loose waves before rushing over to where she waits at the door.

She inspects me from head to toe, looking pleased. "Not too shabby." She links her arm with mine and tugs me out the door, locking up quickly. "Let's go be social."

About an hour later, I start to wonder if an alien source has taken over my roommate.

Reason number one: She's chatting with a guy and giggling.

Reason number two: She's giggling. *Giggling.*

As much as I'd like to leave this party and crawl back into bed and watch *The Lake House* again, I know she'll read me the riot act, so I roam through the cute house a few of her class-mates rent and find a reasonably quiet spot by the window over-looking the street.

The leaves have changed colors and fallen onto the lawn. It's times like this when I find myself wondering what Hollis is up to. If he's ever at parties or bored to death at one like I am.

The most painful thought is when I wonder if he's found a girl—one whose family isn't judgmental and who would accept him as he is.

"You look as thrilled to be here as I am."

I jerk in surprise at the male voice. When I turn from the window, I discover a guy smiling shyly at me. His hair is a light shade of brown, his mouth holds a hint of a self-deprecating smile, and he has a lean, slightly muscled build.

When I don't immediately respond, he winces and quickly rushes out with, "I'm sorry to bother you." He starts backing away.

Something makes me stop him. And it's not because he's ridiculously attractive. It's his dark blue eyes. There's something in them I feel drawn to.

"No, don't leave." I muster up a smile. "You just caught me off guard."

He hesitates as if he's unsure whether I'm simply being polite or not. Finally, he relents and takes a seat in the other chair beside me. He leans to offer his hand.

"I'm Grant."

I accept his hand and give it a brief shake. "I'm Magnolia."

"Nice to meet you, Magnolia." His warm smile puts me at ease. It's different from the more common *I just want to get in your pants* smile other guys employ.

He turns to gaze out the window, and I follow suit. We sit in oddly comfortable silence for a long moment before he finally speaks.

His voice is low, hushed, and sympathetic. "I have to admit that when I saw you sittin' here, I felt compelled to come over."

I turn to look at him warily, wondering if I read him wrong and this is fixing to be some awful pickup line.

"I recognize the look." His smile has now vanished, and in its place is a look of understanding. "You...lost someone who meant a lot to you?"

My breath lodges in my throat and I can only manage to nod.

He turns his gaze back to the window. "I had that same look for the longest time," he murmurs softly.

"How'd you get rid of it?"

A sad smile plays at his lips, and his eyes appear almost haunted. "It took a while. A friend forced me to get my ass in gear and stop mopin'."

A little laugh escapes me. "You just described what happened to me tonight."

He turns, and this time, his smile isn't laced with sadness, eyes clearer. "I reckon we might just be kindred spirits."

I match his smile, and it doesn't feel quite as brittle or as forced as it has these past few months. "I reckon you might be right."

TEXT FROM HOLLIS

Greetings from the Salt Flats in Utah, Shortcake.

27

MAGNOLIA

JUNIOR YEAR
DECEMBER
AUBURN UNIVERSITY

"Y'ALL ARE CRAZY!" I LAUGH, BARELY STAYING UPRIGHT ON MY ICE skates. Stephanie and her boyfriend skate by me so fast, I swear I feel a breeze.

Grant suggested a trip up to New York City since I'd never been, and we'd asked Stephanie and her boyfriend, Tommy, to join us. We've had a blast exploring the sights, and I'm thankful the weather has been far milder than usual this time of year.

Now, we're skating in Central Park—or, rather, I'm attempting not to fall flat on my tush. Grant holds my hands, guiding me along the ice. It's not as crowded, thankfully, since it's nearing closing time, so my chances of knocking down other innocent skaters is far less.

He skates backward flawlessly, holding my hands with a bright smile on his face. I can't help but match it with my own because good *Lord*, I love this man.

Sometimes, I think he singlehandedly brought me back to life.

He's incredible, and not a day goes by when I have any doubt in my mind that I'm the only woman he has eyes for. His gaze never lingers on anyone else.

Grant comes from a family of commercial developers, and of course, my family loves him, simply because his family is well-to-do in their business. And even though he comes from wealth, he never acts like it. He's always incredibly humble and sweet.

"Ready for a hot chocolate break?"

I grin up at him. "Absolutely."

He guides us out of the rink, helping me step carefully off the ice and over to a bench. "I'll be right back."

I turn and watch Stephanie and Tommy skate hand in hand. She waves when she sees me watching, and I wave back. A moment later, Grant slides onto the bench beside me and hands me the steaming cup.

"Thank you." I lean forward, placing a light kiss on his lips.

His smile is one I've come to know as *mine*. Strictly reserved for me. I take a small sip of hot chocolate and return my attention to the rink. Grant drapes his arm along the back of the bench, and I settle against him comfortably.

I let out a content sigh. "I'm havin' the best time." I turn to peer up at him. "Thank you."

His eyes crinkle at the corners, his affection evident as he studies me for a beat. "You look happy."

Caught off guard by his remark, I let out a surprised laugh. "Because I am."

Grant's expression turns tender. "I know." He presses a kiss to my temple before we turn our attention to the rink. "It makes me happy knowin' that," he murmurs.

I know what he's referring to. When we first met, I was drowning in pain. Little by little, day by day, the memories began to fade like the color and print on a dollar bill that's been folded again and again, and handled countless times.

My hurt is still there, imbedded deeper now, like the minuscule fibers of the paper money, but Grant has helped me create new, happy memories to overshadow the pain.

That party was pivotal in my life because I met him. We talked through the night and found ourselves confessing what we'd never told another soul.

He spoke about his girlfriend, who was killed by a drunk driver days before they were due to start at Auburn. She was the girl he always expected he'd marry.

Though I never specifically mentioned Hollis' name, I told Grant that I loved someone who left me even after I pleaded with him to stay. We spoke about how devastating the pain can be when someone leaves your life—regardless of the circumstances—whether it's willingly or if they're taken from you.

We formed a bond that night, one unlike any other I've had. Even Hollis. Grant has become one of my best friends, my "kindred spirit" as he says.

And, eventually, the man I found myself falling in love with.

"Where do you want to end up after this?"

His question draws me from my musings. "Well, it's late, so maybe we can grab somethin' small to eat at that—"

He chuckles softly. "No, I mean, after graduation."

I consider it briefly before shrugging. "Honestly, it's expected that I'll put my name in the runnin' for one of the local spots. Maybe city council."

"Is that what you really want?"

"Yes." *No.* But no one's ever really asked me what I want to do with my life after graduation. It's always been one huge unspoken expectation.

Can I see myself running for city council? Eventually working my way up the government's hierarchy? Of course.

But I'd be lying if I said I was passionate about it. Not the way Grant's passionate about following in his father's footsteps and finding new opportunities for properties.

Grant takes a sip of his hot chocolate, his eyes trained on the rink. Even though his tone is casual, there's a touch of something indecipherable in his expression. A nervousness, maybe?

"We've been edgin' our way into the Eastern Shore, and there's a lot of opportunity there. After I graduate in May, I could start overseein' things…" He lets his words settle between us, the insinuation clear.

We could make a life together in Fairhope.

I falter because…well, because we've never really talked about the future. I mean, sure, we've done the joking around comments of, "When we're married, maybe you'll finally learn not to talk to me before coffee," or "When we're old and gray, you'd still better hold my hand."

But that's all I took them for—jokes.

He turns to me, blue eyes tender, a loving smile gracing his lips, and I realize I never once considered this. I've never considered a future with Grant.

I never let myself because a part of me has been holding on to the past.

To a man who's all but completely detached himself from my life.

Now, as I sit here with the man who loves me, a man I know without a shadow of a doubt would love me forever, I let my mind play out what a life with Grant might look like.

It's…nice. Comfortable. Safe.

I lean in and dust my lips to his. "Plannin' to woo me, huh?" I tease.

His lips curve against mine. "I reckon I could use an old ball and chain."

When my lips part on a half-laugh/half-protest, his hand

cups my nape and his mouth captures mine in a kiss that has me melting.

A kiss that soothes most of the rough, battered edges of my heart. Most, but not all.

But it's enough.

It has to be.

TEXT FROM HOLLIS

Greetings from the Atlanta Botanical Garden (and your namesake flower), Shortcake.

28

HOLLIS

MARCH

AMELIA ISLAND CONCOURSE D'ELEGANCE
HOSTED BY SOTHEBY'S
AMELIA ISLAND, FLORIDA

I'M BONE-TIRED. AND JET-LAGGED. EVEN THOUGH THE CAR EXPO IN France was a great experience, and I doubt most guys my age would ever have the opportunity to go to an event at a chateau and call it work, I'm glad to be back in the States.

We've just finished a long-ass weekend here in Amelia Island. If I felt surrounded by wealth back home in Fairhope and at the country club there, this surpasses that on all fronts. Let's just say when the words "Sotheby's auction" are spoken, it's a whole different ball game.

Uncle Johnny tried to prepare me for it, warning me I'd see some cars up for auction that'd give serious car restoration enthusiasts "massive hard-ons," but I had no idea it would be —*could* be—on this grand of a scale.

Now, I'm seated at the bar in the Amelia Island Plantation Resort, nursing a beer. Now that the event is over, this place has thinned out considerably. I should be celebrating with the other guys and my uncle, who are in the billiards room playing a game of pool and partaking in friendly shit-talking, like usual. Instead, I'm here, scanning the countless liquor bottles in front of the mirrored wall of the bar, wondering if my eyes were just playing tricks on me.

It's happened before. First, a few weeks after I got to Atlanta. Then in France. In my periphery, a woman with long blond hair, the shade of Magnolia's, will catch my eye. It's never her, though.

She haunts me, but I have no one to blame for it except myself. But I needed—*need*—this. To try to make something of myself. To try to be worthy.

To try to *feel* worthy.

I reach for my back pocket and withdraw the small, thin item like it's some sort of priceless artifact. It's fucking ridiculous since it cost me less than a dollar, but I always keep one with me. Having a packet of cherry Pop Rocks makes me feel closer to her somehow.

The guy beside me slides off his barstool after scribbling his signature on the credit card slip. Within seconds, someone new takes his place. Distractedly, I run the pad of my finger over the edge of the packet and take a sip of beer. The bartender sets a fresh pint of the pale ale on tap on the coaster in front of the guy beside me.

I wonder what Magnolia's up to. I haven't been able to bring myself to search for her on social media. I've steered clear of creating a Facebook account of my own, but I created one on Instagram. Granted, it's more to drum up attention for Uncle Johnny's shop because I tag his business' Instagram page when I post. Which reminds me...

I reach for my phone that sits on the lacquered bar surface and snap a pic of my beer and the coaster. I tag Custom Motor-werks and mention the auction, and within seconds, notifications pop up with people liking it or commenting. I take another drink of beer and toy with the edge of the Pop Rocks packet.

"What's her name?"

My head snaps around at the question from the man beside me, his Southern accent thicker than molasses. From Texas, maybe?

At first, I'm caught off guard by how physically intimidating he is. Sure, I jog and do push-ups to stay in shape since I'm lugging around heavy equipment daily and logging long hours on special restoration projects, but this guy has serious bulk. Yet the thing that stands out to me most are his sharp blue eyes. They give me the impression he doesn't miss much.

He lifts his chin in my direction. "That expression on your face is a dead giveaway." One edge of his mouth turns up. "Gotta be a woman."

I shake my head and turn my focus to my beer glass, the condensation beading on the outside.

"Let me guess. Sweet Southern belle. Her daddy chased you off with a shotgun."

I shoot him a sharp look. "You always like this with people you don't know?"

"Yep," a male voice answers from behind us, and a dark-haired man steps into view, sliding into the spot beside the other guy. "He won't shut up till he bleeds you dry of your life story."

"Not feelin' the love, cuz." The man's tone says otherwise, voice dripping with amusement.

The dark-haired man meets my gaze. "I'm Jude, and this behemoth here"—he tips his head, gesturing to the blond man —"is my cousin, Kane."

Begrudgingly, I offer my name. Good manners and all that. "Hollis Barnes."

Something flashes in Kane's eyes that looks like recognition.

He cocks his head to the side. "You're Johnny Barnes' nephew, huh?" His eyes survey me.

"Yes, sir," I answer carefully.

Kane's lips stretch wide into a grin. "You just sir'd me." He leans against the back of the barstool, looking over at Jude. "You reckon I'm an old man, now?"

Jude lets out a low grunt and smirks. "*Now?*"

Kane's hand flies to cover the center of his chest, and he feigns hurt, his Southern accent growing thicker. "That wounds me deeply, darlin'."

"Yet somehow you'll move on, I'm sure," Jude answers drily.

Kane shakes his head with a smile and turns his attention back to me. "I served under your uncle. He's a good man."

It takes me a moment to get on track with the shift in topic. My uncle Johnny had been in the Army for a while—specifically a Green Beret—until an injury took him out of the game. He'd battled with TBI, traumatic brain injury, until he finally called it quits.

"That he is." I take a drink of beer.

"Word on the street is you're the best guy for body work aside from him. Impressive for your age."

I shrug, uncomfortable with the compliment. My uncle doesn't cut corners and actually takes his time with projects. His work is top-notch, and I've learned more than I ever expected by shadowing him.

I've graduated from my apprenticeship, and I'm proud to say I've earned my title of Auto Body Restoration Technician. I'm still on the lower ranks, but I know I'll move up quickly. I'm good at my job, and I love it. It's something that gives me pride, especially when we auction off our work through a prestigious company like Sotheby's.

The more I learn and the better I get at this job, the closer I get to being good enough.

For her.

It's always at the back of my mind even though I'm sure she's moved on by now. No way could a girl like Magnolia Barton stay single forever. I know there's no chance she'd want to be with me, but at least I feel closer to being good enough.

"You from Georgia, too?" Kane's question draws me from my thoughts.

"No, I'm from Alabama."

"And the girl you left behind's there, too?"

"Ye—" I stop myself abruptly, jaw clamping shut. Damn, he's slick.

"Well played," Jude mumbles.

Kane nods, and his eyes flick to the Pop Rocks lying before me. "You got a sweet tooth?"

A small laugh rushes out. "Not really." *Shit.* My voice sounds all sad and pathetic. I'm hoping he won't notice.

"But she did." It's not posed as a question.

I just nod.

Jude flashes Kane a sharp look before turning to me with a sigh. "I hate to leave you with him, but I need to talk with your uncle about my foundation's upcoming charity auction." He thumbs toward Kane. "Just ignore him if he starts prying." He settles a knowing look on his cousin. "He's a prier."

Kane grins proudly as if he's just been given a compliment. "Why, thank you."

Jude shakes his head with a laugh. "Nice meeting you, Hollis."

"Great meetin' you."

I turn back to my beer, hoping this unexpected interaction will fade.

"I'm a good listener, you know."

I don't respond aside from a sharp side glance. You'd think he'd take a hint.

He doesn't.

"I'm dyin' to know the story behind the Pop Rocks."

Jesus. This guy doesn't let up.

I'll pay my tab and move on. Because the last thing I want to talk about—least of all, with a stranger—is Magnolia.

"It's her favorite candy." The words are out before I realize it, and shock settles through me.

What the fuck is wrong with me? Have I sunk so low that I'm becoming one of those pathetic barflies who moan about their sad life? *Shit.*

I reach up to pinch the bridge of my nose and release a long, slow breath.

"And where might this lovely lady be now?" A more serious tone has replaced his earlier lighthearted one.

"Auburn University."

"Huh," is all he says for a moment. "You still love her? Or just miss her?"

I swallow hard before my response comes out, sounding hoarse. "Both."

"And how does she feel about you?"

I huff out a humorless laugh and shake my head. "Not sure."

I find myself telling him the entire story, and surprisingly enough, Kane lives up to his claim of being a good listener. Once I finish, we both fall silent.

"Want my advice?"

A hoarse laugh escapes me, and I hate how emotional I get just thinking about her. "Sure."

Why the hell not? It's not like I have anything to lose.

He fixes his blue eyes on me. "You've gotta get rid of that shit-ton of baggage you're luggin' around first."

My brows slant together in confusion. *What?*

He continues. "You've had it jammed down your throat that

you're not good enough for her to the point you believe it." His features turn intense, and I struggle against the urge to fidget under his scrutiny. "I'll let you in on a secret. If you really think hard on it, no one'll ever be good enough for your Magnolia. Not even you."

He levels me a look. "And definitely not some guy who works on Wall Street, wears a three-piece Armani suit, and rakes in millions. But if you"—he points his index finger in my direction —"feel good enough about yourself and know you'd move heaven and earth to do right by her, that's enough."

He turns his focus on his beer glass, appearing thoughtful. "When you see good people get run through the wringer, it puts things in focus." He glances over at me. "My buddy Hendy came back with scars all over his body. Went from bein' a stud to what he saw as a monster."

A faint hint of a smile forms. "He found a woman who saw more than the surface shit. She understood that money and material things don't hold up in the long run. It's what's in here"—he taps the center of his chest—"and here"—he taps a finger against his temple—"that'll keep you in the game for the long haul."

I mull over his words quietly as I finish my beer.

"This woman..." I toss him a glance. "She's still with your friend?"

He nods, and the edges of his mouth tip up affectionately. "Sure is. They've got a little girl now. Couldn't be happier."

Leaning back in his seat, he settles his laser focus on me. "You're the one who needs to figure out if you're good enough. Not for her. But for *you*. Until then, you're no good to her."

~

The next day, I decide to try something different. In addition to the usual postcard and cherry Pop Rocks I send in an envelope, I also send a text.

Hollis: Greetings from Amelia Island, Florida, Shortcake. I miss you.

I don't get a response.

Until three days later.

Shortcake: Looks beautiful out there. Have fun and be safe.

Hollis: Greetings from Rome, Italy, Shortcake. I miss you.

Again, her response comes a few days later.

Shortcake: Looks amazing. Eat some good pasta. Have fun and be safe.

With each message—my stupid way of testing the waters—she never reciprocates. At least not the way I stupidly hoped. At best, we're friends, and I need to come to terms that I've lost my chance.

But if friendship is all she's offering me, then *by God*, I'll take it.

If I can be in Magnolia Barton's life in any capacity, then it's enough.

It has to be.

29

MAGNOLIA

Senior Year
AUBURN UNIVERSITY

Grant continues to talk about the future—more specifically, our future—and I suspect he plans to ask me to marry him after graduation. Everyone adores him, and I'm not sure there's a soul on God's green earth he couldn't hit it off with.

His lovely family welcomed me with open arms, so warmhearted that it caught me off guard. It's the opposite of the cool, guarded greeting I've come to expect from people with any form of wealth. His mom shared her recipe for her "famous" cornbread, and I divulged the secret our housekeeper, Miranda, taught me when making her delicious collard greens.

I can imagine myself marrying Grant and having Grandpa Joe officiate. Maybe starting a family a few years after, once I'm established in my job. Yet there's a fine tether that holds me back.

Hollis.

I've only allowed myself to look him up on Instagram a time

or two, but I've only found photos of sights or spots he's found during his travels while working for his uncle. Or the latest car restoration—before and after photos—which are impressive even to a person who knows next to nothing about that sort of thing. I don't follow him on there because once he left, a line was drawn, an unspoken agreement that we would keep in touch in the most minimal way.

Then he sent those two text messages and completely threw my world off-kilter.

I miss you. Three words he hasn't included at any other time sent a mix of anger and near debilitating pain rushing to the forefront. Anger, because how dare he suddenly tell me he misses me when he's the one who left *me*. When he hurt me so badly. When I wasn't sure I'd be able to put the pieces of my heart and soul back together again.

Suddenly, he decides to change things, and I don't know what to make of it. I've come so far, finally dredging myself out of the miserable abyss from his absence, and now it seems as if he's trying to pull me back under.

I couldn't bear to respond initially. I just couldn't. I stared at those texts so long and so many times, I swear, if I close my eyes, they're still imbedded on the insides of my eyelids.

Maybe it's time to finally let Hollis go. Lord knows I've let this drag on enough, this hold on my heart I've continued to let him have. Even though the idea of closing the door on any prospect that we could ever be together, that he would come back for me and want a future with me, sends a sharp stab of pain radiating through me, the more rational part of my brain knows it's for the best to lock it tight and throw away the key. He can have my friendship but nothing more.

Nothing more? an inner voice questions while I ignore the piercing anguish that follows.

Nothing more. Just friendship.

Because when it comes down to it, Hollis never did the one thing I'd hoped for him to do.

He never chose me.

30

HOLLIS

AUBURN UNIVERSITY
Magnolia's Graduation Day

I reckon I shouldn't be here, but I couldn't stay away. Least of all, on a day as important as this one.

As I watched Magnolia Barton walk across that stage and accept her diploma, a feeling of utter pride filled me from head to toe. I'm so damn proud of her.

Once the ceremony ends, I linger even though I know it's dangerous. I'm not sure what her response would be to me being here.

Fuck. I scrub a hand down my face and over my short beard and release an inward groan. This is another sign of how fucked up I made things. Before, I wouldn't have hesitated in being here, in letting her know I came.

"Hollis?"

I startle at the male voice calling my name. When I turn, I find a guy about my height wearing a button-down shirt beneath a sport coat and a pair of pressed slacks. He regards me with a mixture of surprise and recognition while I have no idea who the hell he is. He steps closer with a smile.

"Sorry to catch you off guard," he apologizes and holds out his hand to me. "Grant Stevenson."

I shake his hand warily. "Hollis Barnes." I pause before adding, "But somehow, you already knew that."

He grins, and if I'm being completely honest, I don't detect any douchebag vibes. "I recognized you from one of the photos Magnolia has in her room of the two of you."

It takes all my control to suppress the jolt that zigzags through me at his words. *She still keeps a photo of us?*

His eyes crinkle at the corners, and he lifts his chin to gesture to me. "Although I have to be honest, the ink and beard initially threw me off."

A surprised laugh escapes me, and I slide my hands into my pockets.

Grant steps closer and glances around before lowering his voice. "I'm actually glad you're here. I know you and Magnolia haven't seen one another in a while, but you're her oldest friend..."

Oldest friend. Not best friend. I don't miss the phrasing. Although I don't feel it's intentional, it cuts deep just the same.

"I'm nervous as hell, and I'm hopin' you can tell me if she'd like this."

It takes me a moment to realize what he's pulled out of his pocket.

A velvet ring box and a packet of Pop Rocks.

Fuck, fuck, *fuck*.

I resist the urge to rub at the center of my chest, where searing pain radiates.

He flicks open the box to reveal a ring with a large diamond that's fancy as hell. Something Mrs. Barton would love and deem appropriate. But Magnolia? *Hell no.*

"Her mom helped me pick it out."

Exactly.

"And I know she loves Pop Rocks since she always has a pack."

Not the strawberry flavor.

But he's trying. I can see the nervousness in his expression. The hope. The excitement.

I can't crush this guy. He's exactly what her parents have always wanted for her. The kind of guy who doesn't get his hands dirty. The one with money and connections.

The one who can give her the future her parents expect her to have. The one who won't come home with rough hands, callused to hell and back from working on a project that's for a high-end client or due to be auctioned off to a car collector with more money than they know what to do with.

The man who wears button-downs like they're second skin. Designer clothes.

So caught up in my thoughts, I don't immediately realize that he's pocketed the items and is gazing in another direction. When I turn and follow his focus, catching sight of her weaving through the crowd, I take advantage of the moment and let my eyes drink her in. She's...so goddamn beautiful.

Her long blond hair spills down her back, and even beneath the shapeless graduation gown, her sleek, tanned legs peek out from the bottom hem, her heels accentuating her toned calf muscles.

When she catches sight of Grant, her entire face lights up, and...*goddammit.*

I can't do this. This was a fucking mistake. It's like someone's performing open heart surgery and just cracked my chest open without anesthesia.

I spin around, my eyes trained on an exit. I can disappear,

and she'll never know. I'm sure in all the engagement excitement, he'll forget to mention to her that I came.

I barely make it two steps when I hear it. The voice I've dreamed of every night since I left.

"Hollis?"

Fuck.

My eyes fall closed, and I battle against warring emotions. Slowly, so damn cautiously, I turn around.

Seeing Magnolia from a distance was both heartbreaking and wonderful. Up close, though, it's downright devastating. Like an invisible hand reaches into my chest and rips out my heart.

I force a smile that feels brittle as hell. "Congratulations, Shortcake."

31

MAGNOLIA

AUBURN UNIVERSITY
GRADUATION DAY

"CAN YOU BELIEVE IT?" STEPHANIE SQUEALS, DOING A LITTLE SIDE-to-side happy dance. She jostles me in the process, and my hands fly to keep my cap from shifting too much. I know my parents will want to take pictures, and Roy will likely post one on his social media pages, so I need to look presentable.

I knew I should've used more bobby pins to keep it in place.

Also, I'm not sure I've ever seen my roommate this bubbly before. Tommy's had quite the influence on her. He's softened a lot of her edges, and it's nice to see her like this. She still dyes her hair fun colors and dresses how she wants, but she's more affectionate and energetic and just so...happy.

If I'm being honest, I'm a smidge envious.

My parents and Grandpa Joe are here with Grant somewhere in the large crowd. Stephanie and I are milling around, trying to find our respective families in the crowd now that the graduation ceremony is over.

"Do you think Grant's going to propose tonight?"

I jerk to an abrupt stop, causing someone to run into me from behind.

"So sorry," I offer automatically before turning back to Stephanie. "Did he say somethin'?"

She gives me an odd look. "Um, you've been dating him for a while, and you two are like an old married couple." She snorts with a smirk. "If the apocalypse happened right now, I'd be more surprised about that than if Grant proposed."

She's right. Grant and I get along so well that our relationship has been flawless. But still, something's been holding me back.

I miss you.

Lord, help me, but I just can't seem to escape the presence of those words from Hollis' text messages. They stubbornly linger in the recesses of my mind, haunting me.

Inwardly, I shake off my distracting thoughts and finally spot Grant in the crowd, my family standing off to the left of him, speaking with a few people I'm not familiar with. Merely seeing his handsome face smiling at me lifts my spirits.

I smile and wave back, intent on making my way through the crowd to him. I take a few steps when something—or someone, rather—to the right of Grant draws my attention. All I see is the man's back, but something about him strikes me as familiar.

White shirtsleeves rolled up to just below his elbows reveal dark, intricate swirls of ink. His khakis fit him well, and he looks fit, lean but muscular. He's tall, and his hair is dark, yet longer on top while the sides are close shaven, and—

Hollis.

My heart lodges itself in my throat and a faint whimper spills from my lips. *Is it him?* Or am I making a fool of myself, mistakenly seeing him in a crowd? Lord knows, I've done that dozens of times before, only to feel devastated in the end.

"Hollis?" The man falters at my raised voice as I advance closer.

When he slowly turns, as if resigned to do so, I'm utterly robbed of breath. *He came.* Hollis came to my graduation. Tears well in my eyes as I now stand a foot away from him.

He looks so different yet the same. He's grown a beard that's neatly trimmed, dark like his hair. Tattoos peek out from the small view of his upper chest granted by the button-down shirt. He looks like a devastatingly handsome stranger yet also like the boy I loved.

His smile seems brittle at the edges. "Congratulations, Shortcake."

Good Lord, I've missed his voice.

I continue standing here, hating the uncertainty plaguing me about whether it's okay to hug him or not. Finally, the urge is too strong to resist, and I rush forward and wrap my arms around his waist.

"I missed you," I breathe against his neck. He smells crisp, clean, and just like...Hollis. It's comforting, unlike anything else.

"Magnolia?"

At Grant's voice, Hollis stiffens beneath my touch. Too caught up in this moment, I don't respond. Easing away, I drink in the sight of my best friend.

"We're headin' to an early dinner, if you want to join us." There's no mistaking the hopeful tone in my voice.

He offers a smile that doesn't quite meet his eyes. "Thanks, but I don't wanna be in the way." His gaze flicks to something over my shoulder. "I reckon other things might be more important."

His smile makes my heart ache because I know him. I know his smiles, and this one holds so much sadness, it makes me want to hold him tight to me.

"Congratulations, Shortcake." He dips his head to dust a

featherlight kiss to my forehead, and I close my eyes to savor every ounce of his touch. "On everythin'."

He shifts to move away, and my eyes flash open in panic. I part my lips to call after him, his tall form already making quick work of weaving through the crowd, when I hear my name called.

"Magnolia Mae Barton."

I spin around to see what Grant wants, and as soon as I face him, he drops down to one knee and opens a small black velvet box.

TEXT FROM HOLLIS

Greetings from Monterey, California, Shortcake.

32

HOLLIS

SIX MONTHS LATER
Fairhope, Alabama

It was bound to happen eventually. Especially since the housekeeper, Teresa, I hired to keep up with the house had told me as much.

After Dad's death, my mom had taken to the bottle. *Hard.* I knew she'd dabbled in drinking before, but she'd stepped it up to a whole other level once Dad was gone.

Maybe it makes me a terrible excuse for a son, but I hadn't stepped in even though Teresa had given me updates periodically. Not because I wanted Mom to drink herself to death, but because I knew it wouldn't make a damn bit of difference. My mom's always done what she wanted, and I'm the last person who could've had an impact on her choices.

I'd done a hair above the bare minimum and allotted those funds Dad had appointed for her living expenses. She had a roof over her head and food in the pantry, a company regularly scheduled to take care of the yard and landscaping, and Teresa ensuring the place was kept clean on the inside. But I couldn't bring myself to do much more.

Her liver gave out minutes after poor Teresa had received a tongue lashing about whatever rant my mother had been going off about. The housekeeper discovered her unresponsive when she'd gone to check on her before she was due to leave for the day.

I hired cleaners to come in and deep clean the house, and I either donated all furniture and furnishings or had them hauled to the dump. I really don't know what I want to do with the place. It holds so many memories, both good and bad, but I know I should sell it and move on.

That would be the smartest move.

But then there's the backyard. Hell if a damn treehouse isn't holding me back from putting this place on the market.

I stand in the middle of the living room and glance around the empty house, now gleaming; the cleanest it's been in years. The knock on the front door catches me by surprise, and I take another look around, wondering if the cleaners left something behind as I head to answer the door.

I haven't seen him since I left after Dad died, and staring into his eyes now leaves me unsettled as hell.

I fix a polite smile on my face. "Mr. Barton."

He nods. "Hollis." With a cursory glance past me, he asks, "May I come in?"

Without a word, I step back and open the door wider, allowing him to pass before quietly closing it behind him.

He hovers in the small foyer, surveying the empty house, before turning to face me. At his somber expression, I realize this is the first time I've ever witnessed him without an air of confidence.

"Hollis, I"—he breaks off to run a hand over top of his thinning hair—"I, uh, owe you an apology."

Wariness settles through me. Unsure of how to respond, I stay quiet.

"I'm sorry. I didn't realize who you were until..." He trails off, averting his gaze. "Until much later."

"But you knew." *He knew before I did.* I stare at him as anger rushes to the forefront.

His dark eyes meet mine, the shade so similar. "I suspected. I just wasn't one hundred percent certain until recently." He drags his hand through his hair again, this time mussing it. "Your mother had too much to drink and showed up at my door, demandin' I admit the truth."

His sigh is long and defeated, and right now, he's the polar opposite of the man who's always impeccably dressed with a confident smile plastered on his face. "I tried to calm her down and managed to walk her back here before my wife got back from her Women's Club dinner."

"She doesn't know." I don't pose it as a question because I can read between the lines.

He shakes his head slowly, remorse and a hint of fear lingering in his features. "No."

I back up to lean against the wall and shove my hands into my pockets, attempting a casual pose. Inside, though, my emotions riot. "Why are you here?"

The split second of hesitation, the guilt that bleeds into his expression, has me regretting my question. Because it all becomes clear.

Even before he reaches into his pocket.

"Get out." The steely tone has him freezing in mid-motion, the neatly folded paper halfway out of his pocket, pinched between his two fingers and thumb.

A check. More specifically, hush money.

He continues to withdraw the check and unfold it, yet he can't bear to meet my eyes. Staring down at the piece of paper in his hands, looking defeated, he murmurs, "I have to do this." I'm not sure if he's saying it to me or to himself.

I straighten, drawing my hands from my pockets, and stand tall. My fingers curl as I fist my hands.

"I don't want your goddamn money." His head snaps up at the fierce intensity of my tone. "I never wanted it."

Fury grips me and it takes tremendous effort to get the words out. "You might be able to pay your way with others, but not me. So, you can"—I lift my chin, gesturing to the check—"shred that because I already have a father." I press my lips thin before managing to finish with words I force from between clenched teeth. "And it's not you."

"But this could help you with—"

I tug open the front door with so much force, I'm surprised it doesn't fly off the hinges. "Go home, Mr. Barton." My stony stare settles on him, and he swallows audibly before nodding and tucking the check back in his pocket.

He steps to the door but pauses at the threshold, turning his head slightly, yet still not meeting my eyes. "For what it's worth, Hollis, I'm sorry." Then he's gone, leaving those words in his wake.

I shove the door closed and lean my forehead against the cool surface, letting my eyes fall closed. I'm not sure how long I stay like this, willing myself to get my emotions under control. It shouldn't hurt, the dismissal from a man who was never a father to me. It shouldn't.

But it does.

It serves as yet another indication, a glaringly bright sign that I'm not—nor will I ever be—good enough for the Bartons.

Never.

33

MAGNOLIA

Tomorrow night is the engagement party, and everyone seems to be teeming with excitement.

Except me.

That realization inflicts tsunami-like waves of guilt, but I can't deny it. Because I want one person to be there, and I'm not sure if he'll come.

I pick up my phone and pull up the last text message I received from Hollis. It was a photo from Wisconsin, where he'd traveled for another auto expo and auction.

Hollis: Greetings from West Bend, Wisconsin, Shortcake.

He'd forgone the "I miss you" in his texts ever since my graduation day. I can't explain it, but the absence of those three words lingers even now.

I draw in a deep breath and type out a message to him.

Me: Are you around?

I'd only seen him briefly when he'd been directing cleaning crews and other workers who removed the furnishings from the house now that his mother has passed. I'd walked over, much to my mother's dismay, to offer my condolences, but with all the bustling around us, it hadn't been conducive to much talking.

I can't deny the moment I stopped a few feet away from him in his driveway, the sight of him made my stomach flip. In a simple cotton short-sleeve T-shirt, his tattoos were on display, an intriguing mix of black ink and more colorful designs covering the top of his forearms and spilling onto the backs of his hands. They mesmerized me, and I found myself dismayed by my thoughts of wanting to see his bare torso and investigate the patterns peeking out from his tanned chest, unencumbered by clothing.

It was a fascinatin' difference, that's all, I tell myself again. Such a contrast from the boy I once knew to the man today.

My phone vibrates with an incoming text.

Hollis: Yes, ma'am.

Me: Can we talk for a minute?

I stare down at my phone, waiting anxiously for those three dots to appear. They never do. I wait and wait until my screen times out and goes dark.

A moment later, it lights up with an incoming call.

"Hey," I answer quietly.

"Hey, Shortcake." Even his voice sounds different. It's more gravelly, rougher than it used to be. I lean back on my bed and close my eyes.

"It's so good to hear your voice," I confess.

There's a hint of a smile in his tone. "Same."

I press a hand against my chest over top my racing heart. "I wanted to see if you'd be around tomorrow." When he doesn't immediately respond, I rush on. "I know it's last minute, but tomorrow's the engagement party, and I'd really love for you to be there." My words are hurried, spoken so fast that I'm nearly breathless by the end.

When he doesn't say a word, I prompt, "Hollis?"

He clears his throat. "Sure." The single-word response

sounds slightly tortured, and I wonder if he doesn't want to come and share my special day with me.

The thought of that sears my heart.

"I'd love for you to be at the weddin', too. If it's possible with your schedule, of course." I hate how stilted this conversation is. It's downright painful.

"If you want me there, I'll be there." His low, husky tone holds undeniable affection, and it warms me through and through.

"I do."

"So, what kind of weddin' will it be?" There's a hint of a smile in his voice. "A backyard one with Grandpa Joe officiatin', like you always planned?"

I let out a soft laugh. "Kind of."

Mother has taken the reins and increased the guest list, to my dismay. It'll include far more people than I ever wanted or intended, the bulk of whom will be there for my parents, not me. But, as the saying goes, you have to pick your battles.

"As long as you get your convertible with the tin cans at the end, right?" The tenderly spoken reminder has me welling up with tears and emotion clogging my throat.

"And cherry Pop Rocks."

"Can't forget those."

We fall silent for a beat.

"I should get some rest. Tomorrow'll be brutal. So much beautifyin' and so little time." My attempt at injecting humor into my tone falls flat.

"Go rest up, beautiful. 'Night."

Dismay ricochets through me at the thought of our call coming to an end. "Hollis?"

"Ma'am?"

The words spill out before I can even give it thought. But I can't regret them. I haven't spoken them to him in so, *so* long. "Love you."

"Love you, too, Shortcake."

He quickly ends the call, leaving me with the startling realization that he didn't say the same words we'd repeated to one another countless times over the years.

But not like that.

34

HOLLIS

THE ENGAGEMENT PARTY

I WALK INTO THE PARTY A SHORT TIME AFTER IT WAS SCHEDULED TO start, ensuring the large crowd would serve as a buffer of sorts. They would demand her attention, and that would hopefully mean less awkwardness.

Approaching the table nearly overflowing with wrapped gifts, I deposit mine on it carefully. I'm already second-guessing it, but it's too late now. I'd stayed up late finishing it for her and hope she appreciates it.

"Hollis!" Before I can turn and fully face the person who called my name, a petite woman with blue-streaked hair latches on to me.

Stephanie.

I laugh. "Good to see you."

She leans back with a smile. "Hey, stranger." Her eyes survey me. "You look all…" She struggles with how to finish. "Manly."

I grin. "That so?"

"Do I need to worry about y'all?" a male voice interrupts. Up steps a guy with a friendly smile. He places a hand at the base of

Stephanie's back and offers his hand. "I'm Tommy. Nice to meet you."

We exchange a brief handshake. "Hollis Barnes."

His eyebrows rise. "Whoa. *The* Hollis Barnes?"

I'm at a loss at how to respond because I've never received this kind of reaction before.

"Yes, honey," Stephanie answers for me. "*The* Hollis Barnes."

I glance between them warily. "I'm afraid to ask why I'm not *just* Hollis Barnes."

Tommy shakes his head with what appears to be awe. "I'm a huge fan of your work. I follow you guys on Instagram."

Oh. Well, that changes things.

I nod. "I appreciate it."

"Are you in town for long?" he asks.

"No." I attempt an expression of remorse when, in truth, I can't wait to get out of here. Being around Magnolia when she's due to marry someone else is flat-out torture. "I'm fixin' to head back tomorrow."

We make small talk for a few minutes before Stephanie's attention shifts to focus somewhere behind me to my right. It doesn't dawn on me until the small hand rests on my arm. I turn and, *fuck*. She's breathtaking. There's not a doubt in my mind that she'll be a gorgeous bride.

Seeing her now, in the sleeveless knee-length dress that brings out the blue in her eyes, it's undeniable that she's become a beautiful woman. Merely stopping for gas or grabbing a few toiletries from the local grocery store had me overhearing the locals chatter on about how "the Barton girl is fixin' to take over city council and make things right."

Everything's falling into place for her, and I should be happy for her. No, I *am* happy for her.

I just wish with every molecule of my body that I could be the one by her side instead of Grant.

"Hey, man!" Her fiancé greets me with a warm smile and a handshake. "Glad you could make it." He sobers, then leans in and offers, "I'm sorry to hear about your mother's passin'."

I nod. "Appreciate it."

A lady I don't recognize materializes beside Magnolia. "Your mother needs y'all at the front."

"We'll be right there," Magnolia says. Then she turns to me. "Thanks so much for comin'." She gives me a quick hug, one that has me closing my eyes to memorize the feel of it before she backs away, accepting Grant's outstretched hand.

"Please don't leave without sayin' goodbye, okay?" Her eyes plead with mine, but before I can offer a noncommittal answer, someone else calls out to her, drawing her attention.

I back away and grab one of the offered glasses of champagne from a passing server. Grant and Magnolia are now at the front of the room, thanking everyone for coming. Then Grant begins retelling how the two of them met and fell in love. It takes all I have in me not to toss back my glass of champagne in one gulp.

When the awws and smattering of applause come at the end, I leave my unfinished champagne and sneak out the exit, unnoticed.

I feel like a fool for leaving that present. It's juvenile and not sentimental like I'd originally thought.

I don't wait until the morning. I think I had an inkling earlier, which is why my bag is already stowed in my truck, ready to go.

I hit the interstate in record time, and the pressure on my chest doesn't ease until I pass over the Alabama-Georgia border, bringing me that much closer to Atlanta.

The text comes in within a few hours after I leave Fairhope, but I can't bring myself to read it until two days later.

Shortcake: I wish you would've stayed so I could say goodbye to you. Thank you for the present. I love it, Hollis.

The selfie taken with the pink convertible model car isn't what has me throwing myself even deeper into my work these days.

It's the large, sparkling diamond ring on the hand holding the car I'd painstakingly painted **Just Married: Grant and Magnolia Stevenson** on the back bumper. On the hood, a small print version of Shakespeare's Sonnet 130 glued to the surface. She sticks out her tongue playfully to show me what's on it.

The cherry Pop Rocks from the packet I'd taped to the bottom of the car.

35

MAGNOLIA

THREE MONTHS LATER
WEDDING DAY

STEPHANIE HAS GONE ABOVE AND BEYOND. SHE'S STILL PROVING that even now. After my hair and makeup were complete, she assisted me in getting into my dress. When I whisper to her that I need a quick moment alone, she jumps into action with no questions asked.

"Let's give the lovely bride some air and a moment to herself." She shoos everyone from the room, and to my amazement, she handles my mother with ease. "Mrs. Barton, I think the mayor was asking to speak with you, dying to know more about the caterers you hired."

I stare sightlessly at my reflection in the mirror, my lips curving up at my friend's blatant fib. But it works. Soon, the room is empty aside from the two of us.

She steps up behind me, and I focus on her reflection in the floor-length mirror. "Thank you," I offer softly.

"Anytime." She fusses with the ends of my veil one last time before she lets out a sigh. "God, you're gorgeous." With a quick squeeze of my hand, she disappears, closing the door quietly behind her.

Once I'm finally alone, I exhale loudly. My cell phone lies on the dresser, playing welcoming background music to all the chatter while I was restricted to the chair where the makeup artist and Michelle, the woman from the salon I frequent, had done their best work.

My childhood room no longer holds any of my belongings since everything's been packed up and delivered to Grant's house.

I gaze at my reflection, my eyes flicking over the sparkly headband with the attached veil cascading down my back. My hair is twisted in sections and weaved in an intricate style I could never manage to recreate on my own. My lips are a unique blush color I've never worn before.

I reach up to touch them and freeze when I catch sight of the man standing a few feet behind me.

"Hollis," I breathe softly.

HOLLIS

I SHOULDN'T BE DOING THIS, BUT I HAVE TO. MUCH LIKE THOSE IN twelve-step programs, I need to complete this final task.

When I sneak up to her childhood room, Stephanie slips out the door the instant I approach. She eyes me with a mixture of wariness and curiosity. "She wanted a moment alone."

"No problem. I'm, uh, droppin' somethin' off really quick."

She studies me for so long that I expect her to refuse. Finally, she nods. "Just don't be too long," she says, already rushing down the hall.

I reach for the door, ignoring the slight tremor in my hand, before I tap softly. "Shortcake?" I murmur.

She doesn't answer, but I know she's alone, so I tentatively open the door.

And promptly lose all ability to breathe.

Magnolia stands in front of her floor-length mirror looking too beautiful for words with a pensive expression on her face. I quietly close the door behind me, now realizing the music playing from her phone on the dresser must have prevented her from hearing me at the door.

I take a few steps closer to her, unable to tear my eyes away from the sight of her in that dress. The way it leaves her shoulders bared, showing off her tanned flawless skin, and her hair done up in some fancy way that displays the elegant curve of her neck, does me in.

When her eyes catch sight of me in the mirror, she freezes.

"Hollis."

"You're"—I step closer, and it's a monumental challenge to force the words past the growing lump of emotion in my throat —"absolutely breathtakin'."

A slight flush spreads across her cheeks. "Thank you."

She turns slowly to face me, and I feel like a damn fool dressed like I am. I can't bear to spend money on brands like Armani, especially clothes I'll never get use out of, but this is the nicest suit I own. Hell, I'm still probably an embarrassment to her.

"I wasn't sure if you'd be able to make it."

She wasn't the only one. Hell, even *I* hadn't been sure.

I offer a small smile. "Wouldn't miss it for the world."

Gazing down at her, I realize this will be the last time we'll be together as just Hollis and Magnolia. The last time she'll be my Shortcake. Because in a few minutes, she'll belong to Grant.

I move over to the window covered with a gauzy curtain that looks out onto the backyard, where countless guests have gathered. It's not quite like she'd wanted, but then again, she'd been a young girl who'd wanted a small backyard wedding.

Things change. So do people.

With my back to her, I reach inside my suit jacket and withdraw the letter and the packet. In one hand, I fist the letter tight in a punishing grip. This damn letter holds my words—words she'll never see, because no way am I fixing to be the bastard who confesses his feelings on her goddamn wedding day.

It's the end of the line for me. This is goodbye.

Suddenly, someone knocks loudly on the door in three

demanding raps of their knuckles. "Magnolia?" a woman's voice calls out. "Are you still in there?"

Magnolia crosses the room and opens the door just a crack. "Yes, ma'am."

"We need to get you downstairs in about ten minutes, sweetie."

I walk to the small wastebasket at the side of the dresser and set the packet of cherry Pop Rocks beside her cell phone before I toss the crumpled letter in the trash.

"I'll be ready," Magnolia promises the woman before closing the door. She turns around, and I drink in the sight of her one last time, knowing I need to leave. I shouldn't even be here.

But now it's done. It's over.

I draw to a stop in front of her and carefully place a light kiss on her forehead. "Love you, Shortcake."

Without waiting for her response, I step from the room and close the door softly behind me.

37

MAGNOLIA

I FIND GRANT IN THE SPARE BEDROOM. ALONE, THANKFULLY.

He turns at the sound of the opening door only to comically spin back around, covering his eyes. "Magnolia! I'm not supposed to see you in your dress."

A faint smile tugs at my lips. Good grief, do I love this man. "It's okay, I promise."

Hands still covering his eyes as I approach, he asks, "Is everythin' all right?"

The affection and worry in his tone compound my guilt because, well...he's a peach, as Mother would say. Grant is genuinely a good man.

But I need some answers, and as painful as it might be to ask them, it needs to happen. Otherwise, I'll have what-ifs hanging over me and plaguing me every step of the way.

I draw to a stop in front of him. "You can look at me, Grant," I say in a gentle tone.

Cautiously, he lowers his hands and opens his eyes. His gaze surveys me slowly, as if he's taking in every detail, his expression morphing into one of wonder before his eyes return to mine. "You look beautiful."

I step closer and smooth down the lapels of his tuxedo jacket. "And you look quite dapper yourself." I busy myself by straightening his tie, avoiding his gaze while I drum up the courage to ask him.

"Hey." His tone is low, cautious but gentle.

I lift my eyes to his. "I have a question for you."

"O-kay," he answers slowly.

I press my lips together firmly before I ask, "Do you love me?"

His eyes go wide in surprise before he regains his composure. Expression turning fiercely tender, he takes my hands in his. "I wouldn't be here if I didn't."

I search his eyes, his features, for any indication his words are untrue and come up empty.

It makes my next question that much more painful to ask.

I swallow hard past the lump of riotous emotion. "Am I the person you can't live without? The love of your life? Do you feel passionate about me?" His lips part, but I rush on to finish. "If I walked out that door"—I gesture to the closed bedroom door I came through—"right now and never came back, would you be devastated?"

His mouth opens to answer, but the words don't immediately come.

And I have my answer.

My face falls, and I withdraw my hands from his, curling my fingers inward at the painful realization.

Grant wears a tormented expression. "Magnolia, you know what I went through."

I hold up a hand to stop him, resignation threaded in my tone when I quietly say, "I know."

He moves to cup my face in his hands, eyes pleading. "I love you, Magnolia. I do. But I don't think I'll ever be able to love someone the way I loved her."

Anguish etches his features, and I know he's not saying this to hurt me, but because it's the truth. When he lost her in that car accident, he lost much of his heart, too.

I reach up to cover Grant's hands with mine before gently lifting them away. When I release his hands, they drop limply to his sides. "I know, I just..." Emotion clogs my throat, and I look away.

"I found a kindred spirit in you that day. That was my first thought," he says in a hushed voice.

My eyes cut to his, and the sad smile playing at his lips sends pain lancing through my chest.

"I knew just by lookin' at you that you were where I'd once been. And it took me a hell of a lot longer to claw my way out." He drags a hand through his hair, mussing it slightly. His voice rises with urgency as he continues. "Spendin' time with you and gettin' to know you, I fell in love with you—"

"But not the kind of love you had before," I finish for him, my voice cracking. "Not the kind of love you can't live without."

He holds my gaze for a long moment before resignation settles over his features. "No."

I mash my lips together, willing away the sob that threatens to break free. Turning, I face the window, vying for some semblance of composure.

"But Magnolia..." he says, his voice hurried, laced with unease. "I *do* love you, and I've—"

"Ask me," I blurt out, still staring out the window, vision blurry.

There's a slight pause. "Ask you...what?"

"Ask me if I could live without you if you walked out that door right now and never came back." Slowly, I turn to face him. "Ask me if I'd be devastated."

Blue eyes survey me cautiously as if he's trying to figure out if I've lost my ever-loving mind.

Maybe I have.

With obvious hesitance, he asks, "If I walked out that door and never came back, would you be devastated?"

Tears fill my eyes as I finally admit the truth.

There's only one man who left me in the midst of devastation. Yes, I managed to pick up the pieces and rebuild my world with help, but it's never been the same.

I've never been the same.

When someone who owns your heart and soul leaves, you're left to repair the wreckage. To somehow make due with a heart that's never again whole. One that's weaker and more vulnerable than before.

And the portion of your heart that's left never stops yearning for its missing piece.

"No," I whisper raggedly. Guilt settles inside me like a thousand-pound weight.

Instead of being furious or appearing hurt, Grant's expression hovers between sympathy and remorse. "It's always been him." He doesn't ask this but states it.

I can only nod.

His eyes fall closed and he inhales deeply before releasing a long, slow breath. Once his eyes open, he slides his hands into his pockets.

"Well, then I reckon we have two options."

I furrow my brow in confusion but listen as he continues.

"You can walk down that aisle today and marry a man who will love you for the rest of his life." He cocks his head to the side. "I promise I'll be the best husband I possibly can and I'll always support you," he implores. "I would never do anythin' to bring you shame or make you feel anythin' less than the amazin' woman you are."

A single tear escapes and spills down my cheek. "And option two?"

His smile is tinged with sadness. "We part ways as friends, and you go find yourself the man you can't live without."

I lower my chin in defeat, staring down at the carpeted floor, and whisper hoarsely, "I'm not sure I can."

Fingers lift my chin and he forces me to meet his gently admonishing gaze. "Don't tell me Magnolia Mae Barton isn't brave enough to go after true love."

I let out a pathetic excuse for a laugh. "But what about you?"

"You don't need to worry about me," he chides. "I reckon if we announce we changed our minds at the last minute down there, in front of everyone, I'd undoubtedly be the talk of the town." He flashes me a knowing look, his lips forming a smug grin. "The sympathy from women everywhere would tide me over for years to come." Even though he smiles, I know him well enough to detect the glimmer of unease in his features.

Shaking my head, I gesture wildly in the direction of the backyard. "But I can't just—"

"Magnolia," Grant affectionately scolds me. His heavy palms settle on my shoulders while his eyes bore into mine. "Listen to me. You need to stop worryin' about everyone else." He lets a long, quiet moment settle between us, as though allowing me time to soak up his words. "Always go after what you want. Go after your passion. The one thing—or person—you can't live without."

Those kind blue eyes I've come to know so well crinkle at the corners with his affectionate smile. He leans in to press a soft kiss to my temple, leaving his lips to linger there when he whispers, "Whatever you decide, I'll always support you. And everyone who loves you will do the same."

38

MAGNOLIA

AFTER LEAVING GRANT, THE DECISIONS AND EXPECTATIONS OF ME weigh me down more than the thick, oppressing humidity that plagues Fairhope during the summer months.

Just as I lay a hand on the door handle of my room, the wedding planner rushes my way.

"Magnolia, sweetheart. You have only two minutes." She singsongs the last two words cheerily.

"Yes, ma'am," I say with a smile. "I'll be ready."

She must detect something on my face that she's seen while dealing with countless brides because her expression clouds. "You let me know if you need anythin', all right?"

I nod with what I hope is a more convincing smile and slip inside the room, securing the lock behind me. "I just need a moment," I mutter to myself.

I should also turn off my phone that's still playing music. Turning, I take two steps to reach where my phone rests on the dresser and—

The object sitting beside my phone stops me dead in my tracks. Cherry Pop Rocks.

"Oh, Hollis," I say softly.

There's no way I can resist having some before it's time for me to leave the room. Just as I pluck the packet from the dresser and tear it open, shaking a few pieces onto my tongue, something catches my eye.

The wastebasket off to the side of the dresser now has a wadded-up piece of paper on top. This wouldn't be noteworthy in itself, except that I recognize a small portion of the handwriting. The familiar masculine slashes of inked words.

It belongs to the man who had been here just moments earlier.

Carefully setting the candy packet on the dresser, I reach down to withdraw the paper from the trash and smooth it out on the dresser's polished surface.

Dear Magnolia,

I'm writing this with the delusional hope that maybe it'll finally help me let go. You're about to marry the guy who's perfect for you. The one who can give you everything. The perfect house, family, and future just like your mom always wanted for you. And you deserve it. You deserve happiness.

The truth is, I've never once been able to forget about you. Never been able to forget about the way you kiss, the way you felt in my arms. I've never been able to erase the memory of the night I had the honor of making love to you. And that's what it was for me. Making love.

I think I've loved you as long as I can remember. Sure, it started off as friends, but at some point, it became more, and it never stopped. God knows I tried to stop it, but dammit, you're ingrained in my soul. You own my fucking heart. It's that simple.

Saying goodbye to the woman I love more than anything else in this world has to be the hardest damn thing I think I've ever had to do. But I have to do it once and for all. You don't

need me in your life anymore, and God knows I need to get a damn life and move on.

It's so stupid that I'm writing a letter I'll never give you, but maybe this shit will work. Maybe I'll finally be able to get over you.

I love you, Magnolia Barton. I'm honestly not sure I'll ever be able to stop. I just wish I'd been man enough to admit it, to tell you myself that you're not just my best friend—you're the woman of my dreams.

Maybe in another life, I'll get a do-over, and I'll do everything I can to be enough, to be worthy of you. I won't be gutless and let a day go by without telling you how I feel. I won't be the bastard wishing he had the fucking nerve to ask you to go against everything expected of you and do one thing: choose me.

Go have beautiful babies with blond hair and blue eyes and gorgeous smiles that take people's breath away, just like yours. Make sure they have a treehouse that's their haven, they find a favorite Shakespeare sonnet, and they experience the joy of Pop Rocks.

Most of all, be happy, Shortcake.

Love,

Hollis

(Yes, like that.)

39

MAGNOLIA

JITTERS. THEY'RE NORMAL...OR SO I'M TOLD COUNTLESS TIMES BY my mother. She picks up on my agitation when she arrives with the wedding planner in tow to escort me from my room to the backyard.

After scolding me and demanding I get my emotions under control so the photographs won't be a "godawful mess", Mother finally stops fussing, so I suppose I've managed to stifle my nerves enough to her satisfaction.

Nervous agitation has given way to a dazed detachment from my surroundings and it clings to me, adhering like moss to a tree, while my mind attempts to process everything.

With a warm smile, Roy waits for me to approach. He loops my arm through his and when the violin quartet begins playing the wedding march, he guides me toward the rear aisle. Everyone's attention turns to us. My eyes immediately search for him in a near frantic and needy way.

Hollis.

As soon as I find him in the very back, leaning against one of the posts of the pergola, my spine relaxes a fraction. It's bittersweet to have him here. Sweet because out of everyone else, aside from my grandpa Joe, Hollis has always grounded me. He's made me feel safe and accepted.

The bitter comes from the realization that our friendship will be forever altered after today. With Grant as my husband, I expected Hollis would eventually fade from my life. It's just his way. He's always been a gentleman, wanting to do the right thing. But after his letter—a letter he never intended for me to read—there won't be anything close to a fade.

Hollis plans to disappear from my life forever.

Roy and I draw to a stop, and he and Grant shake hands. My stepfather presses a light kiss to my cheek before finding his seat beside my mother in the front row. I hand my bouquet to Stephanie before I turn and place my hands in Grant's. His palms are warm and comforting. Familiar.

I know Grant loves me. Even if I'm not the ultimate love of his life, we still have a solid relationship.

But is it enough?

Grant said it was okay to call off the wedding, but could I really follow through?

Could I do that to him? What kind of woman does that? And to a good man, no less?

I draw in a breath in a desperate attempt to calm myself, to quiet my racing mind.

This is it. My wedding day. Aside from the increased number of guests Mother invited, this day is nearly what I've dreamed of since I was a little girl. A backyard wedding. My grandfather officiating. The man who loves me ready to pledge his life to me in front of these guests.

Grant's blue eyes crinkle at the corners as he gazes at me, a tender smile playing at his lips.

"We are gathered here today..."

While Grandpa Joe begins the ceremony, I lose myself in the eyes of the man who's been by my side for most of my adult life.

The man who will love me forever.

The man who will support me in anything I do.

Yet one thing lingers.

Edging its way into my mind is the awareness that the cherry flavor has faded from my taste buds.

And it serves to signify that I'm losing something far bigger than the flavor of the Pop Rocks candy Hollis left in my room.

40

HOLLIS

At barely ten past three in the afternoon, the diner holds only a few customers. I tug open the door, noting the *Seat Yourself* sign, and find that I'm a glutton for punishment.

Because I slide into the booth. *Our* booth.

"One last time," I mutter the promise under my breath.

A young waitress I don't recognize comes by, and I only order a coffee. Once she delivers it, I discreetly pour in some of the whiskey from my flask and recap it, stashing it back in my inner pocket.

I stare into the black brew, and my goddamn chest feels hollow. How the hell is my heart still beating?

This is it, I think. Once I finish my final cup of coffee, I'll say goodbye to this place forever.

There's nothing left for me here.

41

MAGNOLIA

"...JOIN THESE TWO IN HOLY MATRIMONY..."

"...two souls become one..."

As Grandpa Joe continues with the opening of our ceremony, his deep voice fades into the background while I gaze up
at Grant. His hands hold mine, offering what they always do.

Comfort.

Security.

Love.

Affection.

But is it enough? Especially now, when I know there's a
chance I could have more. That I could have the love of a man
who's always had a hold on my heart.

My focus drifts over the backyard to the spot where Hollis
had stood against one of the pergola posts.

The wooden post stands alone. The man who'd been there
only moments ago is now gone. His absence ricochets within me
before the loss settles, embedding itself deep. It serves to finally
shake me from my stupor, as realization and resounding shame
simultaneously engulf me.

You need to stop worryin' about everyone else. Grant's earlier words echo in my brain, serving as a much needed rein-forcement.

I can't deny that I've never truly stood up for myself before—not in the full capacity of any kind. I've never been brave enough to speak up about what *I* want from my life.

Though I'm adult now, I reckon I've never really outgrown feeling like that little girl whose gap between her front teeth displeased and embarrassed her own mother. The girl whose hair wasn't perfect or even the desired shade of blonde, and who never managed to be ladylike or refined enough. The one who wasn't friends with the "right" people.

It's been practically drilled into my brain that I need to be exactly what my mother and Roy expect of me, even at the expense of my own happiness. My life has consisted of me desperately trying to gain their approval and acceptance—ulti-mately, their form of love.

And I'm not sure I ever fully succeeded in gaining it.

I turn back to Grant, and the shift is subtle. His eyes change to brown, his hair darkens and is a little longer on top, the sides cut shorter. A dark beard covers his face, one I imagine will rasp against my skin in the most delicious way. Tattoos peek out, flowing from beneath the cuffs at his wrists, and I itch to trace each curve and swoop of ink lovingly. And those familiar lips curve up at the corners in a smile meant solely for me.

He'd whisper, "Love you, Shortcake," so softly that only I could hear him.

I'd whisper back, "Like that." Then we'd smile at each other throughout the ceremony, unable to look away in fear that it was all a dream. A fantasy. The most perfect vision of our future.

My eyes fall closed as emotions batter away at me, piercing my heart, and when I open them, Grant's blue eyes watch me carefully.

Knowingly.

Tears gather in my eyes, and he dips his head in the faintest nod. His hands give mine a gentle squeeze.

I turn to my grandfather. "Excuse me."

Grandpa Joe's eyes meet mine and he doesn't say a word for a moment. His focus briefly darts past me before settling on Grant and something passes between the two men. My grandfather lowers his Bible, setting it on the small podium, while one hand drops to his side. He holds out an upturned palm to me.

I place my hand in his, and he raises it to press a soft kiss on the back. His eyes never leave mine as he brings his other hand up to tuck his car keys in my palm. "Go get 'em, Shortcake."

Grandpa Joe's voice is loud and clear as he announces, "Thank y'all for attendin', but there's been a slight change in plans."

I offer a bright smile as I face everyone, feeling lighter than I have in a while. "If y'all stick around, I plan to bring back a special guest. Then the celebration'll truly begin."

Please, let Hollis be where I think he is. Please, I plead internally.

I wrap my arms around Grant and give him a quick hug. "Thank you," I whisper before backing away.

I barely make it two steps before my mother darts up from her seat, blocking me.

"Young lady, you get back there and—"

"No, ma'am." My tone is firm.

Roy darts up from his seat, glancing around anxiously, likely concerned for how this all might look to others.

I clench my hands tight while straightening my shoulders in an attempt to fortify my courage. "With all due respect, I've let you manage my life for far too long. It's time for me to start livin' it and findin' my happiness."

Mother leans in, her upper lip curling in a sneer. "You *will*—"

"If y'all don't plan to bear witness to a true love match when

my granddaughter returns, then you'd best be on your merry
way," Grandpa Joe's voice booms loudly. His stern expression is
fixed on my mother, and her mouth parts in shock. It's probably
due to the fact that no one normally challenges her.

I take advantage of her speechless state and sidestep her.
Down the aisle I go, avoiding most everyone's gazes until I lock
eyes with Stephanie. Her wide grin and thumbs-up bolster my
confidence.

I rush through the yard as fast as my heels can carry me and
practically dive into Grandpa Joe's car.

Starting the engine, I drive like a bat out of hell, praying my
instincts are right. A lungful of breath expels from my lips when
I see the truck parked in the diner's lot.

I pull into a space, park, and hike up my dress to retrieve
what I'd folded and tucked beneath the snug blue garter belt.

My something old.

Hollis' letter.

42

HOLLIS

GOD KNOWS HOW LONG I SIT, HOW MANY REFILLS THE WAITRESS pours me, until I finally register the sensation of someone staring at me.

I tense because the last thing I want or need is to chat with someone about Magnolia's wedding. But when I turn my head, no one inside the diner is paying me any mind. Yet that eerie feeling lingers. Finally, I turn toward the window.

The sight I'm faced with robs me of all ability to breathe, let alone form words. Shock reverberates through me to the marrow of my bones. I force myself to blink, sure that it's a figment of my imagination.

Magnolia stands on the other side of the window in her wedding dress. Her features are etched with nervousness, and I skim the length of her, worried that she's hurt or something has happened to her grandpa.

Then I notice what she's holding.

"*Fuck*." The hushed expletive spills from my lips at the sight of the letter I wrote her.

She steps closer to the window, her eyes never leaving mine.

Then, with what seems like aching slowness, she raises her left hand, fingers splayed wide.

No rings in sight.

As if in a daze, I rise from the booth and quickly toss down cash to cover my coffee and tip before striding outside to where she stands.

I stop about a foot away while my unease and fear of giving in to hope war within me. The slight breeze picks up the hem of her dress, causing it to billow in a ripple at her ankles.

"What're you doin' here?"

"I wanted to talk to my best friend." She holds up the letter. "The one who wrote this."

I swallow painfully. "You got him, right here."

She steps closer. "Why didn't you tell me?" Unshed tears glisten in her eyes. "I've loved you my whole life." A tear escapes, tracking down her cheek.

"Because I need to—"

"*No.*" She cuts me off fiercely. "I've only ever needed you. I've only been happiest with *you*. I've never"—her voice cracks, more tears trickle down her beautiful face, and it fucking guts me —"cared about the money or your job." She takes another step toward me. "It's always been you, Hollis. Alw—"

I grip her nape and tug her mouth to mine, capturing her lips in a kiss I've been dying for. She wraps her arms around me, pulling me closer, and I pour everything into the kiss—every single ounce of my love for her.

We finally draw apart, and I rest my forehead against hers. Eyes closed, I take a moment to breathe her in, to bask in the feel of her in my arms.

"Feel like gettin' married, Barnes?"

I let out a surprised laugh and lean back to peer down at her. "I reckon we need a marriage license first."

"True." Blue eyes gaze up at me with so much love it makes it hard to breathe. "But maybe we can practice. There's a perfectly good cake and everythin'." Her lips twist mischievously. "I may have told the guests to hang out for a bit. That I was plannin' to bring someone special back with me."

"Pretty sure of yourself, huh?"

Her expression sobers, and she shakes her head. "No." With affection and love etched on her features, she whispers, "I was just really hopin' you'd choose me."

43

MAGNOLIA

LATER THAT NIGHT

"Hollis Barnes," I tease playfully. "Is this where you bring all the ladies?"

He helps me up the ladder and tugs me inside the treehouse. "No, ma'am. Only one lucky lady's ever been up here."

"That so?" I grin up at him before his mouth finds mine once again, and I get lost in his kiss. I tug at his clothing and his fingers encircle my wrists, stopping me, before he backs away.

"I didn't plan on this, so I need to get things situated." He tips his head in the direction of the sleeping bag he'd tossed inside seconds ago along with the air mattress stowed on the shelf.

Within a few minutes, we have everything set up. He's shucked his suit jacket and unbuttoned his cuffs to roll them up, baring his muscled forearms to offer me a view of the inked skin beneath. Those slacks of his accentuate his strong, firm thighs and backside.

He turns and catches me in my pathetic attempt at removing the headband-veil combo from my head and stops me.

"Let me."

With gentleness that makes my heartbeat stutter, he removes countless bobby pins, releasing my hair from their confines, as well as the headband and attached veil, before setting every-thing aside. I turn around, gathering my hair in hand and draping it over one shoulder.

"The zipper and the hooks are—"

"I've got this." His husky voice sends a rush of shivers through me. Roughened fingertips lightly abrade my skin as he carefully unfastens my dress. Soft lips press to the side of my neck, his beard rasping at my sensitive flesh, before his tongue darts out for a quick taste.

He continues unfastening, landing tender kisses, taking tiny little tastes with his tongue, until he finally eases the dress off me, leaving me completely bare. Fiery hot need pulses through my veins. I turn to face him, and his dark gaze locks with mine.

"Shortcake," he says hoarsely. "Tell me you weren't like this the entire night."

I can't resist the mischievous grin that forms on my lips. "I took off my panties earlier, hopin' you'd..." I trail off with a blush.

"Hopin' I'd what?"

He tugs me close, and I make quick work of the buttons of his shirt, which is a feat with his hands caressing my body, leaving a blaze of searing heat in their wake. When he dips his head, his playful nips along my neck have me gasping.

"Hopin' I'd touch you here?"

One hand skims between my thighs, his thick fingers teasing my entrance, causing my breath to lodge in my throat.

"Or..." Hollis places my palm over the impossibly hard ridge of his erection. "Maybe you wanted this?"

A rush of breath escapes my lips. "*Yes.*"

I unfasten his pants and hastily shove them down. He kicks them aside before my hand dives beneath his boxers to wrap around his thick shaft. His fingers close over mine, guiding me to slide down to the base before gliding back up his steely length.

Releasing his hold on my hand, he drops his arm to his side. His fists clench, his struggle for control evident. Heavy-lidded eyes watch me while I stroke him. The harsh groan that erupts from his lips, the guttural way he says my name when I graze the pad of my thumb over the slit, gathering the moisture there, intensifies the needy ache between my legs.

An edge of desperation colors his voice. "*Fuck*, that feels good."

His hips arch into my touch, silently begging for more. Then I shove his boxers down past his muscular thighs, letting them drop to his ankles before he kicks them off. I help him remove his shirt, leaving him perfectly bare.

Now, I get to look at him. *My* Hollis. The man, not the boy.

Intricate tattooed designs cover his arms and chest and I trace them with my fingertips, in awe of the beautiful abstract art displayed on his skin. He cups my nape, fusing his mouth to mine before gliding one blunt fingertip inside me. I gasp at his touch, the throbbing between my legs becoming incessant. His beard rasps against my skin in the most delicious way possible while his tongue dives inside to tangle with my own.

I clutch at him, one of my hands moving to sift through his hair. His touch, his kiss, is so different yet so familiar. My body burns for him, my nipples hard against the firm wall of his muscled chest.

He breaks the kiss, his breath coming in harsh pants. Leaning away just a fraction to gaze at me, his expression is raw and fierce. "You won't regret this."

At the vulnerability in his tone, I move to cradle his jaw in my hands. Eyes locked, I whisper the truth. "I could never regret you."

I hesitate, and he seems to somehow understand, waiting

patiently. "You're the only one I've ever been with..." I trail off, a blush rising on my cheeks.

"Bare?" His voice is low and gravelly. His eyes flare, turning molten, searing me with heated lust. "Is that what you're sayin', baby girl?" He adds a second finger, the long, thick digits sliding inside me languidly. "My cock is the only one you let inside you without protection?" His words incinerate me from within.

My answer comes out as a whimper. "Yes."

He groans against my lips, nipping gently, before lifting and carrying me to the mattress now covered by the sleeping bag.

With such reverence it nearly brings tears to my eyes, he lays me down before covering me with his hard body. Resting his weight on his forearms, he tunnels his fingers in my hair and buries his face in my neck, leaving a trail of hot, wet kisses in his wake.

"Same goes for me," he whispers hoarsely.

Then, catching my lower lip between his, he sucks gently before releasing it. I groan and arch my body, desperate to relieve the incessant pressure between my thighs.

"Tell me what you want." His tone is raspy with need.

"You." I gasp when the tip of his arousal brushes against my clit.

A slight grimace flickers across his face. "This time'll be short." He ducks his head, capturing my nipple between his lips and sucking hard before pressing a light kiss to the very tip. Shivers skitter down the length of my spine, and a rush of wetness floods me between my thighs. "But I swear I'll make up for it."

When I take his heavy length in my palm, he lets out a tortured-sounding groan. I guide his flared head to my entrance and drag the tip through my wetness before lining him up. His heated gaze bores into mine as he nudges my opening, teasing me briefly before sinking inside the slightest fraction. I arch on a gasp co-mingled with his throaty groan.

He stares down at me, eyes glazed with lust, and presses deeper. I clutch at him with a tiny whimper.

"More," I demand.

He fuses his mouth to mine, our tongues colliding in a devouring kiss a split second before he fills me with every inch of his rigid length. My inner muscles instinctively grip him and his guttural moan vibrates against my lips.

Once he begins moving, driving deep in a seductive rhythm, I break the kiss and bring my focus to where our bodies join. Slick with our combined arousal, he slides in and out of me. His abdominals flex and ripple with each thrust.

I drag a finger down the center of his chest to trace the light dusting of hair leading from below his navel to his groin. His body tenses, his eyes falling closed as though to savor my touch. A low growl rumbles in the back of his throat and his eyes flash open, a wildness in the depths.

Capturing my bottom lip between his teeth, he tugs playfully before soothing it with a kiss. Then he drapes one of my knees over the crook of his elbow, and the instant he does, the angle allows him to slide even deeper.

"Want you to come hard for me." My inner muscles clench around him in response to his seductive words, and he sucks in a ragged breath.

I clutch at him. "*Hollis.*"

Panting breaths rush from his lips. "I've got you, baby girl." He murmurs this a split second before his mouth lands on mine in a hot, hard, possessive kiss that makes me frantic for more. His thumb finds my clit, applying the perfect amount of pressure while circling it. I whimper against his lips as I grow wetter and wetter, coating him with more of my arousal.

Powerful thrusts combined with his thumb working my clit

drive me closer to the edge. The instant he tugs at my sensitive flesh with his thumb and forefinger, it triggers my orgasm. Hollis continues driving deep, working me through my release as my inner muscles spasm around him, pleasure coursing through my body. He goes taut a split second before a powerful shudder overtakes him and he releases inside me in wet, hot spurts.

He shifts, rolling us to our sides, his arm still securing me to him. His lips find my forehead and linger there. "God, I love you." His words, whispered in a panting breath, hold a hint of wonder in them.

I tug the sleeping bag over us, snuggling closer. My eyes remain closed as a blissful smile lingers on my lips. Exhaustion from the day pulls me under, and I distantly register Hollis' words, spoken so softly, in the barest whisper.

"You won't regret this, Shortcake." His voice cracks with emotion. A featherlight kiss grazes my forehead. "I love you. Like that." He exhales slowly, his warm breath soothing me.

"*Always* like that."

44

HOLLIS

THREE MONTHS LATER
Atlanta, Georgia

It's great to be home after being out of town a week and a half for work. I don't reckon I've ever been so thankful for Face-Time and getting to see Magnolia. Still, nothing's better than having her within arm's reach.

She would've gone with me on this work trip, but she's taking marketing classes in order to eventually join the Custom Motorwerks team.

After telling her how much we struggle to balance everything and still have a reasonable marketing plan in place, Magnolia offered to step in and help. She convinced me it was what she wanted to do, insisting she was more than content to leave politics—a career she'd never been crazy about to begin with—behind. Since starting her courses, she's been doing well and has already come up with some killer ideas.

Magnolia's hand is in mine as we approach the large, newly constructed treehouse in our backyard. Then she whispers words I'll never tire of hearing.

"I love you."

At the base of the ladder, I turn and take her face in my hands. The light from the nearly full moon illuminates her beautiful features. "I love you." With a tender kiss, I briefly rest my forehead to hers and murmur the words we've since changed. "Like that." Then, I step back and gesture for her to precede me up the ladder.

Once we're inside and I've closed the hatch door behind us, we lie back on the soft sleeping bags. The two battery-powered lanterns cast a faint glow over the interior.

As soon as we moved into our new house, only a short drive from where the shop is, Magnolia and I went to work on building this treehouse. It was pretty labor intensive since I decided to add a skylight so we can look up at the stars.

It's wired for electricity and we've included an air-conditioning window unit, just like Dad had done. We took a board from the back of my old treehouse and nailed it on one of the inside walls of this one. It's the board Dad insisted we carefully carve our names into long ago.

Built by: Dad, Hollis & Magnolia

Maybe it's odd to have a treehouse when we're in our twenties, but we don't care. This brings back treasured memories for both of us.

We lie back and gaze at the sparkling night sky above us. She curls up along my side, our fingers laced together, and we have the pillows propped beneath our heads.

"You know what's missin'?" she asks suddenly.

I laugh softly. "Got you covered." I reach into the pocket of my shorts and hand her the packet of Pop Rocks.

"You're the best." She sits up and carefully rips open the top, ready to shake some out of the packet when she goes utterly still.

I study her reaction carefully. Then, her lips part before her gaze slowly lifts to mine, eyes brimming with tears.

"Hollis?"

"I wanted to do this right. But still our way." I sit up slowly. "This is your choice. I'll love you forever, regardless of your answer—that's a known. But I'd be honored if you'd choose to marry me and be my wife. Take my name." A hint of a nervous smile tugs at my mouth. "It's only a three-letter change, if that sways you any."

I sober, clear my throat, and dart a nervous glance at the packet she holds. "That ring in there, it's a promise. I'll be with you, by your side, through everythin' and anythin'. If you choose me, I promise you won't regret it." My voice breaks as my eyes burn with unshed tears.

She reaches inside and plucks the ring between her thumb and forefinger. It's the closest I could have made to what she talked about as a little girl. A two-carat oval-shaped diamond surrounded by tiny diamonds on a simple band.

Tears spill down her cheeks as she holds the ring and looks at me. "Oh, Hollis," Magnolia murmurs softly. She leans forward, pressing her lips to mine, and whispers, "*Yes.*"

Her response sends relief coursing through me, and I carefully slide the ring on her finger. Our eyes lock, and I take the candy from her, setting it on the small shelf, before I tunnel my fingers in her hair and capture her lips with mine.

Within a moment, she's beneath me, and I'm kissing her— my fiancée. My best friend. The woman I plan to spend the rest of my life with.

The only woman who owns me, heart and soul.

45

HOLLIS

EIGHT MONTHS LATER
ATLANTA, GEORGIA

THE BRIDE IS BEAUTIFUL. BREATHTAKING, ACTUALLY. I'VE NEVER seen a more stunning sight before in my life.

Her dress is simple, white and lacy and ankle-length. It's strapless, baring her tanned shoulders and arms. One sparkly hair comb holds one side of her blond hair back, and her loose waves tease the tops of her shoulders. Her blue eyes lock with mine, and a sweet, soft smile plays at her lips.

The best part of all of this is that she's planning to marry *me*.

This backyard wedding might not be exactly how she saw it playing out years ago, but from the look on her face, she doesn't mind one bit.

The hand that settles on my shoulder gives it a quick, comforting squeeze, but I can't bring myself to look away from Magnolia as she approaches. Once she's within two steps from where I stand with her grandpa Joe, a sense of awe stutters through me.

She takes another step, her eyes never leaving mine.

My emotions become a turbulent upheaval and my eyes grow wet. My throat is tight. The final step she takes, drawing to a stop beside me, has me dragging in a much-needed breath, my lungs burning.

Blue eyes still locked with mine, Magnolia carefully hands her bouquet to Stephanie. My soon-to-be wife smiles wider and a tiny tear trickles from the corner of her eye. I carefully smooth it away before taking her hands in mine.

Grandpa Joe begins the ceremony while Stephanie and her husband Tommy, Grant, my uncle Johnny, and a few other close friends we've made since relocating to Atlanta, look on.

"I love you," she silently mouths.

And, of course, I respond the only way I possibly can.

"Like that."

EPILOGUE

MAGNOLIA

"MOMMY! COME AND SEE WHAT DADDY AND I MADE!"

I walk down the hall to where my husband and six-year-old son, Jase—or J, as we've nicknamed him—have been quietly working at the dining room table. When I see what they've built, I can't help but smile at the rush of memories that hits me.

Hollis grins up at me from where he sits with our son. "Might look a little familiar." He winks as I survey the light blue convertible model car they put together. Much like the one we drove off in after we got married, although ours was pink.

"I love it, baby." I press a kiss to the top of J's light brown hair. "You did such a great job."

"Thanks, Mommy." He concentrates on the car before looking at Hollis. "I think that bumper's a little crooked, though."

My husband's eyes narrow as he surveys the car. "Hmm." He leans in close and speaks in a hushed voice. "I won't tell if you won't."

J grins, one bottom front tooth missing. "Deal."

The doorbell rings, and our son practically vibrates with excitement. "Uncle Grant's here!"

Feet pitter-patter on the hardwood floors, and a little voice calls out, "Uncle Grant!"

I turn and scoop up our four-year-old daughter, Ella, propping her on my hip. She grins at me with that gap between her top front teeth, her blonde hair tumbling around her sweet face.

I hold out a hand, and J fits his in mine. "Let's go see your uncle, then."

"Yes, ma'am!" they say with such eagerness it has both Hollis and me chuckling.

Although Hollis will be away at a car expo next week, thankfully, once he returns, he'll be home for a month before he has another one overseas. It's hectic, but we make it work. I manage the marketing aspect for the business, which allows me a flexible schedule so I'm able to volunteer in J's classroom and at Ella's preschool.

My mother and I are still not on the greatest of terms, but we're at least speaking—mainly on birthdays and Christmas when we call her. Her refusal to fully accept me and my choices, as well as the man who makes me the happiest woman on earth, has been a bitter pill to swallow. It's unfortunate, but in the end, she made the decision to not be a prominent figure in our lives.

Things between my stepfather and I remain stilted. After Hollis revealed the truth about Roy being his biological father and the offer of money to keep that fact secret, I lost so much respect for my stepfather. Afterward, the letter I'd stumbled on in Mrs. Barnes' sewing room all those years ago made much more sense. It had been meant for Roy.

We're blessed, though, because Grant, Stephanie and Tommy, Grandpa Joe, and Uncle Johnny spoil our kids rotten with love, which helps to take away some of the sting of my mother and Roy being absentee grandparents.

Grant is seeing a nice woman, and though I'm not sure if it'll go anywhere, I'm thrilled for him. He's a wonderful friend and loves our children to pieces. He and Hollis have grown close, which I initially expected to be awkward. But when I asked my husband about it, he said, "We both love you—just in different ways." Then, in typical Hollis good-hearted fashion, he added, "I reckon he needs us—people who don't expect anythin' from him." And that was that.

Our little ones barely allow Grant a chance to greet us, instantly chattering with their uncle about everything that's happened since his last visit. Our dear friend takes it all in stride, indulging them with unmistakable affection on his face.

When our sweet boy darts off to his room to grab his newest favorite model car to show Grant and Ella rushes to hers to grab her favorite fairy tale for him to read to her, it allows him a quick moment to catch up with Hollis.

I lean against the doorway watching the two men, their conversation so natural. Something Grant says has my husband tipping his head back on a laugh, his dark beard framing those familiar lips I love.

While I watch Hollis chat with Grant, my husband so comfortable and undeniably confident in his own skin, I can't help the surge of pride at how far we've come. We've successfully moved on from being those two people reeling from the mental and emotional wounds of inadequacy and self-doubt that had plagued us for years.

Hollis' eyes suddenly catch mine, and that secret smile graces his lips. The one that's only for me. The one that silently says, *I love you.*

And I'm reminded yet again, even though it took us a while to get our lives sorted, I did the right thing in choosing Hollis Barnes.

There's a saying that sometimes beginnings are hidden in what we're certain is the end. And in our case, it's true.

We may have gotten our happily ever after, but that doesn't mark the end for us.

It's the most beautiful beginning.

"To be someone's first love is extraordinary, but to also be their last is exquisitely magical."
　—*Unknown*

ABOUT THE AUTHOR

RC Boldt enjoys long walks on the beach, running, reading, people watching, and singing karaoke. If you're in the mood for some killer homemade mojitos, can't recall the lyrics to a particular 80's song, or just need to hang around a nonconformist who will do almost anything for a laugh, she's your girl.

RC loves hearing from her readers at rcboldtbooks@gmail.com. You can also check out her website at http://www.rcboldtbooks.com or her Facebook page https://www.facebook.com/rcboldtauthor for the latest updates on upcoming book releases.

Find RC here:

Facebook: https://goo.gl/iy2YzG
Website: http://www.rcboldtbooks.com
Twitter: https://goo.gl/cOs4hK
Instagram: https://goo.gl/TdDrBb
Facebook Readers Group: https://www.facebook.com/groups/BBBReaders

Be sure to check out my other books:

Standalones
Out of Love
CLAM JAM
Out of the Ashes

ACKNOWLEDGMENTS

This book ended up going through edits right when I had something unexpectedly happen: I had to undergo emergency surgery on my eye to fix a detached retina as well as a few other issues. Without having my vision restored, I suffered from brutal eye strain in my good eye and had to have my husband (who's typing this as I dictate to him) step in and help with things he had no idea about. Talk about a crash course. My assistant Melissa, my publicist Nina and the team at Social Butterfly PR, and my close author friends have helped me out while I've been unable to read and be online to post to social media.

Without the help of these gracious individuals, there's no way this book would have been published on time like I'd planned. Nor will a heartfelt thank you ever come close to being enough. To my ladies, my dearest friends, thank you for helping me through this and keeping me sane with your messages and thoughtfulness. I love you to pieces.

I'd be remiss if I didn't also thank the following (in no particular order):

My beta readers—Thank you for offering feedback and helping me fine tune this story.

My readers—Without your support, your sweet emails and reviews, and you sharing my books with others, none of this would be possible.

My readers group—I am beyond grateful for your support, excitement, and feedback when I share my ideas with you.

All the book bloggers & reviewers—Please know that the time you take to read and review my books and/or do promo posts is appreciated beyond words.

Made in the USA
Columbia, SC
03 November 2019

82403875R00191